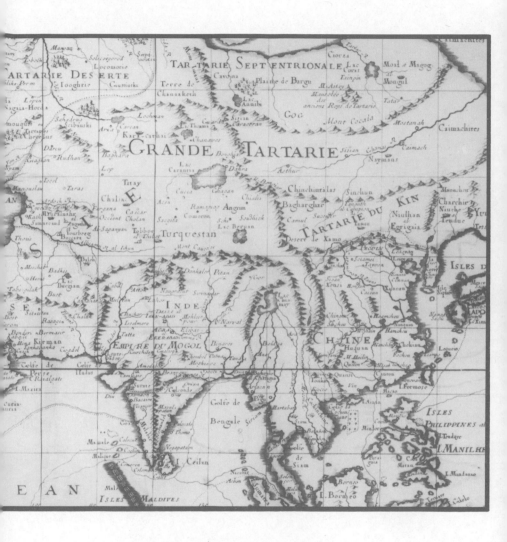

MARCO POLO'S TEARS

The author wishes to thank his agent, Peter Tauber,
for his encouragement.

MARCO POLO'S TEARS

ANDREW JOTISCHKY

PETER HALBAN
LONDON

FIRST PUBLISHED IN GREAT BRITAIN BY
PETER HALBAN PUBLISHERS LTD
42 South Molton Street
London W1Y 1HB
1989

British Library Cataloguing in Publication Data

Jotischky, Andrew, 1965–
Marco Polo's tears
I. Title
823.914 [F]
ISBN 1-870015-29-0

Phototypeset by Computape (Pickering) Ltd, North Yorkshire
Printed in Great Britain by
WBC Ltd, Bristol

To my parents

1

She died on a winter's afternoon; February, to be exact. It was Ben who called me with the news:

'Amanda is dead. Another attack, a couple of hours ago. She has peace, at last.' And, like Agave when she sees her son Pentheus' head bleeding under her arm, I could only stammer and ask, 'Where? And when?'

'In the hospital. Here, in Florence.' He sounded surprised. 'I told you, a few hours ago. I'm sorry, Alex, I didn't check the time precisely.'

I could hear his voice breaking over the line. He grieved at last, with the anger of years of waiting for this moment; helpless in the face of grief. I said, 'I'll fly out at once. Can you meet me at the airport? You know how the trains are down to the country. Oh, Ben, I'm terribly sorry. It seems so sudden, after all this time.'

After all this time—does mental illness protract time? Ben had replaced the receiver; there seemed nothing else to say. She was his wife, and she was my sister.

My wife said afterwards, 'I think none of you knew all of her, least of all Ben. You always insisted on treating her like a mental patient.'

'Martha, she lost her mind. It was scattered over the plains of Central Asia. And you never knew her as we did, in the old days.'

'Because I came later? Will you never forget that? Perhaps I saw more clearly for that. Madness is relative. What was sane, when Amanda was mad?'

1

This came back to me, sitting on the aeroplane taking me to the funeral. I was alone: Martha had no part in this and no desire to come. She liked Ben well enough, and had liked Amanda, but for my sake. 'Because I came later . . .' It was her perpetual condition. Later than what? What was this dance of four, among so many? It was four at first, solemn, precocious undergraduates, aesthetes, separated later but never apart; then three (or, as Ben said once, two and a half, Amanda both there and not there), and now the two of us left. Ben and I were friends as long as either could remember, as schoolboys and students. We discovered Giles in Trinity Great Court; he had been up a year before us. Amanda, I suppose, was more than half a part of it; we were always close. Ben fell in love with her on a long, listless summer, at the end of our last university year. That time was the gem we held between us, like Alexander's stone of paradise. Ben, the historian, the antiquarian, told me the story: Alexander never found the gates of paradise, though he searched the breadth of the world for them. Instead he found the gem, beautiful beyond comprehension, which weighed far more than its size would suggest. But when dust was sprinkled on it, it became suddenly weightless. An allegory of the man himself: we are all weightless in death. Our stone has collected the ashes of half the original company, and still the memory of that time hangs heavy around my neck.

Ben was waiting for me at the airport. Grief had made him leonine, where age had merely drawn lines of grey. He was my size, but thicker, the head square, the jaw firmer. He still had great physical charm, the look of a man who had captained his school's Rugby XV. But he had been a cricketer, rather; he was a man of rhythms and easy spaces. We drove in silence through the cobbled Florentine streets. In February there are few visitors. The Duomo, a vast redundant cake, wept in the rain, soggy marble streaked with dirt. Normally I would stop a moment to go in and pay homage to the Hawkwood shrine. The Florentines promised the old English

2

condottiere a tomb in the new cathedral, but the dead cannot argue, so now he looks down obliquely from his horse, two-dimensional in fresco on the wall. It is a better painting than the tomb he might have got. Today we pass it by. How would Amanda look in profile, on the wall of the little church in Santa Clara? I knew the answer; like Filippo Lippi's Madonna in profile, but dark-haired instead of golden.

Ben told me once, 'When I see Amanda, it is from the side, sitting next to her, looking in wonder. Her hands are folded in her lap.' They were strong arms and hands, for a girl, but not too strong.

The car ride seemed as long as the aeroplane journey. We left Florence and drove in silence towards Siena, climbing sharply at the end. A wedding procession, a dozen cars long, streamed out of the gates of the old city, each honking its horn to celebrate the occasion. Joy expected; grief at last realized.

'What a miserable time of year for a wedding.' I was hoping, at least, to provoke him. Ben had wept and railed for months after Giles' death, and literally torn his clothes. Then he shut himself away, after they returned, and spoke only to himself. Did Amanda deserve such calm?

'Perhaps they can choose their time no more than we can,' he said.

'Oh, fate,' I mocked. 'We were never mystics, you and I.'

'And we're still here.'

'Yes.' I had been trying to say, ever since he called me to give the news, 'She's better off than we, Ben.' It sounds trite and pious, but I believed it, in a way I did not understand. Now, sitting helpless in the car on this cold Tuscan day, inexorably approaching her grave, and her stone-faced white self, unliving, it was as if I became suddenly aware of the distance that was between us. Her death was a guillotine slicing asunder the webby skein of our contact. ('I have learned to love you late, Beauty at once so ancient and so new! I have learned to love you late!') It was Ben's saying, 'We're

3

still here,' as if we two had not yet found words to break a spell.

It is much later now, and Martha is here, and I could tell you something different, that it was a matter of having the right question to ask; like Perceval the Grail-Seeker in the Hall of the Fisher King, standing by the old king's sick-bed, hunted, puzzled: why had they brought him here? What was the old man's disease? Why was the land so barren, the cattle sick, the women wailing? What had this to do with him, or with the Grail? Ah, there is the question—where did the Grail fit in? Well, with Amanda it was paradise on earth, her own quest for the Grail.

Still I cannot say how much Ben knew. He drove impassive through the frosty vineyard-country of the Chianti. It came to me how when we were boys he would sometimes look up suddenly from a game, or from a knot of people, and walk away, as if struck by something incongruous with his activity. He was considered a dreamer for this—and for other things, like losing money, or forgetting his books, or leaving a record playing when he went out. Perhaps he simply stepped outside the range of our experiences. Or, I thought now, he removed the self from its environment. Then he was closer to Amanda than Martha suspected. I was never capable of this, although I tried, as I tried most things he did: wearing silk scarves, walking alone in the early hours to look at the stars, smoking tea-leaves (and getting sick).

'There isn't much food in the house,' he said. 'I haven't had time to do much.'

'It's all right, I shouldn't think I'll stay long—just for the funeral.'

4

'And I haven't made up a bed for you or anything. I suppose the guest-room linen will all be there; I haven't checked.'

'Don't worry, Ben.'

'How long are you staying? I mean, it's pretty dull here at the moment.' I looked across in surprise. I suppose a wife's funeral could be dull: how would I know?

'I'll stay as long as you want me.'

'Oh God, Alex! Now you say it—why couldn't you say it twenty years ago, when we needed you?' He was actually smiling.

'I didn't think you'd need me in paradise.' And now he was laughing, his distorted guilty laugh, starting in his bowels and moving up and down at the same time, so that his arms and feet shook simultaneously and uncontrollably. The laughter of the gods, Giles had called it. (He said, a man who laughs like Ben is a follower of the Tao, even though he does not know it. Now, Giles, if you were alive, I would tell you it was Amanda who was the Taoist.) Ben said it was genetic, this laugh, the only family heirloom of any value. It missed a generation, for his father had been a taciturn man. I saw him laugh once, when a tree blew clean over in a storm and fell across the road. It was a delightful laugh, all the better for being reserved for this special occasion, like a child's delight at the sea-side. But Ben's laugh came from his father's father, old, foreign, out of joint. Grandfather laughed often and at people. Ben's laugh was always unexplained, a thing that stood alone. It made me nervous.

'Why do you laugh?' This, I knew, was a futile question, like asking, 'What are you thinking of?' Usually he did not answer; once, to the latter, he simply said, 'Burial patterns.' It seemed apt now. He laughed all the way through the vineyards and between the rows of olive trees, all the way to the village of Santa Clara.

The village clung to the sides of the hill, its fingers dug deep into the rock. It was named after a nun of a nearby convent

5

who, according to legend, suffered death rather than be-smirch her chastity. During the wars between Florence and Siena, at a time unspecified (and anyway outside my com-prehension), a troop of pillaging merceneries broke into the convent to loot the church of its silver, for which it was celebrated throughout Tuscany. One of them found his way to the cell of a young and particularly beautiful nun, and tried to force her. Level-headed in crisis, Sister Clara held him off by offering him a jar of magic cream that would render him invincible in battle. The soldier was intrigued but not con-vinced. Clara took some cream from the jar and smeared it on her neck.

'Strike here with your sword,' she urged, 'and judge for yourself its effectiveness.' He struck; Clara's head rolled to the floor, spattering him with the blood of her sanctity. The convent is long since crumbled and forgotten (except, perhaps, by Ben); Clara's cream gained her immortality.

This story Ben told me long ago, climbing the autumn mountains of the Chianti. He knew it from the elderly priest, for Ben had spent summers in the house in Santa Clara ever since I could remember. Once I had been, with a school party, to Rome; that summer, our gem, Amanda and Giles and I spent in Santa Clara, and much of the autumn too. It was an incredibly lovely autumn, the first, I suppose, that I really noticed. Those vineyards and forests held their own private festivals, bringing out banners of gold and russet, sometimes even a deep crimson, waved like a declaration of freedom. Embers glowing against a hard blue sky. It is a combination of colours found only in the natural world; they match nowhere else. Earth is a woman, said Giles, vast, round-bellied and laughing mysteriously and continuously. We climbed slowly, emerging at last between lines of trees at the summit. I remember my first sight of the village from above. In the breeze, the trees showered us with their funeral leaves. It was like receiving largesse from hermits: their possessions already sold, essentials packed, ready to

6

head with ever-increasing strides for the caves and the deserts.

That autumn we were alone in the house. There were no German neighbours, no swimming-parties at the lake. In the afternoons we often heard gunshots as the villagers went out to shoot the birds and hares; sometimes we joined them. We walked and read, and in the evenings drank *grappa* on the terrace and listened to Vivaldi.

How could I avoid those memories as we followed the same route, years later, the last survivors of that summer? Even Ben's old priest had died. But it was from between choked and naked vines that I saw Santa Clara again.

Amanda's body lay in the tiny chapel adjoining the church of Santa Clara, there being no funeral parlour or chapel of rest in this village of forty families. I do not know what I hoped for when I went up that evening to pay my last respects—no, not to pay respects, but to see her again. Deep sorrow transfigured into poetry? Well, I am a civil servant; I found nothing. But I wept, and that night wished Martha were with me. Loneliness was something I had not expected.

She asked me later to describe the service. What I recalled most clearly was how, after lowering the coffin into the fresh grave, Ben drew me aside and handed me a letter. His face was streaked; it made him look dreadfully old.

'Amanda wrote this, about twenty years ago. I have never shown it to anyone. But you should see it, if anyone should.'

'Gladly, Ben. But will it change anything?'

He looked at me steadily and rather coldly and said, 'I would change nothing, even if I had the chance. Nothing.' So I took the letter and read it standing by the new grave in the dark February light.

7

Dearest Ben,

I have been wondering, why do my moods change so suddenly, and to what purpose? Is it always an exterior event, however small, that upsets a balance—or does the brain (or soul, I suppose—really I mean 'anima') have its own motor for controlling emotions? I wish it did, anyway. People who don't know me very well think I am calm and level-headed and not at all temperamental (which they expect me to be, as an art student!). But you know I have *angst*, Ben! Buckets of it!

What does it consist of, you asked me. Well, I don't know whether I can say. But on the off-chance that I can, and that there is not more virtue in keeping silent, I will try to put it into words. The root is discontent, but not with anything or because of anything, just plain discontent, of itself. Giles said something once about some people who are 'becomers' and others who just 'be'. I'm a becomer; I suppose you know that. I just wish to God I didn't keep stepping out of the moment. To enjoy the moment! But that means 'be-ing' in the present, and every moment is the present. How terrifying, never to take refuge in anticipation!

But Ben, I hate where I am, always, it seems. It is as if I am perpetually chasing a vision of the future—no, not of the future, but the ghost of the present, in a different time. (Do you understand, or are you already calling for a doctor? I thought you might understand, if anyone would.) Sometimes I wonder whether we have to exist properly in the here-ness. I mean, are we real if we refuse to participate in here-ness? (You can ignore this part if you like. I don't even dare to read it over again.) And where will I be when I have caught up with the ghost? Will she recognize me?

There was more, but I was getting very cold. Everyone had left now, except Ben and me. It was all most informal.

'Why are you showing this to me?' I asked him. 'Is there

8

more to understand about Amanda?'

'Let's go back and warm up. I just thought you might want to see it.'

'When did you say she wrote it? There's no date at the top.'

'After we were engaged. She wanted to break it off, you know.' At this I caught at his sleeve, surprised: 'Did she? I never knew, Ben! Why?' But he walked on into the house.

It had the sanitary sheen of a house only sometimes lived-in, though it had once been a barn attached to a larger and older one, now demolished. A balcony ran around two sides of the upper storey. Inside there were few doors; Amanda tore them out when they wrested the house away from Ben's cousins. It had once belonged to his Italian family, on his mother's side, but now the doors had been replaced with Amanda's curious Mozarabic archways. It could only have belonged to them, for it contained everything; everything had the capacity to interest them. (Perhaps entrance would be a better word.)

Ben had been assembling, like a museum curator, objects to be shipped away. Pacing about the open spaces, he stopped to look at an astrolabe, or a skull, a wooden flute, a Venetian mask.

'These treasures,' he murmured, 'I have shored against my ruin.' (It was a phrase he used often and fondly. I recalled afternoons in the long grass, reading Eliot.)

'Ben, did you say shipped away? Are you abandoning Santa Clara?'

'I couldn't stay now, alone. There are too many memories.'

'There are too many memories to let it go!'

He looked at me strangely, fondling in his arms the ivory cat, Zengi. His name, of course, from the Seljuk warrior. Ben considered Saladin greater, but Amanda thought Zengi the more appropriate name.

'You know, Alex, here's a funny thing,' he mused. 'You stand there, clinging to the past as if it still held the present in some pincer-grip.'

9

'But it does, it always does. It affects me. I was formed by it.'

'Well, don't be so proud of that. I can't figure this out about you. You are the sanest, calmest person I ever knew. You always were stunningly normal. But inside you are an emotional castaway.'

Oh, very fine to say that, Ben, standing four-square in the room ennobled by your (our) loss. I cannot say fine things like that, I have not your stature. I only said,

'But I love my memories.'

'Oh, God save me from you, Alex! You should have been in the earthly paradise with us!'

'Careful, Ben. You'll drop Zengi—if you don't throw him at me first.'

'Amanda always said it was impossible to argue with you.'

We walked around the little house together, he trying to cast away each step he took, I preserving and filing carefully away. Both were futile journeys: what control have we over the past? We sat up late that night, subdued. Neither wished to turn inwards alone; I missed Martha. But in the morning, cold but bright, a morning of hoarfrost on the branches, he came into the kitchen where I was eating breakfast. His eyes glistened.

'I had a dream,' he said, 'coated in honey and almonds, bitter-sweet.'

'Of Amanda?'

'Yes. Of all of us.' He sat down and took the coffee I had prepared. 'We were here, the summer after leaving Cambridge.' Behind the half-smile I saw memory exposed. It seemed that he had shouldered, voluntarily, the burden of a world newly-created since those days. These sudden razor-sharp snatches of memory pierced through to the bone. But more than twenty years ago, on this very balcony, the four of us had sat over late breakfasts and passed memories between us like a bowl of sweets. Once, returning from a hike in the woods, Giles and I were greeted with a young local Chianti

10

and one of the delightfully amateurish lunches we took turns in preparing. Ben and Amanda had stayed behind that morning.

Giles bellowed, his mouth full, 'Is this what you have to show for a morning's work? A fine Tuscan mess!'

'There were no peppers. But I compensated with the garlic,' said Amanda.

'And anyway,' Ben explained, 'We only just got back ourselves. We've been down to the lake for a swim.'

'And how was the water today?' Giles asked pointedly, 'Or did you not take the plunge? Perhaps you simply dangled your feet over the edge, blissfully aware of an embrace too painful to break?' It was always Ben who blushed at his taunts; Amanda enjoyed them, and actually liked to embarrass him. I said, 'Amanda is afraid of water since May Week.'

'Trust her to fall in while punting!' Ben laughed, alluding to an occasion of recent memory.

'It is a spiritual exercise,' Giles explained gravely. 'In this way young ladies are enabled to immerse themselves, at one plunge, into a world otherwise beyond their reach. It is a surrogate degree. The case of Amanda, for example . . .'

The strong brown river carried us, unknowing, in its bosom. It was a humid afternoon; the willows on the bank drooped with moisture. Green leaves, green fields, green bottles. Amanda opened them with inexpert panache, the corks scattering a procession of ducks. The river was empty this far down; we could hear only ourselves: Giles singing lewdly, my rather pompous interventions, Ben's laughter, incredible, formless. (How often that laugh must have echoed across the haunted Afghan sands, like a Mayday call!) Pretty, voluptuous Amanda taking her turn with the pole, Giles and Ben wobbling the sides to make her lose her balance. She teetered for long moments on the edge in a posture of self-conscious abandon. Clearer than a photograph I have that image still, of her limbs embracing the flat landscape.

11

'And you want to preserve that,' Ben said, shaking his head.

'I only want to remember Amanda in the good days,' I said quietly. 'We had something precious then, maybe too precious for me. And it wasn't just a friendship of students— it lasted. For Giles, and now Amanda, it lasted forever. And we are still here, together.' He was silent, and I added, almost to be tactful, 'What came after, that I could easily throw away.'

' "He is no great man who thinks it a great thing that sticks and stones should fall, and that man, who must die, should die." Plotinus said it. If I thought it were true, I would wallow in memory. But Amanda has died and it is not true.

'The tragedy is not in the decay, but in our blindness when the sun is shining hard on the walls. I feel like an old man clutching to his chest a cup of water, careful not to spill a single drop. When we were younger, we flung that water about freely. That is what I resent, Alex.'

He brought out a bundle of papers and envelopes, tied together with string. I could see him pause, as if weighing them in his hands.

'Perhaps you wouldn't be interested, Alex. That's why I showed you that letter first. I don't want to spoil your memories. But I know how close you were. These are her personal memoirs.'

'Amanda's?' I was surprised. 'I didn't know she kept a diary.'

'It's not really a diary. But the dreams are all in here. I'd like you to have them, Alex.'

The dreams . . . I spent an afternoon among her dreams. Then I rang Martha in England and asked her to join me in Santa Clara. I told Ben we wanted a holiday in the house before he sold up. He was on a term's sabbatical anyway, because of Amanda's poor health, and I had leave owing.

I understand what Ben meant when he fought the past. But there is something to be said for flinging water about freely.

12

Would he have had nothing to resent if he had been so careful of the moment, so sparing with himself because of what might happen later? Some men can train themselves to pare the soul clean, cutting off emotions like slices of meat from the bone. But they are wrong to think themselves better-equipped to live in adversity. And besides, we have no foreknowledge; we are not gods.

Amanda dreamt unceasingly. The hours passed in sleep could be years, lifetimes. How many generations could she span, arched and still in bed, while poor Ben lay sleepless beside her? Once he asked her, 'Who were you before this lifetime? Did your soul migrate?' We had often discussed the journeys of the soul; Giles, the self-appointed mystic, considered himself an expert.

'Each night it may cross years as though they were mountain ranges, Ben. After all, who can tell how many people we may really be? It's just that we refuse to give them existence outside sleep.'

'You cannot be whom you see in dreams. Those people have no ontological reality.'

But she only laughed at this, and said, 'Why not more existence? And greater reality?'

He could out-argue her, any time, but he could not apprehend what he saw of her mind. (At least, that is how it seemed at the time, and Martha is still convinced of it.) Later, he told me in despair, 'When I am closest to her, then is she the furthest away. When I can feel her trembling against me, there are centuries and continents between us.'

I remember watching her asleep once—no, twice, if I go back far enough. As children, we slept in adjoining rooms, but I was usually awake before her. I had left something, perhaps a book, in her room, and risked her annoyance if I woke her to fetch it back. The sleep-darkened room, a little

Victorian parlour heaped with girls' things—she was an embryonic collector—frustrated my search. But she was a deep sleeper. I watched her: her mouth was slightly open as if, in her dream, she was perpetually about to speak. Waves of dark hair, unbrushed, invaded the still face. There were rabbits on her nightdress; I knew this although I could not see beneath the sheets. She was perhaps twelve or thirteen, I two years older. How did I not wake her then? She seemed to have been asleep forever; interrupting her then, I saw a cross-section, caught her in one moment of sleep. She looked so perfect, lightly freckled, prettily still, that it was all I could do not to wake her.

And another time, ten years later in Santa Clara, I went into the room where the young lovers were sleeping, to wake them. It was the morning of our departure; we had an early train to catch. She was fuller and softer by now, especially in contrast with Ben's square head. But he slept as if being enlightened; the eyebrows quizzical, the breath even and slow. She, I am sure, was not there at all. The vessel of her body held only water. She soared and leapt over plains, surveyed migrating thoughts from her great height. She was an idea, her body a mere fact. I remembered a line from somewhere: Matter has no reality, it is only the darkness where the light gives out.

I left the darkness intact, and went out into the morning light. Giles was waiting, impatient and fully-dressed, but there seemed no purpose in stirring empty shrouds.

She had a recurring dream. On an unlikely hot medieval day she stood on the quay in front of the Doge's Palace as Marco Polo returned to Venice with his father and uncle. He was forty years old, half his life spent in a world beyond the constraints of geography. From the lands of dragons and salamanders he returned to the half-known Venice of his

14

childhood. But it can be told better than this; I have her own notes.

'. . . a busy quayside, noisy and hot, crowded with sailors, traders, idlers. I am a quiet man, I like peripheries. Are these my people? These tall, white hawks of men? How they stare as we tread uncertain on our Venetian ground! It must be our clothing: we travel light, but we are wearing heavy furs, for it was cold coming over the Taurus mountains, at the last. But it is a bright day here, brighter than I remember. And these beards, of course—no one in Venice wears a beard like this, thick and square. (Although I have seen beards and hair of all colours and shapes imaginable, and some unimaginable.)

'What am I to make of this old home? Colours—coloured bundles, coloured hats, blue and red and green tunics, dirty, brown, harbour water. Square Venetian buildings, falling sheer into the water, impossibly slender. The tongues on idlers' lips sound old and unfamiliar. Uncle Maffeo steps forward laughing, his arms aloft. A thousand cracked veins split his puffy face.

'Fellow-citizens! Tell all Venice! The Polo brothers are home!' Swivelling round slowly, he breathes in the dirty seaweed smell. 'You remember us, don't you? You must have thought us dead!' The crowds press closer, amazed to hear unsteady Venetian from this outlander. There are questions, insults, jokes. Who are we, and where from? What do we bring to Venice, the queen of cities, the richest in all the world? What exotic luxury can we show that is not already known, and packed to the roofs of their granaries? This is not how I had pictured our return. These people are ugly, deformed, awkward. How complacent they are!

'Maffeo, old and round, is talking again. We bring our-selves, he says (too courteously), returned at last from the land of the silk-growing Seres, from the edge of the world. We have come to spend our last days with a Venetian sun on our faces! What have we seen? And now Father presses forwards also, his thin dark face suddenly warm and light. He was

15

more nervous, and happier, at the prospect of returning home. Now listen to him! A torrent pours out of their eager clumsy mouths, they outdo each other in telling the fantastic truth. Streams of Chinese and Brahmins and Mohammedans tumble out into the alien air, Buddhists and Tartars, wind-worshippers and idolaters, cannibals and dragons, sala-manders and fur and gems, rice and fireworks and gun-powder, and the men with no heads, but two holes in their breast which serve as eyes! The people are delighted and laugh louder: what absurdities we talk! Safe with their island churches and stinking narrow canals, what need have they for the lands where the sun rises? What should I say to them of seventeen years spent among a small round-faced yellow people, for whom this Venice would be no more than a suburb of Kinsai?

'So I say nothing, but step forward and tear open the front of my fur gown. My eyes are blurred with tears; I am weeping profusely as I pull the pouch from around my neck and loosen the string. Over the cobbles, with my tears, I let fall a cascade of gems: emeralds, rubies, amethysts, jade, topaz. Now they are silent, pressing still closer, some on their knees or crouch-ing low to see the jewels. My thick hot beard is wet with tears, as I hear a man whisper with reverence,

"This one alone, this would buy the Doge's Palace, and the Doge himself, if he were for sale!"

'Now the people believe.'

What could this mean, we wondered, as we sped towards the Alps? (The train, like some fantastic insect, raced for its mountainous lair before the darkness fell. We had missed the early train and decided to spend a final morning with Masac-cio in Florence.) Giles kept us entertained with speculations, each more improbable to my stolid mind than the last. He had a fine sense of the ridiculous and the absurd. That sharp ugly

16

face and matted blond hair concealed a wild, busy mind. Of all of us he was the most obviously talented. Perhaps, *The Times* obituary noted after his death—for he had already published by then—he had genius also.

'Amanda is a bearer of truth to the ignorant,' he said. He spoke quickly when excited, big bony hands following the words with jerky movements. 'But it is a truth unwanted and misunderstood, like pearls cast before swine.'

'Yes,' she said slowly, 'there were pearls. Many of them.'

'But wait,' I interrupted. 'At first she was only a spectator. Then by the end she is Marco Polo himself.'

'Yes, yes. But Marco is a spectator,' said Giles in high excitement. As he warmed to his task he became more than ever a caricature of himself, a large ungainly bird. 'He is part of no society, neither the Venetian he hardly remembers, nor the alien Chinese. He is a transitory figure. It is very important that Amanda saw herself as Marco, a man of no fixed pole. It is the clue to the dream.' We looked expectantly at her. I think she was less concerned than we were to find a meaning. She was smiling and frowning slightly at the same time.

As if to rescue her, Ben said, 'Steady on, Giles. Marco was seventeen when he left Venice. That's old enough to remember one's childhood home, even if the next twenty years were spent on the other side of the world. And there's no evidence that he found it hard to come back to Venice—in fact, he was an ordinary, successful merchant and a public dignitary.'

'Ah,' Giles warned, shaking a finger, 'but did he choose to remember what he left behind?'

'You're just taking refuge in mystical ignorance.'

Giles ignored this. 'Perhaps the break, and the years of travelling across the world, were enough to snap his memory cleanly in two. Perhaps he became a schizophrenic?'

Now Amanda asked, 'Have you read his "Travels"? Surely they shed some light?' I had not; Ben, the historian, probably had, but Giles cut in, sarcastically, 'Oh Lord, the "Travels" of

17

Marco Polo! Dull as rain! Dry as a grasshopper's wings! Forget them—you might as well stare at your navel in divine contemplation.' He said it with an almost personal rancour. I looked over at Ben, who said nothing but raised his eyebrows in mild protest. Giles had not finished; near Milan he was well into his stride. 'My dear Amanda, the gems you flung so movingly to the ground were a kind of Holy Grail. In your dream *persona*, you sought the Grail. The journey to China is just a symbol—it could have been anywhere. Marco Polo is also a convenient symbol.' The other occupant of our compartment, a young German traveller, got up and went into the corridor. He left behind a vague smell of having travelled for days without stopping. I gesticulated towards his retreating back:

'Another Grail-seeker, do you suppose?'

'Oh, Alex, please don't try to be facetious. Seriousness suits you much better. As a matter of fact he may be Perceval himself. The point is, you search for something whose value even you cannot appreciate. That happened with the Grail. And in Amanda's dream, she doesn't know the value of the travelling until she reaches Venice again, and finds that it all means nothing to the dull Venetians.'

'But what is the Grail?' Amanda asked simply.

'A stone, in the "Parzival", Wolfram von Eschenbach's version,' said Ben. 'Or a cup, the chalice used at the Last Supper, in the French versions.'

'No.' She shook her head. 'It's more than that, it's . . . well, it's knowledge.' At this Giles got up and solemnly shook her hand. His thin face was animated; he seemed to want to expand to fill the whole compartment.

'Amanda, my dear,' he murmured, 'we are fellow seekers, you and I, fellow knights of the Grail. Don't try to deny it, you may not know it yet. But one day you will.' Ben and Amanda exchanged conspiratorial looks, as if they had long since ceased to take him seriously but continued to indulge him. In fact I think this was almost true of Ben. It was a reflex

18

defensive action. The two intellectuals were already jealous of their territory.

The discussion could go no further, for we were beginning to roll into Milan, through decaying fields of iron girders and stale railway flotsam. The German came back into the compartment to collect his rucksack. Giles too took his suitcase; he was leaving us here. He had decided this a few days before:

'I don't think I'll come back to England with you. Not yet, anyway. There doesn't seem to be much there to call me back.' Of all of us, his immediate future was the most uncertain. It was the way he liked it.

'What will you do?' Amanda asked, 'Stay in Italy?'

'I believe I will go to Venice for a bit. All writers seem to have to live there for a while, and I intend to be a writer.' We knew this, of course, but it was the first time he had stated it explicitly.

'If you need somewhere to stay, I think I have a cousin in Venice,' Ben suggested.

'You think? An imaginary cousin?'

'I'm not sure they still live there. My mother's cousin. Her husband died, but I think she stayed in Venice with the children. I probably have the address, if you want to look them up.'

'Thanks, Ben, but I'd rather be on my own. I have some money; I can rent something for a few months.'

He seemed to shrink in stature as he spoke these lonely words. His own father had died when he was very young, leaving him a trust fund and a guardian uncle. Always more independent than us, this would not be the first time he had been alone. He promised, as he stepped on to the grey station platform, to come back for Christmas. We watched until we lost his hunched shoulders in the crowd. During the rest of the long journey, I paced the corridors while Amanda and Ben grew closer together.

The holiday was over. We returned to futures secure and defined: Ben to Oxford to begin his research, Amanda to her final year at Art School, and I to the caverns and passages of the Foreign Office.

Like an avenger of some obscure and forgotten wrong, Marco Polo continued to haunt my sister's dreams. He pursued her as she commuted, most weekends, from London to Oxford, to be with Ben. To her modern friends at the Art School she said nothing (the Sixties were just beginning; who had time for dreaming?), but among the staid cobbles and towers of Oxford she probed Ben for explanations and understanding. The brilliant thick-set undergraduate had acquired a scholar's air. When he took her to the Botanical Gardens he strolled easily, tweed-clad, hands clasped behind his back, absorbing and unseeing. The vague wayward charm of the English don had settled on him already. This he later sought to disown, but it never wholly left him.

Among the scattered remnants of Eden she told him, in mellow, enchanting tones, her dreams. She looked tired, as if the dreaming were not sleeping but a second day juxtaposed with the first, so that she was never at rest.

'Recently,' she said, 'I have been dreaming of a large room. The walls and floor are hung with tapestries, but there is little furniture. It is clearly the room of a wealthy family. There is glass in the windows and a large fireplace at one end. Sometimes a boy sits alone in the room, curled up in the window seat—they are casement windows. He is dressed like the boy in my old school history text-book, from the chapter on "Life in the Middle Ages". He is looking out through the window.'

'How old is he? Can you see what he is looking at?' Ben asked. These dreams are familiar to him now; she tells them like bed-time stories.

'Oh yes, he can see. Outside the window is a small stretch of pavement, and then the canal. Steps lead down into the

20

water, and a flat barge lies in the water. It is secured by ropes to a pole on the quay. On the quay are some bales or packages, with written labels stuck to the sides. Water laps against the side of the barge; it rocks gently at its mooring, like an animal at rest before the hunt. Once the bales are loaded, the boy knows a boatman will come and guide the barge to the greater canal, on the open sea, where the ship is waiting for its cargo.'

'Can you see all this? I mean, the boy—can he see?'

'No, but he knows very well what will happen. He has watched it all before, sometimes from this same spot, some-' times from the church tower or an upper window of the house. From there he can see everything: the crowds gathered on the piazza by the sea-front, streaming slowly and chaotically in many directions; the wind tugging at the banners on their flagpoles in the piazza and on the palace, and at the sails on the ships. He can hear too, but only shouting and the noise of winches and pulleys without distinguishing words.'

'Why is he sitting downstairs now while all this excitement is going on in the piazza?'

'That happens next, Ben,' she said, a secretive smile slowly growing on her face. Ben, watching her, felt his own facial muscles relax involuntarily. He could not have clenched a fist or grit his teeth, for the softness that took hold of his body, beginning in his guts and creeping upwards. ('She was irresistible then, Alex,' he told me. 'She could ask anything of me and I would have to grant it because my insides were melted, like hot wax.' I have a book he gave her, inscribed with the words from the Irish legend of Étain's wooing as a dedication: 'as white as the snow of a single night, her wrists, as slender and even as red as foxgloves her clear lovely cheeks'.) She continued the dream: 'As the boy waits and watches, more bales are carried out from the cellars under the house. Eagerly he opens the window and—he is only a boy of twelve or thirteen—clambers through, dropping to the

21

ground in front of the porter. They are old friends: the porter, elderly, bent almost double, puts down his bale with a cry of delight and sets the boy on it.

'"Well, young Messer Marco you're loitering here again?" He speaks the Venetian dialect roughly, heavily accented; a squint is set permanently into his face: he is a native of the cold northern regions of the Tartars.

'"Where are these packages going, Peter?" asks the young boy. The Tartar laughs his cracked high-pitched laugh:

'"If Messer Marco could read these labels, he'd know well enough."

'"I'm learning to read, Peter. But these are too long; I don't recognize the words."

'"Well, it's no good asking me. You know household slaves don't read."

'"I bet you know anyway. You always know about Father's business." The Tartar smiles and pretends to be searching his memory. He sighs, scratches his head.

'"Ah, Messer Marco, what with all these far-off places and strange lands, I get confused easily."

'"Tell me, Peter!" the boy urges. "Tell me, or I won't let you have this bale back, and you'll be in trouble."

'"In trouble, will I? Let me see then, Messer Marco." He uses the manly title with good-natured irony. Pretending to make out the characters on the labels he spells out names: Constantinople, Trebizond, Samarkand. Marco's eyes sparkle as the magical words drop from the servant's mouth.

'"Where are Father and Uncle now, Peter?" he asks suddenly. "When are they coming back?" Peter, rumpling the boy's hair, lifts him off the bale.

'"They'll be home soon, without a doubt. Who knows where they are now? Bukhara, I heard someone say."

The boy continues to watch as Peter loads the cargo into the barge, then steps into the boat and with a final wave punts it down the canal. Through a junction and under a bridge, then round a bend and lost to sight. By nightfall the big ship will be

22

loaded and checked by the customs men, and then at dawn, before Marco is up from bed, it will slink away and towards the unattainable treasure-houses of the East, perhaps to Peter's country and to Father. His eyes remain fixed on the canal, but instead of its dirty brown water and the green slime clinging to the walls he sees brown scrub burnt by the sun as a distant caravan winds slowly across an imagined plain, and rocky paths clambering between the mountains, and turbaned brown merchants sipping sherbet as they rest in gaily painted tents. And beyond it all he sees golden domes and narrow spires shimmering above pristine walls, the silken cities of the East.'

They had reached Ben's college again, as if by instinct. Arm in arm they wandered past the spires of his tangible present. Still in her own, Amanda asked him, 'Will you tell me about Marco Polo?'

'What can I tell you, my dear? It is you who dream of him, not I.'

'But I know nothing about him. Can't you tell me some historical facts, at least?'

'Almost all we know,' said Ben donnishly, 'is in his own book, the *Travels of Ser Marco Polo the Venetian*. If you read it, you'll know as much as I do.'

'I have meant to,' she sighed. 'But every time I'm about to pick it up I remember what Giles said: dull as rain! What if he's right, Ben? What if it really is dull? I'll feel let down—as if I'm dreaming the same thing, night after night, and it all means nothing. Can it all mean nothing, Ben?'

'I don't understand. You can't be responsible for what you dream. No one can.' Frowning in bewilderment, he failed to acknowledge the greetings of begowned figures flitting across the quad.

'Oh, Ben, don't you see? I know Giles was wrong. The "Travels" can't be dull because I can see their outlines in my dreams: elusive, hinted at, but pounding away at poor Marco's brain. It wasn't chance that made him leave Venice

23

and travel to the end of the world, it was . . . well, something unexplained, but a thing that worked in his brain like a cyclone, until he just got up and left, because he had to.'

'It was money, darling. His father and uncle were business partners, jewel traders. They just happened to be more ambitious than most, and Marco just happened to be taken prisoner, years later, after he returned to Venice, in a sea-battle against the Genoese. Sharing his cell was a man called Rusticello, a writer of romances and adventure stories. Marco gave him stories he couldn't resist.' Back in his rooms, Ben searched his bookshelves and took down a copy of the 'Travels'. 'And you're not the first to dream of him.' He began to quote from memory:

'In Xanadu did Kubla Khan
A stately pleasure-dome decree:
Where Alph, the sacred river ran . . .'

'Through caverns measureless to man
Down to a sunless sea . . .'

Amanda finished for him. 'I know that, but I thought Coleridge was just drugged when he wrote it.'

'He took opium for his medical condition. But when he fell asleep he had open on his lap Marco Polo's description of the Khan's summer palace at Shangtu. China was his drug.'

In his comfortable leathery rooms the embryonic don tenderly beguiled my sister, drawing tighter the web of her dream world. He did it in love, and unknowing. Afterwards, though, he said, 'I had a choice, and I was blind. I could have told her what Giles told her. Perhaps then she would have begun to dream of the Beatles or space flights.' But he knew, when he said it, that he did her wrong. So when Amanda asked again, 'Tell me about Marco Polo,' he told her calmly,

'In 1260, Maffeo and Nicolo Polo, jewel merchants, left

24

Constantinople, where they had a warehouse in the Venetian quarter, to try their luck further east. They sailed to Sudak, on the far shore of the Black Sea, and sold their gems. But once they were there, they thought they might as well go further. They fell in with some Tartars, whose Khanate of the Golden Horde controlled the Caucasus, Georgia, Armenia and Soviet Central Asia. They traded in Bolgara and Sarai, becoming wealthier by the week. War between the Golden Horde and the Ilkhanate of Persia prevented them from going back the way they had come. They had to go east, and back by a different route. But it didn't work: they found Bukhara, the finest city of Persia.' Ben opened the book and read slowly: ' "When the brothers came here, they could neither go on nor turn back. So they stayed for three years." Now Maffeo I suspect was a bachelor, or a widower, and a heartless old pirate, but Nicolo had a wife and young son back in Venice. What can a man be thinking of, sitting in an alien caravan city learning to speak Tartar while his son is fatherless half a world away? Well, perhaps his wife drove him out in the first place.'

'No, Ben,' Amanda interrupted, 'she is in my dreams too, a gentle delicate creature, like a captive bird.'

'The brothers went east and still further east. They reached Khan-balik, in China, and met Kublai Khan, the noblest of all rulers. They visited Kinsai, capital of the Sung Chinese, and returned to Europe, on the Khan's instructions, to collect a hundred great minds and a flask of oil from the Holy Sepulchre, both for his edification. Well, since they were in Jerusalem, and it was nearby, they went back to Venice. Nicolo found himself a widower. I wonder if he mourned. He took seventeen-year-old Marco back with him. They collected two friars, rather than a hundred, and set off north from Acre, into Armenia, where they lost the friars, east to Mosul, Baghdad, down to Hormuz on the Gulf, north again because the Persian ships could not be trusted, over the plains of Iran, the Pamir mountains, Balkh, Kashgar, Yarkand, the Desert of

25

Lop, Tangut, Cambaluc, Sugui, Khan-balik again. A three-year adventure.'

'And then?' Amanda wondered. 'What did they do in China?'

'That you must judge for yourself,' said Ben, handing her the book.

'All I want to know,' she mused, 'is why they did it. What was Marco looking for?'

Amanda, if only you had been content with the question alone! I believe Giles, in his way, tried to warn you—all of us—about the danger of answers. With Martha, in Santa Clara, I read the notes and memoirs over and over again, while Ben went out to hunt rabbits. Martha had the idea of preparing them for publication, if we could shape them into a coherent whole. After all, she said, Marco Polo did the same, to pass the time in a Genoese cell. And did Amanda deserve less from us, who had failed to make sense of her while she was alive? (Martha acts as duenna as well as wife; how could I ever be complacent while she is there to remind me of guilt?) I pointed out that Marco had the fortune to share his cell with a writer of adventure stories, at which dear Martha said she didn't think much of his style anyway. ('Dull as rain! Dry as a grasshopper's wings!' Has Giles said everything, so long before us?) But Amanda read the book Ben gave her, and saw its heart at once.

Reading her neat entries, those astonishing words inscribed with rounded matter-of-factness, we knew also where to look. I could see then how he stood on Mount Ararat, high in the windy grasslands of Armenia, the first and strangest of the Christian kingdoms; how he saw the natural oil wells spurt out of the sands at Baku. I could listen with him as he stood on the dusty quay at Hormuz, while all around a thousand tongues droned like the bees in the cloister bee-

26

hive at home. Watch as Maffeo argues, red-faced, with the saturnine Persian shipmen, and Nicolo inspects the frail trading ships, with their flimsy ropes to hold the planks together, instead of nails—they would have split the wood rather than making it fast. Follow as they turn north again, across the bitter salt Desert of Kerman to the cities of Khorassan and Badakshan, where young boys, the descendants of the Medes, ride before they can walk, on horses sired from Alexander's Bucephalus. Draw in the air of these cities whose domes and towers echo with their sonorous names, an air heavy with the aromas of spices: cinnamon, nutmeg, ginger, molasses, scented woods. In this land of mountains and plateaux, of hunting and hawking, the Venetians stayed a year while Marco recovered from an illness caught in Kerman. A gust of fresh mountain air rustles the page where he describes how his health was restored among the winds.

Leaving behind this place of dark-skinned sages they climb the highlands of Pamir. On the roof of the world they see great hairy sheep, whose horns are used by the tribesmen as drinking-bowls. They follow the Oxus as it twists back almost to its source; listen for the distant dash of waves that signals, deep in the lowlands, its apotheosis. The trail continues: Kashgar, Yarkand, Khotan, outlandish jade-bearing cities of regions unknown until 1860. The hidden Lake Lob, undiscovered until Russian explorers stumbled upon it in 1871. And at last to the wastes of the Gobi, the Desert of Lop, whose narrowest point stretches to a month's journey. Mountains and valleys of sand, brackish water: no beasts or birds. At night they cling together like blind men as the spirits laugh in their faces, luring them off the path with phantom cavalcades. Even in daylight the invisible gongs and drums resound across the empty miles, while Marco listens for the little bells on his horse's harness, and guesses at the true path.

On the great throne at Khan-balik the Great Khan Kublai waited for them, as if all in that miraculous land was frozen until Maffeo and Nicolo returned. Marco was befriended by the Khan, became his companion, envoy and governor of a province in Kara-Jang, superintending twenty-four cities. He travelled on the Khan's business in Cochin China, lived in frozen Tangut for three years. The Tartars became his friends, and even the native Cathayans: Chao Meng-fu, the artist who became the Khan's minister of war, and his wife, the Lady Kuan, who watched the shadows of the moon on rice-paper windows, and transposed those elusive outlines to paper in a few tantalizing strokes. So does Marco Polo with his pen: on every sparse page he leaves a thousand images undrawn; each must speak for years.

2

he marble floor absorbed her, opaque and impenetrable as the sea. Following a vein as it swirled and cavorted in the heart of the stone, she lost it in myriad others, until the whorls became a shape of their own: a circle, or square, a house, a tree, a face gradually disappearing, like the Cheshire Cat, before her eyes.

The great hollow of the cathedral was almost empty at this evening hour. Each visitor was lord of an airy vault the size of a small church. But they huddled together, as if the ancient empty space itself had power to beget. Amanda stood alone, the queen of a hundred marble flagstones. The cathedral reminded her of a refurbished Victorian railway station, remote, on a two-track line, serving gentle semi-suburban towns on late summer afternoons. Where was it? She could not be sure; its very familiarity confounded her. It seemed that she had been there before, but on that occasion, sidetracked by the frescoes and side-altars, she had hardly noticed the space. One could almost swim in it; fields of air captured and sanctified by the architect. She knelt on the sleek marble, and felt it surprisingly soft.

From behind a column a masked man approached, cloaked in dark wool, his head covered by a broad-brimmed hat. He stood before her and said,

'Come with me. I will show you how to climb into the space.' The voice was familiar but distant, as though a ventriloquist was throwing it from hundreds of miles away.

She asked him, 'Do I know you? I feel as though I should.'

29

'Well, do you? We don't have time to stand and think. The stars are waiting.' She followed him towards a side door, and up a flight of steps, then the climb started, up spiralling stone steps whose edges were smoothed by travellers' feet. They climbed in silence, so that she could hear his asthmatic breathing. Her temples began to throb; the air was hot and stuffy. They came to the top, and she followed him out on to the ledge. She saw that they were standing on a narrow balcony that stretched all the way around the inside of the dome. They were at the top! She felt the air now, making great circular sweeps of the inside of the cathedral.

'Do you feel the wind?' he asked her.

'Yes! I had no idea . . . isn't there a roof?' She looked up and saw that what she had taken, from down below, as the roof, was nothingness: the dome tapered and appeared to vault, but in fact the vault was the roofless sky and went on for ever. She clutched the railing and looked down. All she could see was space, marble-coloured, veined like a cheese. Then something occurred to her.

'Take off your hat. You shouldn't wear a hat in church.' Carefully he removed the wide-brimmed hat, and as he did she saw the little clasp pinned to the front. 'What's that?'

'My pilgrim's badge,' he said defensively. 'All pilgrims wear one, to show the shrine they are visiting, and the ones already visited.'

'And where are you going? Or have you been there already?'

He took off the mask and she saw that the voice belonged to Giles. He looked more hawkish than ever, the sandy sharp face appearing out of shapeless black wool.

'To seek the Grail,' he said, grinning. 'I have been looking everywhere for you.'

'Why? I don't know where it is.'

'Ah, Amanda, you are looking for it too. I need you to come with me.'

She laughed, and heard her own echo, given wings by

30

the wind, swirl around the dome.

'We thought you were in Venice.'

'We?'

'Ben and I. We're married, remember? We invited you to the wedding, but you didn't reply. We didn't know where to reach you.' But Giles stood perplexed, as if something did not quite fit his expectations, and he was unsure how to proceed. Then she saw another figure approach them. 'Look, here's Ben now. He'll be glad to see you.' Ben was walking slowly, as if counting the steps. He had framed his thick-set face with a beard.

'Amanda!' he called out, 'We must leave. This cannot be the place.'

'What place does he mean?' Giles asked her. The centre of the world, she thought. But instead of answering him she said,

'Darling, look who's here. It's Giles!'

'It doesn't matter. This is not the place. I have measured it carefully. At first I thought it could be, because of Gervase of Tilbury. But he was wrong; his calculations were off.'

'Who's Gervase of Tilbury?' Giles asked her. Ben was nearly upon them now.

'I don't know. Ben, darling, you're not paying attention. Look, I've found Giles!'

'Actually,' Giles said, pushing forward, 'I found her, she was kneeling on the marble down below.'

'It doesn't matter,' Ben said sadly, 'We must go on looking.' He raised his eyes and saw Giles for the first time. 'Why, hello! Are you looking for it too? Don't trust Gervase so readily!'

'Of course I'm looking for it. I didn't think you'd be coming too.'

'Well, why not? It was my idea.' Amanda suddenly realized the confusion, and explained,

'Darling, Giles is looking for the Holy Grail. He asked me to come with him.' But her words were lost in a gust of wind that

31

swooped down on them from the night overhead. It snatched at her dress, and she felt cold. The nameless space seemed to hang over her, thickened and heavy, as she interpreted for two dangerous rivals, neither speaking a tongue known to her. As she raised her eyes to the vault the stars descended into the space around them, and the whole empty night entered the dome. Both men were talking now, but she could not hear for the roaring in her ears.

While she ate breakfast Ben leant over the railings of the terrace. It was a fine view; they were lucky to have been lent the flat, in a fashionable part of Jerusalem. They were lucky to be there at all. Ben's successful research (as if research could be unsuccessful!) on medieval Jerusalem had borne fruit: a book, articles, lectures at conferences, and now, most luscious of all, a stay in Jerusalem, at the invitation of the British School, for one term. He taught a little, read a great deal and immersed himself with enthusiasm in the magical cauldron. Every day they took walks, crossing into Jordan (this was before the war of 1967) with the careless impunity of aliens. Ben, in any case, might have been unaware of states and treaties and international status: this was the centre of the earth, the pilgrim's goal, the golden city, the heavenly, figure and metaphor of a thousand sermons and dreams, Jerusalem! For Ben the city was history alive, for Amanda, it was art. She asked him,

'Who was Gervase of Tilbury?'

'A chronicler of the unlikely and fantastic. In the early thirteenth century.'

'Did he find the centre of the world?'

'This, my dear, is it. At least, on most maps after 1100.'

'I dreamt of us last night. You were looking for the centre of the world. In a cathedral.'

'Where?'

32

'I'm not sure.' She concentrated on restoring the scraps of her nightly existence. 'It was a vast cathedral, with a high dome. There was a lot of marble everywhere, but I don't remember too much else about it. We went up into the dome, somehow—at least, I did, and you were already there.'

'Did you recognize the cathedral? Had you been there before, in real life?' She paused. How could she tell? One forgot cathedrals, as they merged into set patterns. That was the cathedral where it rained and we went inside to shelter; that was the one where we had the awful hotel, or where we got lost and drove around aimlessly for hours. But the cathedrals in dreams had no sharp outlines, such as in a photograph. You remembered the touch of a particular stone, or the gargoyle on a capital, and at once you were inside the soft belly of the memory, feeling again the taste of sleep in your mouth.

'I had been there before. But now it was different. The night came right inside the building. There was no roof. We could see the stars among us.'

Ben, whose nature it was to accept the improbable, did not question this.

'And what happened?'

'I met Giles there.'

At this he started violently. He had never appeared in her dreams before; they had not seen him for a few years.

'He was wearing a long black cloak,' she went on, 'he told me he was looking for the Holy Grail.'

Ben believed in her dreams. If she dreamt something of a person, it was likely to be true, in some sense.

The cathedral, as he felt it should, puzzled him. It probably wasn't here in Jerusalem—it did not sound like the Holy Sepulchre, or the Russian Cathedral, or the Armenian, or St. George's, the incongruous misplaced Anglican Cathedral. Ben, typically, was treating her dreams as if they were the precise documents of night-time voyages. They became, like his manuscripts, arguments, cases, evidence. But Amanda

33

had no thesis to present, and asked for no judgment. Giles would have understood better.

Giles—in this teeming navel, amid jostling head-dresses and crazy plethora of beards, we four came together again. For, I should explain, I too was a Jerusalem resident. Although Ben never said it, and Amanda did, I think I was partly the reason they came. We had seen little of each other since their marriage. Ben was ensconced at Oxford with Amanda; I was sent abroad by the Foreign Office as soon as my training was over, to a succession of dull stand-in posts. The Jerusalem posting was an unlikely adventure for me: a raw cutting edge, the old hands said, an impossible field sown with bitter seeds, from which sprang up armed men fiercer than ever Jason faced. What was I to make of the warm, insane splendour of this city? Of horizons crammed with minarets and crosses, of round-topped mosques, and the square little churches of forgotten ancient denominations, of termite streets, stinking ancient cobbles laden with the flotsam of centuries? I fell in love; what else could I have done?

I had already been there for eight months when Ben and Amanda came. We spent a lot of our time together, attending the same embassy functions. We crossed the frontier as if it were a county border, we enjoyed the feeling of tense armed guards, racial division, we even felt a reflected importance. At a consular party one night, the excuse for which I have forgotten, the Intelligence Head, Saddle, whom I knew slightly, called me over. Gravely dropping cubes of ice in his wine and stirring the mixture, he whispered, 'I've been meaning to talk to you—alone.'

'Well, this is a good time.' I was bored and there was nobody around. 'But why don't you talk properly. No one will overhear.'

'Security. I've had a disturbing report about one of our nationals. He has been observed in conversation with known PLO members, or contacts.'

The man pressed himself uncomfortably close, in that

34

confined space. I was already regretting my mistake.

'Here in Jerusalem?'

'On the other side, naturally. And probably elsewhere,' he added with menace.

'Why are you telling me?'

We had moved imperceptibly to the edge of the crowded room, near to the window. I was grateful for the breeze. The night outside enticed me like a bazaar.

'You're in the Press Attaché's office. We don't want this to get out.'

'Why should it? Who is he, anyway? An industrialist? He's probably trying to buy protection for an investment—it doesn't mean he's a terrorist.'

'He's a writer,' Saddle said with scorn. 'Giles Devereux— you've heard of him.' Oh, I had, though not from him for years now. We never quite forgave him for the pseudonym. It was like him and unlike him at the same time. I suppose Saddle took my surprise, when he mentioned the name, as natural. Giles was fairly well known by then.

'Playing at being Byron, perhaps?' I suggested lightly. Saddle looked at me with suspicion. He had little imagination. 'I suppose the Israelis know?'

'Of course. If we know, they know.' Saddle knew, I reflected, because the Israelis had told him. It was hard to picture the man accumulating his information on his own initiative. I had unlikely visions of him, pale-faced, slightly pompous, trampling the Jerusalem streets in his broad-rimmed hat. Did this man know where Giles could be found? I could hardly ask him, though the temptation was strong. Suddenly I had to see Giles again, and the thin sour face that jumped spontaneously into life, illustrating absurd pronouncements. Where in Jerusalem was he? Did he know I was here, and the others? I left Saddle and fetched another drink, but the indolent Foreign Office veneer had become stale. I went instead to my office and telephoned Ben. He had been working late.

35

'What is it, Alex? I'm too tired to go out now, and Amanda's asleep.'

'I've just heard news. Giles is in Jerusalem!' There was a long silence at the other end of the line. 'Did you hear me, Ben?'

'I heard you. What is he doing here? And why now, of all times?'

'What's the matter? Don't you want to see him? When was the last time?' My voice sounded on the brink of hysteria.

'Oh, I don't know. Yes, I suppose so. I can't explain, Alex. Amanda dreamt of him the other night. They were in a cathedral dome, of all places. He was being weird, as usual. You know those dreams. They're so . . . intense. I can't cope with Giles now.' Just that: not even any interest. It was a warning, that brief dismembered exchange. The path had forked, and Ben tried to guide us down one path; but we took the other, perversely. But it was more difficult than that—we had no idea of his purpose.

I did not tell Ben what Saddle had told me. But I told Amanda, perhaps because she was my sister. While Ben was teaching, we met in the Old City. I guided her towards the great Temple compound where the Golden Dome shines on the whole city, but she said she would rather see something quieter, so we wandered through the Armenian quarter. It was midday, and there were few people around. We paid our entrance money for the Armenian museum, inside the estate of the monastery of St. James, and sat in the peaceful courtyard. From the first-floor terrace we could see Mount Zion lumbering just behind the walls of the city. The walls, wheat-yellow now, would glow orange later. The colour was the same as the wooden boards used to support an old decaying house I had passed every day on my way to school, half a lifetime ago, after the rain had been on them all day. Amanda said absently 'Marco Polo travelled through Armenia on his way to China.'

36

'Do you still dream of him?' I was surprised. I suppose I had thought that merely a phase of unusual longevity.

'Oh, yes. But I don't talk about it so much. I think it irritates Ben.' Only here, where she was surrounded by ghosts, did Marco reappear.

'Did he spend time in Jerusalem?' (I was the most ignorant of all of us about him; I am neither artist nor historian nor dreamer.)

'Yes, to collect some of the oil from the never-dying lamp at the Holy Sepulchre. Kublai Khan had requested it.' She recited it not as if from a text committed to memory, but almost from the tangible memory itself. I was becoming dreamy myself in the tender heat. It was spring; hot only if you were exerting yourself. Here, in this mausoleum to a land no longer considered extant, whose only population consisted of priests and tiny frail ladies, our English jarred in alien air. Ben could do some research on Marco Polo, I thought idly. It would please Amanda, and it might even be exciting. Research was a great mystery, but a mystery that flew scholars hundreds, thousands of miles to examine churches and manuscripts. If Jerusalem, why not further? Who had followed Marco every step of the way across Asia? My wild ignorance soared; Armenia was a good place for dreaming. There were small fir trees in the courtyard below, and strange herbs whose scent I did not recognize. Perhaps the unreality of our presence in Jerusalem, Jordan, infected me. She was talking about Giles now.

'So you have no clues about where he might be?'

'Saddle wouldn't tell me; I have no business knowing, after all. I expect he's been spotted in a bar being rowdy.' I said it to allay her anxieties, without believing it.

'Terrorism is too earthly for Giles,' she said. I did not mention simpler fears. I dreaded the day when Saddle might approach me in a corridor and say, 'That fellow in East Jerusalem—it's drug-smuggling, after all. We've got him, or rather the Jordanian police has. Bad news for his career.'

37

Perhaps Ben suspected the same; it would explain his coolness.

'He could be within this half square mile.' Sitting alone in a filthy café watching the old men play backgammon, in fading robes that showed cracked bony legs, drawing on hookah pipes. Or lost in a decaying alley, among these people of infinite variety and prejudice. While he wandered alone and tactless, thousand-year-old quarrels and genetically-inherited hatreds boiled. Suddenly Jerusalem seemed just the place for him.

'Where else would Giles be but in the Golden City?' I said.

Afterwards we stood conspicuous at the back of the dark Armenian church while cone-hatted priests, black-clad, chanted impossible syllables. Amanda, who had not been there before, was fascinated by the little women who brought their own folding stools to perch on. There were no seats inside the church, only dense oriental carpets. From the ceiling and suspended between pillars hung chains, ornamented with Christmas decorations of complex intricacy. In the uncertain light they shimmered like candles. Now, I am told, tourists wander in every afternoon and stare in bewilderment; when I knew it, the cathedral seemed like a garden enclosed. I never knew a word of Armenian, nor did Amanda, yet it was as if a distant aroma settled on us, perhaps the gentlest whiff of an Eastern caravan, of ginger and cinnamon and sandalwood. But with Amanda, you could never quite tell how ideas came to her. Maybe she knew already where her Grail-quest would take her. Mine, I think, could have taken me the same way, but at that time I was looking for Giles, and so I came to follow Martha.

Saddle, that dull wasp of a man, brought us together unwittingly. He irritated me more because of what he knew, or thought he knew, of Giles, than for any trait of his character. Childishly, since he had never again alluded to him, I began to follow the spy. When he left the Consulate, I trailed behind him; I sat on benches in parks, in bars across the street, I took meaningless bus journeys through West Jerusalem. A pattern emerged, for Saddle had the routine of any civil servant. He favoured a café a stone's throw from the Jaffa Gate, in sight of the border. From the other side of the road, at first, I began to notice the young woman who was invariably sitting in the café whenever Saddle was there. Initially I took her for a sabra—a native of the land; she wore dark glasses against a dark complexion. She was always alone, and never spoke except to the barman. After a few days I ventured into the café itself, heedless that Saddle might notice me. But in any case I was doing nothing wrong; and he was working his was through Hardy, oblivious to others. It was she who spoke to me first. She was writing a letter, but ran out of ink.

'Would you have a pen you could lend me until your drink is finished?' she asked, with no trace of an accent. The voice was pure, cool Home Counties.

'I'm afraid not,' I lied. 'But I could keep you company instead.' Not normally bold, I surprised myself, but not, apparently, her. I suppose in London she would have dismissed me curtly.

She said, simply, 'Yes.'

It was a calm face; it still is, whatever her mood. There is the same equipoise in her eyes as Amanda had, but behind Martha's are still pools, reserves of passion never used—and behind Amanda's, I think, were oceans and galaxies.

'I have seen you here often. Do you work nearby?'

'I used to.' She paused a few moments, then, smiling, inclined her head in Saddle's direction. 'You see that man? I am following him.'

'You are?' Immediately I thought: Giles, you should be here; this cries out for you.

'He works at the British Consulate,' she went on.

'So do I.'

'Of course you do,' she said, still smiling. 'Why else would an Englishman be living in Jerusalem?'

39

'Oh, I might be a tour guide. Or an archaeologist.'

'I think not a tour guide,' she mused. 'And if you were an archaeologist, I would know you. There aren't so many about. My fiancé is one.' I had noticed the ring on her left hand but, perversely, it had given me some confidence. There can be safety in constraints so clearly defined. She said, 'Your colleague is M.I.6, isn't he?'

'He is? I didn't know we had any,' I said glibly. She raised her eyebrows, patronized me.

'In Jerusalem? Really?'

'What do you want from him?'

'Can I tell you, d'you think?' she wondered slowly. 'No, not today.'

She finished her drink and we parted. The whole short scene, so alien to my experience, had been like a turn on an ice-rink. I had fallen at the end, but there was the promise of more—'not today.'

Ben would surely know her fiancé, if he taught at Jerusalem. He might even have met her, at a reception or a lecture. But no, she said, the next afternoon, they had never met, and her fiancé did not teach; he had worked for the Government's Department of Museums and Antiquities. Was he English? (I cursed myself for having probed, a moment later.)

'He is a Palestinian,' she said. Almost immediately, she leaned forwards and said quietly, 'I need your help. I'm only asking because you work at the Consulate. He disappeared a fortnight ago. I've heard nothing since.'

'Why don't you go to the police?' I asked.

'He's a Palestinian,' she said again, and I understood what she meant; he supported the PLO.

'I'm in the Press Office. I don't know how to find people who disappear.' My hand, I think, was shaking, though she was perfectly calm.

'He does,' she said, nodding at Saddle, hunched over the Wessex countryside in a corner of the café.

40

'You have to tell me more.' She rested level grey eyes on mine, but not in appeal. I insisted, 'You have to trust me, if you want my help! And you must understand, there may be nothing we can do. As a matter of fact, I'm looking for someone myself—a friend of mine from England.'

'He has also disappeared?'

'No. But Saddle told me—without knowing he was my friend—that he'd been seen here, with . . . undesirables.'

'Like Mansur?' she said ironically.

'We could team up in this—we'd do much better working together, after all—we could both follow him.' Her eyes never left mine while I gabbled this foolishness. She knew perfectly well, of course, that I cared as little about this Mansur as she did about Giles. But she said, 'Meet me tomorrow, Friday evening, I'll be in the procession, on the Via Dolorosa.' Every Friday the Franciscans held a procession in memory of Jesus's last progress, to the place of his crucifixion. It was a good place; the area was always packed with tourists. I should have been excited, that evening, but Martha's own calmness dampened me. She has this quality still, of making me seem a child.

It was my good fortune to run across Saddle as I left the Consulate the next day. He asked me to join him for a drink; suspecting he had further word of Giles, I acquiesced. By some pre-ordained harmony he led me in exactly the opposite direction from his normal route. Near the Post Office we turned towards the frontier, and once across it he led me down the Nablus Road, north-east. Just outside the American Colony we entered the Tomb of the Kings, an empty and unprepossessing quarry. He spoke, almost for the first time: 'Go down the steps.'

No one saw us descend those neolithic stone steps. At the bottom was a complex of shallow caves, facing the street but well below street level. One narrow entrance leads into the tombs. Broken pillars and pediments lay scattered about.

'What's this all about, Saddle? Why are we here?'

He had reached into the pocket of his cream-coloured blazer; I instantly thought it was to pull out a gun, but I was not so important; it was only a pair of dark glasses. He walked slowly towards me, the sun behind his head, framed against the ancient rubble.

'Let's not play around, Alex. This isn't all your fault; you're young. What has Mansur's woman been telling you?'

'Who? I don't follow you.' This was true; I had never suspected Saddle might know what I did. I was indignant, too. The despised Saddle had become a sudden threat.

'Bloody fool! Do you suppose you could sit talking to her unnoticed? While I was in the same café?' He reached forward and grabbed the lapels of my jacket. 'Didn't it occur to you that I might be watching her? You idiot!'

'I had no idea! She asked me to get you to help her—she wanted me to approach you on her behalf.'

'Innocent!' He thrust me backwards, letting me go so that I staggered into the wall.

'It was a mistake, Saddle. I just got talking to her. She just mentioned her fiancé was missing— that's all.'

He seemed to have calmed a little, if ever he had been angry. Surely a spy generated the passion he needed coldly, at his own leisure, preparing for these moments well in advance, alone in darkened rooms.

'I can believe it of you. Your naïvety might save you. What did she say about him?'

'Nothing. Just that he was an archaeologist—and that he had disappeared, two weeks ago.'

'Archaeologist!' Saddle sneered. 'The Israelis have been on to him for months. That girl tried to pass him off as an archaeologist? He's a terrorist, Alex—in the same club as your author friend!'

'How did you know about Giles?' I asked in shock.

'That you're a friend of his? It's easily done.' But he had misunderstood me. Our friendship had never been hidden; here was a thing that was. Saddle took out a handkerchief and

42

handed it to me; I had grazed my forehead on the rocks. 'Nothing need happen to you, you realize. You just got yourself into trouble—put it down to youth. Now you have to help us. I don't suppose I have to spell out the alternative,' he leered. I was still dumb, so he said, putting his face closer, 'The choice is yours, Alex. Prosecution, disgrace, prison. Or a discreet transfer—as soon as things here are cleared up.' I had never noticed before how unsavoury that yellow-tinged complexion was, like butter that has been left out too long.

'Transfer from Jerusalem?' I whispered.

'Don't you see what you have done? What damage, to yourself?' He paused, and explained, as if to a child. 'Mansur, or whatever his real name is, is in Cairo, with friends from the PLO. When he comes back, his briefcase will be full of banknotes, and, more incriminating, letters. You've been seen talking to his girlfriend; you're implicated.'

'And Martha?'

'She is our concern, as a British national. That is where you can still redeem yourself.'

'She knows nothing of this—I'm sure of it.'

Saddle looked at me in astonishment, as if I had told him she were a countess travelling incognito, or a world-famous ballerina.

'Is that what she told you?' he sneered. 'How often have you met? And do you suppose Mansur never told her anything?' But, curiously, I knew he was wrong. In my confusion, this thing remained clear; Martha's eyes are not dead, but nor do they lie. A clear pool can hide no pebbles.

'What do you want me to do?' I asked.

'Since you're so far in, you can make yourself useful. Mansur we can leave to the Israelis; Martha Pollock is your responsibility. Stay close to her. If she leaves town, I want to know. If she needs money, I want to know. Find out who her friends are. I will ask for regular accounts.' The exchange had exhausted him; sweat dripped from his neck down to the collar. It was a warm evening, for spring.

43

'I'm supposed to meet her tonight. Now, in fact.'

'Then go. You will hear from me tomorrow.'

It seemed strange, to walk away free from that place. The whole encounter had lasted only minutes. It could have been anywhere—why amongst those redundant caves? Why not a dark side-street, or even his office? He must have used the place before, to bully and terrify others. Perhaps he had even killed there. I thought of the awkward small talk, ice cubes stirred in white wine. The real Saddle, grimy and sweating, held court, with a kind of poetic aptness, in the empty tombs of biblical kings.

Ben grieves for the lost sense of earth's harmony! Life was once wholly integrated, he says; nothing that was perceptible happened without relation to its place in this order, or without a direct vertical link to another more perfect order. Like the ecology of a pond, I always want to say. Sometimes a snatch of an event, like a half-caught tune, will open up the marvellous skein of paths, forking again and again to eternity, if only for a moment. A line from Amanda's notebook: The space of a hundred heartbeats alters a whole chain of happenings—but only for those who see in a horizontal sequence. Somehow I think this is what Ben is saying, but I am not sure.

After leaving Saddle I plunged into the Old City, through the crowded Damascus Gate. I kept to the main thoroughfares, swimming with Arab women carrying baskets on their heads, sellers of sweets and fruit blocking doorways, boys chasing cats with high-pitched yells, ancient vehicles backing heedlessly into gutters. The side-streets I usually took, emptier of this chaos, terrified me now. I stumbled through the *suq* as if into an oasis: noise and colour were calming; drowning thoughts. Where was Martha? From time to time I thought I saw her ahead of me, but lost her in the turmoil. At the Via Dolorosa, the Franciscans' procession blocked the way. The thin Latin chant carved a space in air already thick with syllables. With impervious grace the bedraggled faithful of five continents, tourists mostly, followed the path of Jesus, led by the brown-robed monks. Traffic does not stop for the procession; rather it makes those narrow cobbled streets impassable as it winds its way past the stations of the cross, to end in the Holy Sepulchre itself. Jerusalem has changed little in this respect since that first lonely walk: the busy shouting, staring Arabs are as oblivious now, as most of Jerusalem must then have been.

Surely that was Martha, near the head of the procession, in a light green dress and straw hat. She was moving, but seemed perfect and still in the commotion. I shouted but could not reach her. A smiling Japanese beside me swung his bandolier of cameras against my ribs. At every stop, while the 'Ave Maria' was sung, I slipped under arms and between bodies, closer to the front, but never quickly enough, before the train started moving again. In the hot Jerusalem sun that baked skins and bricks orange-gold, she was a cool, pale Madonna, painted in pastel shades. This jolting, noisy, whirling procession came to be, suddenly, the whole of things, swallowing in its every movement, its stopping and starting and chanting, the sum of the confused events and thoughts that chased each other around my brain. I felt as though something were slipping between my limp fingers. Amidst the strangers whose rank sweat was in my nostrils I perceived Martha, Saddle, Amanda, Giles, even the unknown Mansur. We followed one another oblivious, separated by anonymous others, linked in a trembling chain, crossed at each link by other haphazard chains, so that the whole makeshift memorial became a dance of souls joined, a giant cat's cradle spun by arbitrary unknown hands. A crazed

45

memory—from God knows what conversation—of the world-soul attached itself, like a limpet, a living thing, to my mind: all our souls the residue of a great wind infusing the tangible universe, like a viscous liquid.

The leaders of the procession were turning now, and climbing steps that would take them to the precinct of the Coptic monastery. Martha climbed too, as if on an escalator. Her head was tilted slightly to one side, and I noticed, watching helplessly and somehow seeing for the first time, that she was beautiful. Not in any clear-cut way, but in perfect freshness of form. Against the grubby walls and writhing figures she shone translucent, as if from a fresco. Then, that was enough for me; the warmth came later, as with a rare plant that yields its aroma only when pressed. I think that, if I had been close enough to touch her, my hand would have passed through her body. As I stood watching, I was shoved aside and lost my place. And suddenly the spell was broken, and I was cut out of the chain, and it had closed over me, as if I had never been a part of it. A voice, calling out, broke it:

'Alex! Over here!' Thin-lipped and square, Ben stood apart. 'What luck, to find you here! I didn't know you followed the procession.'

'I got caught up in it somehow,' I explained.

'What's happened to you?' He had noticed the cut on my head, and torn sleeve, powdered with ancient dust. I told him I would explain later, but I do not think he could have heard. We were trying to speak over the roaring ocean. The noise seemed to be increasing, and more people were being sucked into it, from all around me. Ben took my arm and steered me away, and turning back I had a vague impression of something like an earthquake, that had thrown up bodies upon each other like rocks and concrete. Ben was shouting, 'What's going on? What in hell is going on?' I tore myself free and found a doorway to shelter in. 'Something's collapsed, Alex! On top of the procession! That stairway—look!'

As the crowd cleared we could see crumbling stones

46

hanging free, and a gap in the centuries-old wall. About half of the procession had passed beyond the stairs, but those unfortunates under whom it had crumbled had fallen on the stragglers below, crushing them in the already packed and stinking street. Now, with amazing speed, by-standers were prising boulders and limbs free. Ben charged into the midst of the panic to help. I leant against the doorway; I felt I would pass out. The disaster was less serious than it had looked in the instant of happening; only a few people had been trapped by rocks, and it seemed no one had been completely buried. Watching it, detached, I shook uncontrollably. Then Ben came back, dragging a body by its arms. A seller of souvenirs had the lower half. Before they spoke, I saw the faded cream blazer, the battered fedora. The suddenness had taken poor Saddle by surprise, too; he had not had time to cry out before he was crushed by the weight of falling bodies. But he had not suffocated. A great stone had caught the side of his head, and laid it open. He died with his grimy secrets untold; they were smashed in that horrible skull. Ben must have supposed my insane, frightened stare to be the natural shock of seeing death so close. He almost had to carry me home.

At the elegant flat Amanda was waiting with iced drinks. Even as I sat down I could see that she had something to say, but Ben had begun to talk about the disaster. With Amanda, anyway, it was not as with other people: if she had something to say we were as likely never to hear it. But I always knew when there was something below the surface.

'Sixteenth-century stonework!' Ben exclaimed, 'it should have lasted forever. Damned lucky there were so few hurt.'

'Was anyone killed?' Amanda asked.

'One man, as far as I could tell. A European, in a cream suit.'

'His name was Saddle,' I said wearily. It would come out

47

eventually, so there was no point in feigning ignorance. But I was unprepared for Amanda's startled reaction.

'Did you say Saddle?' she had jumped up in excitement.

'Yes. He was the Intelligence man at the Consulate. Do you know him?'

'Only vicariously. Giles was the one who knew him.'

'Giles? Have you seen Giles?' I almost shouted. 'When? Today? It's important, Amanda!'

'Yes, I know. He came here, a few hours ago. I don't know how he found out the address—or even that we were in Jerusalem. He looked pretty shabby, but he was the same as ever. I was so pleased to see him that I only half-listened to what he said.' Ben, who had been pouring a drink, shook his head slowly, as if bestowing profound disapproval on the events of the afternoon. Spies, collapsing walls, mysterious reappearing friends: against the firm clear outlines of his manuscripts these were bright, unreal baubles.

'What is he doing in Jerusalem?'

'Working on a new book, to be set here. But he had got into some kind of trouble; I'm not sure how. He said this man Saddle had become suspicious and started following him. One day he cornered him in the Old City, and threatened him.'

'What had Giles been doing?' I asked.

'He called it research. He seemed to know a lot of Arabs.'

'Saddle thought he was running guns—or something—for the PLO,' I said baldly. 'He told me so, just a few hours ago.' It seemed days. It was hard even to picture Saddle now, as we sat talking about him. That vulpine face dissolved into split images, like a jigsaw puzzle. Had he ever really been alive?

Ben interrupted with a howl of laughter, 'Giles? A PLO agent? Ha! What a novel that would make!'

'Of course, he wasn't anything of the kind really,' I explained. 'But Saddle had him mixed up with some other business. Did he say where he was going, Amanda?'

48

'He just said he had to leave before this man Saddle got to him.'

'But where? Now that Saddle's dead, he might not have to go.'

'He only said, East.' Amanda was protecting Giles, not from enemies now, but from the unbelief of friends. 'It was just like in my dream: he told me he had to follow the path of the Grail. I understood what he meant. Suddenly, it became clear. He is looking for the earthly paradise. That's why he has to go East.'

Ben looked up suddenly, a hawkish gleam in his eye. 'The terrestrial paradise,' he murmured. 'Who would have thought it? Yet there it is—someone is still trying, after all these years.'

At the time I did not understand his words, and I hardly tried to unravel them. I lost whatever meaning Amanda hinted at in the practicalities. Did Giles leave an address or a telephone number where he could be contacted, I asked her. She handed me a number, and a name: Mansur.

'Who is Mansur?' I asked in excitement. 'What did Giles say about Mansur?' But Amanda did not know: he had mentioned no other name, and she had not looked at the paper with the number written on it. The effort required to decipher this mystery frustrated me. This was Saddle's world, not mine. Was this just coincidence? Had Giles adopted the name as a cover for his activities? He would fool no one; he was as Anglo-Saxon as anyone could be. Then, I reasoned irrationally, it could only be Martha's Mansur—as if there were not thousands within those few square yards! Did Giles know Mansur? Then I was closer then ever to Martha! But Saddle, then, was right after all; Giles must be involved with the PLO. I stood helpless and light-headed, as if plunged involuntarily into the middle of an unknown examination-hall.

Ben said, 'We'd better try the number.' The telephone was in their bedroom; he came back a few minutes later to say, 'No reply. Perhaps he has left already.'

49

'Who else would have known—or suspected—about Giles?' Amanda asked.

'I don't know. There isn't much of a staff here, you know. Saddle worked mainly on his own. Of course there will be records, I should think. But he hadn't got far in his investigations.'

'You may have to destroy whatever records there are,' Ben said.

'Oh, fine! Do you realize what that would mean, if I were caught? On top of the trouble I'm already in?'

'That trouble lasted only as long as Saddle was alive,' Ben pointed out, 'unless he had already opened a file on you; in which case it would be in your own interests to destroy it.' Ben's logic allowed for no argument. he was stirred now—I think the terrestrial paradise had woken him, drawn him from the fringes. 'Giles needs help. You know what an idiot he is when he gets an idea into his head. And he really doesn't know about paradise, though he thinks he does. What an opportunity, if I could get to him!'

Amanda interrupted his rambling: 'There's something else, Alex. A woman came here to see you, this afternoon. She left a message—she won't be able to make tonight's meeting.'

'Martha,' I said. It had to be her. In my confusion I had forgotten our meeting anyway.

'Martha Pollock,' Amanda confirmed. 'She seemed a nice girl. You didn't tell me about her.'

'Did she say why she couldn't make it?'

'She's leaving for Cairo tonight. She said she was flying via Athens.' Martha too, caught out by the sudden hideous death of Saddle. Briefly and tentatively he had linked us together in his web; now that he was gone, could we untangle ourselves?

'Martha is engaged to a Palestinian called Mansur,' I explained. 'Saddle thought he was in Cairo, in a PLO safehouse. But Martha didn't know that—I was going to tell her tonight.'

'Unless Mansur was able to contact her himself,' Ben

50

suggested. But we all knew how unlikely that was; we were driven to the same mad thought, perhaps because it had a lurid and repellent fascination: Giles was Mansur. We talked uselessly for a few more hours, convincing ourselves that the unspoken thought could not be true. When I walked home later I had drunk too much, but I do not think it was that that made me stagger in the street and retch violently into the gutter.

Saddle's accidental death was not investigated by the police; his place as Second Secretary was filled by a newcomer from London, and soon, as the anxious days yielded no further horrors, and I was neither dismissed nor disciplined, both he and Mansur faded like old photographs. If I should have been suspicious that Saddle appeared to have committed nothing of his investigations to file or code, I was too relieved to notice. Weeks later, a letter arrived from Martha: she and Mansur had split up; he would remain in Cairo and she return to England, but first she would go back to Jerusalem, and she looked forward to seeing me again. I looked forward to it too, for whenever I looked backwards I was struck by a buzzing little doubt, shifting almost imperceptibly among the memory of events that were becoming ever more vague. My life until that year had followed a predictable and pleasant pattern, unwritten but decreed by generations of comfortable Englishmen. I encountered nothing whose shape I did not recognize or whose purpose I could not discern. But Jerusalem demanded responses that fell outside my experience and the reservoir of ancestral wisdom. Strands converged there, that years later I was still unable to separate.

3

Untouched, it seemed, by the people outside them, Amanda's dreams began to claim her as their own. We fleshly creatures became shadows flickering on the walls, and the nightly journeys encroached into daylight.

In her dreams, the young Venetian sat motionless among gaily-coloured cushions before the Great Khan, like a swan on its bank of feathers. They were playing chess. Marco sat cross-legged in the Tartar fashion. His uncle Maffeo laughed at him for it, and others he had adopted: Marco resembled nothing but a Latin (and more a German or Bohemian, if the truth be known, with his sharp face and thin sandy hair); his expressive gestures were Venetian, but already he spoke a Tartar that was understood here, and behaved at table like a native. Maffeo would never adapt; he was too old and set in his ways. 'A lifetime of travelling, young Marco,' he said; 'how can I be all kinds of men, wherever I happen to be? They know me here, and if I seem a curiosity, well, at least they honour their guests.' Yes, Marco thought, guests are honoured but a guest is ever an exile. Some men see the same sky in Venice and in Cathay; well, for me the sky will never be enough. He recalled his father explaining to an old acquaintance, back in Venice, 'The same gems and precious stones are coveted, from Ireland to Cathay. We are jewel-merchants, therefore, for us, all men are the same. We understand the desire and the love for beautiful objects, and so we understand all men.' This came to Marco suddenly: they understand, father and uncle, because they are content to look only so far. I, who speak better Tartar than either and am learning Chinese in secret, I who enjoy their mare's milk and ride with them to the hunt, I look further than they.

Kublai the Great Khan looked up from the chess game and said softly, his small old head cocked to the side, 'Tell me about your journey.'

'Great Khan, I have told you many times already.'

'But each time there are new things, and new people. Each story has many re-tellings.' The Great Khan's voice was still deep, despite his age, which made some men's breath whistle and crack, but it had none of the roughness of his people. The head reminded Marco of an old withering fruit, puckered in many places, giving him an amusing air. He wore a thin pointed beard which was trimmed every day. It had been thicker when he was in his prime, but before Marco it drooped pitifully. The magnificent Tartar body, compact and square, was still strong enough to hunt with leopards. He needed no support when he walked, except on those feast nights when he took too much 'koumiss' to drink, and then there was no one who did not sometimes need to lean on a shoulder or grasp a supporting arm. But it was the Great Khan's eyes that set him apart. They were black and smouldered like a molten metal, or, Marco thought, like jet. Even when the face was at rest, the eyes moved constantly. Marco had seen them administer harsh punishment, beat men into submission. But when he faced them they bestowed kindness and wisdom, or, as now, requested stories.

'In my youth,' the Great Khan said, 'the many peoples of the world and their customs hardly existed for me. I rode with the horde—and I was the finest rider in my cohort. In middle age, when I assumed the kingship, my interest extended only so far as those who were still a threat. For the rest, their taxes

53

and their loyalty in war were enough. Now I am old, and the government is secure enough with my sons and barons. Wise men have said that in old age men become children again, and children, as you know, love to hear tales and stories from all parts of the world.'

'When I was a boy,' Marco mused, 'I heard such tales at the knee of my father's Tartar servant. He bought him in the market at Constantinople, and brought him back to our home in Venice.' Marco knew that the reason for his place in the Great Khan's esteem was that he posed no threat, and desired nothing that he could bestow. He talked with this sturdy old man more freely than with his acquaintances in his distant home, or with the father who had missed his formative years. He would now have hissed at him to be silent; surely he offended the Great Khan by mentioning the slave he, a mere merchant, had made of the warrior from the Khan's own people. But Kublai was beyond such offence, which might have angered one of his barons. The small figure seated on his cushions in front of the chess board could summon at a whim the most powerful army in the world, tens of thousands of horsemen with bows and axes, the hordes of hell. In his domain were empires and kingdoms once independent, duchies and cities of gold, cities on junks and cities on stilts. Into them flowed rivers of precious commodities, rare spices from the islands to the south, cloths and furs, carved and scented woods from India, jade and topaz, amethyst and diamonds and rubies brought by such as Marco's father, fabulous beasts, monkeys and leopards and speaking birds of many colours. Caravans of camels and mules staggered under the volume of the riches that trailed in and out of his cities each day; ships were loaded until they sat dangerously low in the water. Could such a man, possessing all this, be offended? Marco thought: it is the way of little men, like myself or the Doge of Venice, to take offence at another's words. But the Great Khan is beyond this because, having everything it is possible to own, he can be touched by no man,

54

and since he knows himself beyond each man's power, he knows their words too are meaningless.

The Great Khan said, 'My empires are unknown to me. With every journey you take, and every story you tell, the frontiers must contract for you, but for me they expand. Things seen are always smaller than when imagined.'

'But, Great Khan, as you have yourself said, there are many ways of telling the same thing. Suppose we were to sit here talking for twenty years; I could then draw for you the circumference of your empires, and they would become as familiar to you as they have become for me. After another twenty years you would begin to pick out from the diversity, like spots of the same colour on a silk screen, the subtle similarities between one city and another, between Kinsai and Karakorum, between Kashgar and Lahore, the Desert of Lop and the waving grasslands of Pamir. After yet another twenty years, you would notice that there are more similarities than differences. Your empires would have contracted for you, and become only the measure of sameness, according to various set patterns. Only the dog-headed islanders of Andaman would elude the remorseless pattern. And maybe after another twenty years even they would find a place next to the men of Cathay. When a man recognizes what he sees, the whole world can be reduced in this way, perhaps to one pattern.'

'When a man has reached my years, Marco, a single stretch of twenty years is an infinity,' the Great Khan smiled. 'Speak, and do not worry about reducing my empires.'

But Marco thought, what would happen if we were indeed to continue to talk and contract reality? He assumed for a moment that the years passed by with no effect to their ages: would it be possible to reduce the vast lands of the Great Khan, from the Volga to the Encircling Sea, not merely to one set of patterns or themes, but to a single pattern? What form would it take? Surely the form of the man telling the story, the shape of his perceptions. Suppose he noticed that in each city

55

of the empire what was most reducible to a universal similarity was the method of waste disposal, or the peculiar angle of a beggar's eyebrows, or the rush matting inside a barber's shop. The empires of the Great Khan become the phenomenon perceived by one man, become one man himself. But not simply one man, because for each man who has travelled and can give the same account, the perception and thus the pattern would differ slightly. Each man is a microcosm of the vast lands of the Great Khan. But this means, Marco realized, that there is not one single empire or conglomerate of empires ruled by the Great Khan but tens of thousands, as many as there are men to see them. Which of these is the real one, which contains the cities and countries to their fullness? Which Khan-balik is the real city, which palace is the one where he sits motionless on bright cushions before the Great Khan? Suppose in another man's empire he was a porter back in Venice, or had never been born at all?

As Marco began to speak, in his immature Tartar, he recalled the things he described. The Great Khan had been interested to hear about the two friars who had travelled with the Polos as far as Armenia. When he let Maffeo and Nicolo go after their first visit, he asked them to bring with them on their return a hundred wise Christians. The Pope had given them two Dominicans, an Italian and a German. The Italian was small and sullen; he was travelling against his will and was always looking out for an excuse to turn back. The German, William, was a huge man with a cheerful laugh. He explained that his father was German but his mother a Norman, and he himself lived in Tripoli, and had travelled widely in the Holy Land. He and Marco became friends; he hoped to interest the boy in Aristotle. They rode side by side, and William lectured him, but less as a master to a pupil than as one riding companion to another, as if they were discussing hawks or the style of a suit of armour. William said, as they left the city of Ayas, 'Aristotle says that all things that can happen, do happen. Why do you suppose he says this?'

'I cannot think. Remember, I have never been to the university, William. I cannot even read Latin fluently.'

'What he means, of course, is that things happen because they had the potential to happen. Nothing can happen without being able to happen in the first place.'

William was a learned man: he had studied in Paris and at Oxford (although he had to leave England, he explained, after a misunderstanding with some of the townspeople of Oxford which had left several students dead); he was an envoy of the Holy Father. But Marco resisted, or ignored, his interpretation. When William said, 'all things that can happen, do happen', he took this to mean simply that potentiality is inevitably fulfilled in every conceivable way, not just in one of the possible resolutions. They had left Ayas behind and were entering the foothills of the mountains of Armenia. When they reached the Euphrates, they would turn south and east, heading for the city of Mosul. But, alternatively, they could turn north, and through the mountainous neck of land between the Black Sea and the Sea of Baku, into the wastes of Scythis, or due south and back to Jerusalem, where they had started, and eventually into the Arabian desert. According to Aristotle, Marco realized, all these possibilities would become accomplished facts, although they would be aware of having made only one decision, and taken only one route. In fact, neither of these happened, for a day out of Ayas they came across a party of warriors who were fleeing from the army of Bundukdari, the Sultan of Egypt, who was ravaging the country of Armenia. Here was the Italian's excuse; immediately he declared that he would go no farther while his life was in such peril. William of Tripoli laughed and told Nicolo and Maffeo that he had no choice but to accompany his brother, for they could not expect him to travel alone in safety. So Marco learnt no more about Aristotle, but he became aware

57

of this resolution of the situation, which he had not expected. But, he told himself, still other possibilities existed: William could have persuaded Nicholas the Italian to continue with us, or Father could have plotted a different route to take us out of the danger zone, or Nicholas could have gone back on his own, or we could all have turned back. According to Aristotle, he thought, each of these resolutions really did take place. How could this be, when he could see clearly that the friars had both turned back, and they had stuck to the same course? As he talked with the Great Khan, years later, he realized that he knew the outcome of the potentiality only because he had been there, and had seen what had happened. What if he had not been there, but only heard from another, suppose from one of the muleteers, who had misled him about the details? What if he were to tell the Great Khan of a solution different in some detail to what he knew to have happened? Then, to Kublai Khan, something different would have happened. In this way his entire journey, a series of fortuitous revelations of thousands of potentialities, would be different according to whose ears it reached. To each man, Marco Polo might have traversed Asia by a different route, or died a hundred deaths on the way. To some, he might never have existed at all. Perhaps, Marco considered, this is what Aristotle meant.

Why did the Great Khan keep returning to his foreign guest, the thin-lipped straw-haired young Venetian with the darting eyes and jerky movements of the hand? The Tartar court had become used to foreigners from the West; Nicolo and Maffeo were not the first. A Dominican, William of Rubruk, had been a guest at Karakorum, ten years before the Venetians reached Cathay, and there had been others, like John the Franciscan —the Great Khan was not not so sure about these, never having met them, but news travelled fast among the Tartar people. Of course, Karakorum was not Kinsai or Khan-balik, the great capitals of the empire, and no Westerner before the Polos had seen the summer palace at Shangtu, which Kublai had built himself.

There was something else, too: the earlier visitors had been willing to talk, but only about gods and religion. These were things that cropped up often when the Great Khan talked with Marco, as was to be expected, but he had noticed in Marco a reciprocal interest for the first time with one of these Latins—and, he had to say, it was the same with them as with the Mohammedans. Perhaps this was because, with Marco, they stumbled upon ideas in conversation, as if considering them for the first time. When Nicolo and Maffeo visited for the first time, they had persuaded him to listen to the services of the Nestorian Christians in his own city. Then they would take him aside and try to explain the words to him. He had heard the same from the Mohammedans and the Buddhists, more numerous among his peoples than the Christians. He understood their tales (though the Buddhist least of all) and appreciated their devotion, which seemed to him in many ways more befitting for a god than the Tartar customs. Many in his own family had secretly been followers of the Nestorian religion, which Maffeo assured him was almost the same as his own, though confused on some details. But it seemed to Kublai Khan, in a way which he found hard to explain to Maffeo—he strained to catch each unfamiliar word, leaning over on his cushions so as almost to be in the old Khan's lap—that only he, the Tartar horseman brought up on the plains, could interpret one man's god-talk to another who did not follow it. Once, he invited the Venetians to a feast at which some Mohammedans and some Cathayan Buddhists would be present. He hoped to hear them discuss each others' gods. And suddenly, before each had time to speak, they were interrupting and shouting, and Maffeo stood up, red-faced, and shook his fist in the face of a Mohammedan, and soon all were on their feet, even the taciturn Nicolo, and

59

shouting in unknown tongues at each other. This seemed stupid to Kublai, for they must be aware that none understood another's language; they should all have used what little Tartar they had. He swung his hammer against the great gong several times, until there was silence.

'You people,' he said, addressing all of them, the Venetians and Nestorians and the dark turbaned Mohammedans and the bald-headed Buddhists, 'you have all despised and scorned the Tartar people amongst yourselves. You sneer at our ways, which seem wild to you, and accuse us of polluting city-life with our customs. And many of us have adopted your beliefs and practise them here as you do. But as soon as I entertain you together, you begin to shout and your beards bristle with anger. And yet when I sit and listen to you, I hear the same thing, but in three or four different tongues. Why is this? Why do you keep your gods so separate, and address them only in your own language? If you put them all together and made peace between them, and worshipped them in the same tongue, your deeds would be favoured by many gods, not just one. Until you learn to do this, you will never be as powerful as the Tartar nation—and until then I will never again invite you to the same feast, for it is forbidden to shed blood at the table of the Great Khan.'

This was all he had said on the subject of the gods, though he continued to listen to their talk for hours, until the rest of the court grew restless and sullen with boredom. Indeed, he encouraged the Venetians to bring back with them a hundred of their teachers. But when none came, he was secretly relieved, as he confided to Marco, for although they interested him greatly, they were inclined to be short-tempered and difficult. They made poor guests too, he said sadly, for in his experience they were seldom good huntsmen or riders, and did not care for singing or making music.

Marco said once, when they touched on the subject of gods, 'When my father was away, which was most of the time, even before he came to your Court, I was brought up by my mother and grandfather. They sent me to the monks to be educated, for, she said, she would not turn me into a merchant too, and deprive another poor woman of a husband and a boy of a father. So I learnt a good deal about Christian worship, though it was very different at home from the Nestorians in your cities.'

He tried to imagine the resonant Latin chants filling the hollow spaces of light Chinese halls, but the idea was impossible. They belonged only in their stone wombs. The Christians of Khan-balik wore saffron robes, like the Buddhists, instead of rough grey wool, and their churches were decorated inside with bamboo matting and fine silk screens, rather than the elongated wall-paintings he used to know so well. When they sang, they were accompanied by strange percussion sounds. He remembered how Brother William of Tripoli had told him that they believed falsehood about the Lord Jesus, and for this had been thrown out of the Roman lands by ancient emperors, but Marco's Chinese was not good enough to be able to discern the subtle distinctions, and these things were impossible to render in the Tartar language, which had no way of distinguishing essence and existence, hypostases and unity in diversity, ideas which were too hard for him to understand even in Latin. Marco knew that the Great Khan would never openly embrace the Christian faith, but however often he might tell this to his uncle, Maffeo continued to pray that he might become a Christian, and instructed Marco to do the same.

'That is our mission, in God's eyes, my boy,' he explained. 'When we left Venice, your father and I took an oath together to do all we could to save the soul of the Great Khan by opening his eyes to the deeds the Lord has done, and his ears to his word. After three and a half years we limped into his presence again, battered and half-dead from the journey.

61

How many times did we escape death by a mere chance? Why do you suppose the Lord preserved your life, when you lay dying of fever? Or when we evaded capture by the thieves of Rudbar, or crossed the Desert of Lop?' Maffeo's eyes enlarged and he thrust his ruddy nose close to Marco. When he was being most earnest, then he seemed the most comical to Marco. 'Our lives have been saved countless times by the angels of the Lord, for it is his will that the Great Khan's eyes be opened, and then the eyes and hearts of all his people. Unworthy as we are, it is our duty to accomplish this.'

'But uncle,' Marco insisted, 'all this talk makes no sense to Kublai. He respects the Christians because he sees they worship a powerful god, whom he does not wish to antagonize. But his ways are not ours; he sees no difference between us and the Mohammedans.' At this Maffeo put his arms around his nephew's shoulders and smiled patiently.

'It is the way of the young,' he sighed, 'to abandon the race before it is won. Recall to mind the words of the blessed apostle, Paul, and persevere. Fight the just fight, my boy.'

Maffeo was delighted when the Great Khan asked him, 'In what way is your god stronger than the god of the Mohammedans, who despise the Christians for their weakness?'

He replied eagerly, the words stumbling over each other as they tripped from his lips, 'Great Khan, if the Christians were indeed weak, as they say, you would not honour us as you do. Moreover they treat us with scorn when we go into their country because we are few and they are many. Who is not weak when outnumbered? But even those few Christians who live under cruel submission to them can call on the true God. I will tell you a story,' he said, cleverly; a story always gained the Great Khan's attention. Marco could see that his uncle had been drinking too much of the 'koumiss', the Tartar wine that is made from mare's milk, left to ferment. His lips were wet, and some food still clung to them. This reminded Marco of the statues the Tartars made of their god Matigai, who watches over the crops. They dressed him and his wife in specially-made clothes, and, when they ate, smeared their brazen mouths with food. Maffeo, without the square beard, would resemble the Natigai. Now he was warming to his story; his hands described eloquent circles. 'In the city of Baghdad in Mesopotamia, there are many Christians, mostly Nestorians like those in your own cities, and Jacobites. Many years ago the Mohammedan ruler, whom they call the Caliph, wanted to do away with the Christians altogether, for he hated them with an irrational ferocity. This man called to him the Christian bishop and interrogated him regarding his faith. The bishop, thinking that God had at last opened the eyes of the wicked Caliph, rejoiced that he should have been chosen as the instrument of conversion. And he told him, amongst other things, that the Lord had said that if a man had faith as small as a mustard-seed, he could cause a mountain to move by his own will. The Caliph's eyes gleamed. He asked the bishop, "Well, old man, and are you able to cause a mountain to move by your own will?" The bishop sensed that he had made a dangerous mistake: he could tell this from the little smile flickering across the smooth dark face of the Caliph. He shook his head slowly, "I have never tried to do it, my lord. It is not for us to put our faith to the test in this way." "Then for whom is it?" "Why, for God alone," replied the bishop. The Caliph studied the face of the bishop, noticing the bald head glistening with the perspiration that comes from fear, the mouth hanging slightly open. "In this city, I am your God," he declared. "If you have less faith than a mustard-seed, which is the smallest of all seedlings, you are not fit to be the bishop of the Christians. Go away, and send me another in your place. If he also is not able to do this thing, then I shall know that your faith is a deceit and a blasphemy." The bishop turned to go, but as he reached the doorway the Caliph added calmly, "and then, bishop, I shall put all the Christians in this city to death. You have ten days to find a man with greater faith than yourself."'

'That,' observed the Great Khan, 'was a dishonourable condition to impose.'

'Thus the Mohammedans sought to trick the Christians into accepting death or conversion to their foul cult,' Maffeo continued. 'For the Caliph issued a proclamation granting an amnesty and freedom from the conditions of the test to all those among the Christians who would agree to turn to the faith of Mohammed. But out of 100,000 Christian souls in the city, not one elected to take the cowardly road of betrayal. This angered the Caliph still more, and he cut the time allowed to the Christians to six days. Now before resigning the episcopal throne, as the Caliph had ordered, the bishop ordained that the cathedral clergy should hold continual services of repentance, and that never-ending prayers for deliverance should be offered up to God by all the Christians in the city. But each night he went to bed troubled at heart. As he slept, there appeared to him in a dream a strange figure, whom he seemed to recognize, but dimly. The man was old and gnarled, like an apple-tree: his eyes were bloodshot, and out of one of them he squinted, his nose appeared to have been squashed, and saliva dribbled from cracked lips. He was a shoemaker: all day he sat with calloused hands repairing shoes by a feeble candle-light. A woman called at his shop, veiled in sleek dark muslin. Old and decrepit as he was, the shoemaker was moved to lust by her obvious and disdainful beauty. His hands trembled as he fitted her graceful foot into a shoe. After she had left his shop, lascivious thoughts chased each other around his confused mind. In shame he recalled the words of our Lord, that if an eye causes a man to sin, he should pluck it out, or if a hand, he should cut it off. And in his passion he groaned, "False traitor that my eye is, I will take vengeance on it." And he took the sharpened awl which he used as a tool for repairing shoes and thrust it into the middle of his good eye, so that it burst inside his head with an excruciating pain. For a day and a night he lay helpless, tormented by the terrible pain, but the Lord took pity on him,

64

honouring him for his noble act of repentance. So he spared his life, although the miserable wretch could no longer see well enough to continue his trade. And then the bishop, waking up, remembered where he had seen him before: surely this was the filthy blind beggar who squatted before the gates of the cathedral each day? Often the bishop had recoiled in horror at the sight of the shrivelled, useless creature. If only he had known what a holy act it was that had reduced him to this plight! In the morning he went out and summoned the beggar to him. "God has revealed to me in a dream your great Christian sacrifice and the devotion with which you have served him," he announced. "Therefore you alone are fit to be the new bishop of the Christians." And he took off his rich vestments and placed them over the shrunken body of the beggar, who could only stand in astonishment before him. And the bishop, relieved, went out to offer prayers of thanks to the Lord for showing him his rightful successor.

'Now when the Caliph heard that the bishop had annointed a successor, he called him to the palace. The beggar, washed and dressed in unfamiliar robes, was led through the marble halls by a deacon. The Caliph, smiling and fondling the ears of a cat that lay in his lap, told him what he had told the old bishop. "But I have become impatient," he said. "Tomorrow, at noon, you will cause the twin mountains outside the city walls to move together." The beggar-bishop despaired for his own life and the lives of all the Christians of Baghdad. "This is a thing that has never been done," he told the deacon, "and am I, a blind beggar, to accomplish it?" But as the deacon led him tottering through the streets, he suddenly took courage. Stopping in the middle of a square he lifted his eyes, one black and sightless, the other bloodshot and squinting, to heaven, and cried out, "Lord remember your servant, and what he has done in obedience to your law!" Then he fell on his knees and began to pray. All through the day he prayed, kneeling where he was in the filth of the gutter. And at night he fell exhausted into the arms of the young deacon who had stayed to support him.

'At noon the next day the whole Christian community assembled outside the city walls, in accordance with the Caliph's command. A canopy was set up on a platform, and on it was placed a throne for the Caliph to sit on, and cushions for his feet. The Christians were made to kneel in the scorching dust with their heads stretched out in front of them, so that their necks were exposed. And by the side of each row stood an enormous black man from the Caliph's bodyguard, resting a naked scimitar on his shoulder. Accompanied by trumpet blasts, the Caliph rode out of the city gates on a pale white horse. Behind him streamed a multitude of idle Mohammedans, for the day had been declared a public holiday. In a festival mood they stood around in groups to mock the Christians in their humiliation. The Caliph ascended the steps of the dais, and had the bishop brought before him. He was in a light good humour, anticipating the final defeat of his enemies. "My lord bishop," he addressed him with heavy irony, "the hour for your demonstration has come. Look around you! See the excited crowd of spectators waiting for you! We are thankful to you for making this such a joyful festival for pious men!" At this the Mohammedans cheered and clapped. Some threw rotten fruit at the Christians. "Let the miracle begin!" the Caliph called, "and let us not be disappointed!"

'Then the bishop turned to face the twin mountains, and kneeling like his people, cried out, "In the name of the Almighty Father, the Son and the Holy Spirit, I command you to move." Barely had he finished speaking when a crash rent the air and from the east there came what sounded like thunder, although it was a clear day and the sun was shining. Everyone turned and saw to their amazement the two mountains beginning to crumble like clods of earth. In only a few minutes the solid rocks had become fine sand, pouring down the valley towards the city. The Mohammedans, terrified, fled

66

like a routed army back towards the gates. The Caliph himself leapt on his horse and, screaming at the heavens in rage, rode pell-mell into the crowds. Many were knocked flying by his horse's hooves. But the Christians all raised their voices in a hymn of praise to God, who had shown his awesome might through the least of his faithful, a man despised and left for dead. And that very evening, as he dined with his concubines, the Caliph was seized by a sudden pain in his head, which no one could relieve. Maddened by the pain, he rushed this way and that, smashing his head into the marble columns until it shattered like a pear, spattering the soft divans with his blood. Thus was the Lord revenged over the mighty Caliph of Baghdad.'

Exhausted by his story, which he had not only narrated but acted out in the presence of the Great Khan and his court, Maffeo sank back into his seat. Many of the Tartars showed their approval by slapping him on the back and toasting him in 'koumiss'. Indeed, some later approached him and asked how they too could become followers of this powerful god.

The Great Khan, whose eyes had never left Maffeo, said in his clear deep voice, 'He is a strong god indeed whom you follow. His vengeance is to be feared as greatly as his commands.' Maffeo made no reply to this, but bowed deeply. Marco, however, left the feast early, troubled by what he had heard. For some days he could not clear from his head the image of the eye bursting in the old shoemaker's head, and at night he would wake shivering with a fear he could not explain.

Later, Marco remembered the story, equally true, he had heard from his father and others at the court: a baron called Nayan, a Nestorian Christian, rebelled against the Great Khan and raised an army to fight him, but was defeated, despite having the sign of Christ's cross woven on his banner.

The Great Khan had him executed by wrapping him tightly in a blanket and dragging his body this way and that, knocking it violently on the ground and against rocks until he was dead. Nayan was a member of the royal house, so his blood could not be spilled on the ground, nor earth nor sun nor air witness his death. After his execution the Buddhists and pagans and Mohammedans mocked the Christians, pointing to the cross which had failed to save them from defeat. But the Great Khan took them aside and berated them, saying that no sign or banner would have won the favour of God in an unjust war, and that Nayan's defeat was the fruit of his treachery. Perhaps the Great Khan's clear-sightedness could be explained by his impartiality in these matters. Or, Marco thought, perhaps that made it more admirable.

Aristotle would say, of course (with a certain self-importance, as Marco imagined him) that in another outcome Nayan triumphed and the Christian God was vindicated, and subsequently revered by the Mohammedans and pagans. (Is this not, after all, what happened to Constantine?) Again, in a possible past, Nayan was himself a Mohammedan, or he escaped from the battlefield and mounted another, decisive rebellion. All outcomes were possible; all, therefore, were true. The one which Marco knew was known in Khan-balik and Tangut and Cathay, wherever Kublai Khan's hand was felt and Nayan's blood spurted, staining a carpet red.

Leaning over the balcony overlooking the Great Khan's formal garden, Marco murmured lightly, to provoke a response,

'How fragile is the base on which all this reality rests!'

'The reality must be sufficient for us, who are close enough to grasp it,' pondered the Great Khan. 'Why should it be the same for the whole world? I am here, the rhododendra are here, the little pond and fountain are there. We are friends, though we might have taken an instant dislike to one another and become enemies; the garden might have been a stable, the gardener a cook or a sailor. Perhaps any one of these is the truth perceived by, for example, your Doge in Venice.'

'If there are a million alternative truths to the one we see in front of us, then there are a million Tartar empires, a million Kublai Khans, a million Marco Polos—or perhaps none,' replied Marco. 'This you may find satisfying, or even enriching. But to one who has traversed almost the entire breadth of the world, it is frustrating to know that he has never left his own threshold.' Kublai Khan laughed delightedly. The boy had become, under his amateur tutelage, a sage. When young Marco had first seen the gardens, with their elaborate waterworks and fountains, the lush grottos of exotic fruit-trees, and beyond, the lake where the young sons and daughters of the nobles bathed alongside the geese, his response had been limited to wonder, like his fathers. But the Great Khan had not let him sit idle in Khan-balik; he sent him abroad to his other great cities, as a courier or ambassador. Now this young man, only twenty when he arrived among the Tartars, was becoming disillusioned. The Great Khan recalled the nights he had spent listening to the detailed accounts of the journey across Asia: a catalogue of cities and towns, temples and mountains, races of people analyzed according to colour and shape and religious custom, the nutritional value of their food, the size and capabilities of their domestic animals. He had fetched a scribe to convert the words of the Venetian into lists and charts, and divided up these charts according to the regions of his empires.

But one night, when Marco had finished emptying his memory and sat exhausted in the darkened palace, the Great Khan said, 'You are drained and empty, Marco. Is this the sum of my empires? And are you their vessel? If they can be contained in the charts compiled from one man's memory, I may as well be king of this,' and he held up a hollowed coconut whose milk they had drunk only hours before. Marco did not understand, but whenever he travelled after that he found that the places were contained, in his mind, within the image of a giant coconut. Sometimes the brown hairy skin became transformed into the withered humorous face of the Great Khan himself, so that cities shone from his eyes, rivers flowed from his shrivelled lips.

In a way unfathomable and certainly inexpressible Marco found the words of Aristotle enshrined in his travels. At the court of the Great Khan they took a shape of their own, separable at last from the great laughing face of the Dominican William. The lands of the Great Khan, so far from contracting, had exploded into thousands of new dimensions. He was no longer able to recall details of his travels that might be useful to the Great Khan; a scribe no longer sat with them as they talked late into the night. He was sorry and glad that this had happened: glad because he saw that he had been wrong to imagine an empire becoming smaller as it became more familiar to him, but sorry because he had hoped one day to write a thorough account of these unknown lands, for the benefit of Venetians who would never travel so far themselves. But as for the Great Khan, Marco could not say whether he was sorry or glad, for his face rarely showed emotion.

On one occasion Kublai Khan said to Marco, 'Tell me the story I have heard from the Christians here, of the birth of your god.'

Marco thought for a long while, and then said, 'You have heard how the Christ was born of a virgin mother, and how he was worshipped by three wise men from the East. This, too, is a many-sided gem, such as my father sells in his shops in the city. There is perhaps no one who has comprehended all these sides simultaneously.'

'Nevertheless,' said Kublai, 'tell me one side, in your own words.'

'In the city of Saveh, in Persia, many years ago,' Marco began, 'three men who were revered in that place above all others for their wisdom and learning went out of the city and journeyed to the west. Their names were Beltasar, who was a young man, Gaspar, who was of middle age, and Melchior, an old man with white hair. These three had seen in the stars a new star which shone far brighter than the others. They conferred and agreed that it signified the birth of a prophet. Then they followed it across the sparse plains of Persia, and travelled by night through the desert of Mesopotamia. At last they came to a small town in a distant region close to the Narrow Sea, which we call the Mediterranean. Here they saw that the star shone brighter than ever before, and seemed to hang over one little house especially. They made enquiries, and found that a child had recently been born there. One by one they entered the house to visit the child. The youngest entered first, and found that the child was of exactly the same age and appearance as himself. He came out open-mouthed, in his pale grey eyes a reflected wonder. Then Gaspar entered, and the child appeared to him of middle age, and very like himself, so that he came out dumbfounded. And Melchior, going in last, saw the child a white-bearded old man, and looked into his own failing eyes. Then all three came into him together, and the child appeared in his own likeness, not twenty days old. Each gave him the gift he had brought. For Melchior had said, "Let us take three gifts: gold, frankincense and myrrh. If the prophet accepts the gold, we will know he is an earthly king, if frankincense, a god, and if myrrh, a healer." But the child took all three gifts, and handed them in return a small locked casket.

The three wise men began the journey back to their own

71

country, weighing up in their minds what they had seen. They decided to see what the child had given them, and opened the casket. Inside they found only a small round stone, so pale as to be almost translucent. They wondered what it might signify, but could not agree among themselves.'

'The meaning seems clear,' said Kublai Khan, 'Since the child-prophet took the gold, the frankincense and the myrrh, he must have been at once a god, a king and a healer. And this is surely what you Christians believe of your man-god, Christ. The stone was a symbol of the constancy with which the wise men should follow this belief, revealed to them so soon after his birth.'

'Alas, Great Khan, the sages were less wise than you. For, not understanding why the stone had been given to them, they threw it into a well they happened to pass by. And at once there descended from the skies a burning sheet of flame, which descended into the well. The three wise men immediately regretted their folly and worshipped this miracle. They took some of the fire and kept it in a lamp and carried it back to their country. There they built a great temple to house the flame, which never gutters or dies out. All their sacrifices and burnt offerings are burnt by this flame, and the people continue to worship it as a god. The child who gave them the stone was the prophet of the fire, but it is the fire which is the god.'

Kublai Khan was silent for some minutes, and Marco began to worry that his story had displeased him. Some of the Tartars, he knew, were still fire-worshippers. But eventually the Great Khan said, 'To each man, his own judgement of what he sees manifested. The same truth is granted to all, but there are many apprehensions of it, as many as there are men in the world. You have told me as much, in other ways, in all that you have said.'

Again, Marco thought of Aristotle. The sage seemed to say, 'Who are you to judge which man's sight is better, and which worse? It is this multitude of perceptions which make up the

72

empire of the Great Khan, the universe, each man within that
universe.'

The Great Khan was attempting to apprehend his empires
through the sight and hearing of a young Venetian, his guest,
ambassador and companion. By defining this microcosm, he
hoped to discover the whole; if that whole proved to be only
one possible account or approach to the empire, he cared less
than Marco. For surely in one lifetime a man could do no more
than grasp the outlines of one universe?

Even within the careful delineations into which he shaped
Marco's stories, ignorance blew like the wind through holes
in a wall. Tracts of land, regions, peoples lay untouched in
Marco's memory like unopened chests, and the dust settled
as new patterns were imposed. Marco himself was aware of
these gaps; when he conversed with the Great Khan,
examples were picked out by a subconscious selective
process, and those left unchosen remained in their boxes,
while the handwriting on the labels faded. The further he
travelled, the more selective he became. For the Great Khan
did not ask direct questions requiring information; he did not
say, 'Describe the walls of the city of Kashgar', or 'How do the
people of Kara-Jang dress?' These details which had once
constituted the bulk of his reports he now hardly noticed. It
was only when recounting a story from the mountains of
Tibet, or describing the sweep of the Yang-tze river, that other
unmentioned minutiae flooded like light through the cracks
in his mind. What remained unsaid in his tales did not
become oblivion. For in the retelling of a story, the narrator
loses it, and the hearer gains. In this way Marco's journeys
became Kublai Khan's; Marco became his empire.

By day, it is possible to instruct the mind to relax its grip on an idea, or latch on to another. But in sleep the will deserts the mind, and, left alone, it escapes the confines of harmony. The Great Khan dreamt at night, and his dreams were the voyages of the Venetian traveller. The accounts once given soberly by Marco became his own vision of the empire, and new and unfamiliar details were added in sleep.

Two days ride to the south of the plain of Hormuz, criss-crossed by rivers and abounding in date-palms, lies the city of Hormuz, dipping its feet in the ocean at its narrowest point. This is where the merchants of India end their journey, blown from the sub-continent by the monsoon wind, to stock the shops and market-stalls with spices and rare fruit, cloths of silk threaded with gold, elephants' tusks and white pearl. Here also the Polos arrive, but their ships are camels of the Arabian desert. In the torrid climate, dripping with sea-moisture, young Marco rocks unsteadily on his mount. Maffeo's red face is afire; his grimy hands leave grey smudges where he has wiped away the sweat. Only Nicolo, small and grave, seems unchanged. This shrewd traveller, to whom each city is no more than the sum of its people, and its people the difference between their greed and the gold in their pockets, arranges for the transport of their baggage to a guest-hostel on the edge of the city. He takes a look at his son, and orders him to go with the baggage and rest, for clearly he has been overcome by the heat. He and his brother must start to look for a ship immediately, for it is the height of the sailing season, passages are hard to find, and no one stays longer than he needs in Hormuz.

Along the harbour the two foreigners cover their faces, right up to the eyes, with cloths, to escape the fetid heat and the mingling smell of fish oil. The men of Hormuz use this, rather than pitch, to caulk their ships, fish being so plentiful. It is not yet summer, but already the fruit on the trees has ripened and is being sold in the streets. In only a few more months, the vegetation will have withered and died in the heat. By open braziers men sell little cakes made of tunny fish and onions, the staple diet of the poor, along with the ubiquitous dates.

The Polos plan to find a passage to the Abyssinian coast, where, they have heard, the gems that are collected from the bed of the Nile can be bought in exchange for the rare stones, amber and jet they have brought from Venice, where they in turn were sold by traders from Scythia and Norway. From Ethiopia it is possible to sail to India, with the right wind. This is common knowledge among traders on the Red Sea, whom the Polos met in Jerusalem. One of the sailors on board a large trading ship eyes up the strangers and calls to the captain, a man like a whipcord burnt in the sun of the southern oceans, whose eyes are white cracks in a lined face. He calls to them, first in Persian, then in his unsteady Arabic. Neither Nicolo nor Maffeo understands, but their guide, the man who has led them from Mosul to Baghdad, and south across the country of Rudbar, replies for them. The captain likes the look of them; Nicolo insisted on their second-best robes and a discreet choice of jewellery. Too well-dressed, and the fares will match the clothes, but no captain wants beggars as passengers. Yes, he tells one-eyed Yusuf, the guide, a Syrian Jacobite, he will take them to Aden. Well, they want to go further, to the coast of Ethiopia itself, Yusuf grumbles. Ah, but a passage from Aden to the opposite coast is easy to find, once they are there. And this ship is sailing tomorrow—the lords will not want to linger in Hormuz unnecessarily? No indeed; it is a poor gem-market, Nicolo thinks. They will do better in Aden.

While they are arguing Maffeo has been examining the boat. He is curious about the long thick ropes lashed around the planks of wood that make up the hull. He steps closer; it is a deep harbour, so that the boats can moor right up to the side of the harbour wall.

'Look, Nicolo!' he points to the hull. 'Where are the nails?' His brother takes a look too, while Yusuf discusses the fare

75

with the captain. He will not be travelling with them, but the lower the fare he can negotiate for these rich Latins, the greater will be his own fee, and anyway, he loves to argue.

'Nails? There aren't any,' Nicolo observes, with some surprise. He has never seen a ship whose hull was held together without nails. What could be holding it together—surely not that rope? Nicolo grabs the guide by the shoulder and points. 'Are we to sail in a ship held together by ropes?' Yusuf shrugs; he is accustomed to Latins making a fuss. The Venetians are the worst, although as a rule less rude than Franks.

'Sir, in this city there are no nails.'

'So we can see! How does the ship stay afloat?' Maffeo asks. 'Doesn't the salt water spoil the rope?'

'Oh no, sir. It is made from coconut husks,' He pronounces the words like a magic formula; now these obstinate Latins will stop interfering and let him finish the bargain. But they are not convinced. He is not to know that they have seen coconuts before, at the table of the Great Khan.

'Coconuts?' Maffeo snorts. 'And I suppose the masts are made of elephant ivory?'

'No, no, of wood,' Yusuf persists. 'They soak the husk of the coconut until it becomes very hard, like the hair of a horse, then they separate it into threads and bind it into rope. It lasts very well. These are good ships, sirs, the best on the ocean.' Maffeo has already turned away. Now the captain of the ship wants to know what is going on: will they sail to Aden or not? Nicolo is undecided. Surely all these ships cannot sink, else they would not continue to make them in this way. And how else are they to reach the port of Aden, unless from Hormuz? But Maffeo, a sound craftsman himself, will not trust shoddy workmanship.

'I won't sail in one of those,' he insists. 'We'd be better off going overland. We've done it before.' They begin to walk away from the quayside, leaving Yusuf still chattering to the captain.

76

'The land journey is too hazardous,' Nicolo objects, 'and we have not been to India overland.'

'Why go to India? We can sell our stones anywhere in the world. Let us try the northern silk cities—Kashgar, Samarkand, Balkh. We could even go back to Bukhara.'

'Still it is too dangerous. Marco is young and soft. He's just a boy, the hardship might kill him.'

'Good for him, more likely,' says Maffeo. But he does not argue. It is approaching that time of the day when it is not possible even to stand in the shade, when it can be found. The quayside is almost empty; they walk to the guest-house through deserted streets. For some hours the very sand will burn feet through to the bone. Such a sun, they have heard, can make a man quite mad.

It is the custom at Hormuz at this time of the day for the people to retire to shacks erected in the spacious gardens of the city. All the houses are built around central courtyards with fountains; the richer ones also have a strip of land at the back, running down to the river or an artificial pond. It is here that these little houses are constructed, of thin canes with a light cloth stretched over them, sometimes of silk, or even sometimes with foliage instead of the cloth. The canes are planted so that some are actually in the water and others driven into the bank. In this way those seeking relief can sit dangling their feet in the water. Some even spend entire afternoons in the water, and hold meetings and conduct business submerged up to their necks.

Marco is resting in such a shelter at the foot of the garden of the guest-house. Their host has prepared a makeshift bed for him, for it is obvious that a fever has taken him, the result of the days of travel across Rudbar. They had to come quick at the last, to avoid ambush by armed brigands; this deprived Marco of rest badly needed. As he leads Maffeo and Nicolo out to the cool of the shelter and the river, the host is recounting the story of how Hormuz was saved from the ambitions of the neighbouring King of Kerman. Glasses of

77

cool sherbet glisten on a silver tray he is carrying; Maffeo's attention is taken up with these, but Nicolo listens. Kerman marched on Hormuz during the early part of the day, in order to reach the city at the hour when it would be deserted, the inhabitants neck-deep in water. But they lost their way in the plains, and had to bivouac in the open, out of sight of the city. Here one of the hot winds blowing off the sea caught them, and stifled them in their tents. Without drawing their swords the army was decimated, such is the power of this wind.

It may have been these words from their host that decided Nicolo to leave Hormuz that very evening, the Great Khan considered, as he woke from uneasy dreams, despite the growing weakness of young Marco. This was the lowest ebb of the journey: ships held together with coconut husks, a city whose population lived in the river to escape the heat, and, to the north, a countryside infested with brigands. Perhaps, for once, Nicolo despaired, with his head sticking out of the warm brown water. The Great Khan could not recall having seen him ill at ease, or disconcerted. He had opted in the end for the safety of experience, though his chosen course was more adventurous than his unpredictable brother's. North again, to the silken cities and the road across the Desert of Lop: it was not an easy journey, especially across the desert, but at least they knew that it was there.

The Great Khan knew that Marco had been weak from this fever for a whole year, and the journey from Hormuz up to Herat, in central Persia, almost carried him off. It was a persistent sickness which was cured only by the blasts of cool air in the mountains of Pamir. This much he knew, but no more; Marco, who alone knew the contours of that feverish voyage, was quite silent about it. When he chose, he gave all of himself, but about those things on which he was silent, Kublai Khan would sooner have asked a conquered warrior how it felt to wear a Tartar slave-ring on his neck than plumb those still waters. And yet, he told himself, that year of

78

sickness was the pivot of Marco's experiences, for a fever is like a high-pitched dream, where one sees as if through a window of opaque coloured glass. Unless he too could mount the steps to that window, unless he could see the monsters and dragons, the adventures of delirium, the Venetian would slip through his fingers. And if Marco Polo, then his empires also.

arco watched as the Lady Kuan tested the thickness of the ink mixture with the wooden knife the servant held out to her. She nodded her approval; he bowed and left. Naturally the preparation was all done by the servants; the Lady Kuan could have done it herself, but what would be the purpose, since servants specially trained had been bought by her husband? There were five colours of ink: black, for basic outlines, a watery mixture over which the other colours, blue, purple, green and yellow could be painted. This paper was not the type made from the bark of the mulberry tree, which was used for the money of the Great Khan's empires, but a special kind, known only to those who had learnt the process at their fathers' workshops; it was made from rice. Even the Lady Kuan marvelled each time she began to paint at the delicate whiteness, the slightly rough texture that absorbed the ink and held it in the shapes guided by her brush.

'This brush is a new one,' she said, 'I had it blessed only this morning. It has never been used before.'

'What is it made from?' Marco asked. 'The hair of the badger's tail?' She smiled coyly, as if revealing a secret.

'That would be too coarse. This is an especially fine hair. The craftsman assured me he made it from the whiskers of a leopard, but I do not believe it. Probably it is mink hair; that is finer than badger's.' Looking at the thin strands of white hair, Marco decided to believe the leopard-whiskers. The Lady Kuan herself was a cat, perched on her painting-stool which had no back but a padded rail at the front to support her legs, so that she leant forward almost in a kneeling position. Her eyes moved slowly and steadily, as if the light that shone from them endowed each object with a form and colour. When she moved, to stretch her arms or dip her brush in the ink, it was a languid, contained gesture, suggesting more. Since he had arrived in this city of Kinsai, called by the Chinese a heaven on earth, Marco had seen many beautiful women, more than he could recall in any other place, but none fascinated him as this large pale cat.

'What am I painting?' she asked. A tree, a wooden bridge over a stream, roses climbing over the railings.

'Your garden, in shadow through the paper screen. But who are the figures on the bridge?'

'Lovers entwined in each other's arms. They are parting, for he must go away.'

'Where will he go?'

'Who knows where his king will send him?' she sighed, lifting her eyes from under hooded lids. Marco was attracted to her subtlety. The Chinese, he had learnt, seldom said straight out the words that came to their minds, as the Tartars did. In part this was because the Chinese tongue had so many words meaning essentially the same thing, but each one expressing a slightly different tone or shade, whereas to the Tartar, the sun was hot, the night dark, the plains beautiful. Among them only the Great Khan had the subtlety of speech that Marco had found among the Chinese. But with Kublai he never felt, as he did now with the Lady Kuan, that behind her words lay a half-meaning, a fancy expressed like a leaf dropping from a tree, that might be caught by the wind and swirl far away, or be plucked by a waiting hand. He was beginning to realize that the words she spoke with her mouth were less important than those in her eyes.

The Lady Kuan's husband, the artist Chao Meng-fu, had been his host on his arrival at Kinsai. It was an honour to have been selected as courier extraordinary, the Great Khan's personal envoy to the capital of the Sung kingdom, newly conquered by the Tartars. The Great Khan's general, Bayan of the Hundred Eyes, spared the city and its inhabitants, on account of its great beauty and fame, he explained, but Marco suspected that the general, a fine old-fashioned Tartar from the Great Khan's own tribe, had simply been taken aback by the lack of resistance. For the people of Kinsai, following the example of their King Facfur, shunned the use of arms, and spent their days either in peaceful industry or, if they were wealthy enough, in the harmless pursuit of pleasure. Many fled the city in the face of the Great Khan's army, either along the river or south into the countryside. But Bayan allowed them all to return and harmed no one. Chao Meng-fu told Marco that Facfur had not even attempted to defend his city because he had been told by astrologers that he could never lose his kingdom, except at the hands of a man with a hundred eyes. Only when it was too late did he realize that the name of the general was Bayan, which, rendered in the Chinese tongue, means 'Hundred Eyes'. And perhaps, Marco reflected, the Great Khan too had known of this and selected Bayan specially for the task of conquest. The Lady Kuan had also said that it was the queen, Facfur's wife, who had surrendered the kingdom, since Facfur himself had already fled to one of the islands in the Ocean. The Great Khan was delighted that no damage had been done to the splendid city and its royal palace and Buddhist temples, since it was his intention to preserve it as a regional capital, under the direct control of a governor and council appointed by himself. It fell to Marco to present the letters of office to the council, one of whom was to be the artist Chao Meng-fu, known personally to the Great Khan because of his reputation as an artist and inventor of certain war-machines. Soon the governor would arrive and Marco's commission would be over. He had already decided—perhaps one day when he was out riding with Kuan—to stay for a while in this City of Heaven.

'What kind of a man is the Great Khan?' she asked Marco. 'Describe him to me and I will paint him.'

'He is unceasingly curious about the peoples and cities of the empire. He sends out scores of envoys for no purpose other than to accumulate information about his lands.'

'I have heard that he is a giant of a man, with fiery red hair.'

'He is smaller than I am, but thicker. His hair and beard are white; he is an old man now, but his complexion is like yours, soft and pale.' This flattery she took like a cat being stroked. Suddenly oppressed by the silent airy room, Marco said, 'Let us walk in the garden.' It was the time of day he liked best: things growing larger in the early evening shadows. They walked over the very bridge the Lady Kuan had painted, he reducing his stride to match her delicate steps on bandaged feet. The Chinese valued smallness in women as a quality greater even than a smooth pale skin. His own appearance, not unattractive to Tartars, was a source of curiosity, and often contempt, to the Chinese, for whom his thin straw-coloured head perched on a long neck was grotesque, like an animal's. Marco considered that he had reached his manhood aeons ago, in Venice, but never since those awkward days had he felt such a clumsiness with others as with these perfect, delicate people. 'One becomes used to being different to other peoples,' he wrote to the Great Khan, 'but to be uglier, worse, that comes hard to a Venetian.' He relived in Kinsai nights he had thought lost forever, illicit moments stolen with girls of his quarter, fumbling on the slimy canal steps, panting between desire and embarrassment. The courtesans of this city, for whom love was an art as rich and varied as the Lady Kuan's painting, giggled among themselves, recalling the weight of his apologetic kisses. He no longer visited them: the satisfaction could not outweigh the trembling of his faltering pride. But Kuan belonged to a different order: among animals there is no pride in love, only nature fulfilled. She led him as if he were blindfolded, an actor on alien boards. Beside him, silent, walked the spirit of his friend Chao Meng-fu.

The gardens of the Lady Kuan nursed a secret path among the rhododendra, which led out to the great lake on the south side of the city. The deep flowers spread a violet carpet for them, as if to cushion their footfall from the listening trees. To the Chinese each act was witnessed, for nothing had been created without ears, eyes, a nose. Marco stooped between overhanging branches. If they saw, he thought, they would not soon forget so strange a guest. Wordlessly they walked down to the beach. Across the water, the island, like a sleeping monster, invited and threatened. In the dying light the surf appeared purple, except where lanterns threw an orange glow. Dancing fire reflected on the water. Shapes and colours with no clear outlines. One of the pleasure-barges provided for the lake was moored nearby, a small one, designed for no more than five people at one time.

'Send away the boatman,' Kuan murmured. He strolled off unconscious of an honour left unguarded. Marco took his pole and pointed the barge out into the lake. The lantern, swinging gently, painted his hair orange as he steered them towards the island. For a moment he was reminded of Venice, but here, instead of the gulls calling to woo men further and further into the lagoon, tall flightless birds stood like young trees in the shallow waters. It grew darker as they approached the island; the fading sun was obscured by trees. They travelled in almost-silence, outlined by the quiet rhythm of the water against the side of the coloured barge, the occasional chuckle of a bullfrog.

They drifted into a cove overgrown with bushes and tall grasses. On this side of the island few people ventured; nearer to the other end, opposite the city gates, stood the pavilions and temples where the chattering rich of Kinsai took their picnics, their women, their pleasures. At this time of the evening only a few lovers wandered through the formal gardens, like the ghosts of a well-filled day. In their secluded arbour Marco and Kuan lay in the long rushes undisturbed, while enormous lilies sagged above their heads. At first she was frightened, pointing to the ancient worn statues of kings gathered in a clearing, like a conference of the dead.

'They have come to hear our nightmares,' she whispered, clawing at his arm. He kissed her green eyes and led her by the hand out of the clearing.

'They are our guardians, against the prying of strange beasts,' he said. But even in the delectable moment of love he sensed them surrounded, as the very grasses strained to hear each whispered endearment, feel each caress. The statues took on the faces of the living, and merged into one, the impassive Chao Meng-fu. Marco pictured him riding alone in his carriage through the streets of the city in his ministerial robes, and felt his deep and sensitive sadness, like an arrow finding its target in the dark.

'Do not try to explain,' she said, putting her small hand over his mouth. 'It is not a thing like that.' She would not let him speak about themselves, as if that might awaken her from a dream. For his own part, words did not come so easily. Even loving was new in an alien language. He thought instead of waters, drifting like desert sand blown by the wind, waters of many colours, like the shades of his love's paint or the gems held in his father's wrinkled hand. All this was like an episode from the city's own history, as if stones and painted wood, the smells of scent and garbage, the sound of the summer rain on temple roofs, had the power to create. When the Lady Kuan said, 'It is not a thing like that,' she meant, 'This has nothing to do with us; the city has created it.' The city: stalls in the streets piled high with fruit—apples, melons, mangoes, pears—and the wineshops where rice wine flowed from silver barrels; the streets themselves, paved with brick, each with a gutter at one side to collect the rain; the statues of the Buddha and ancient heroes, bronze stomachs jutting below proud faces; the light carriages pulled by white horses racing sound-less through the rain, offering clouds of watery spray behind

85

them. Above all the dancing, for Kinsai was a city of dancing people. In each movement of the oldest porter bent under a heavy load, in the playing of children in wide straw hats Marco glimpsed the disjointed steps of the dance of the City of Heaven. The roots of a rhythm infused every square and house, so that every citizen was a part of it, and the city incomplete without a single part. Kuan, sitting triumphant in peacock feathers in her husband's carriage, or observing the shadows of the moon on rice-paper, was also a part of the dance, and the fat lazy Facfur with his concubines, the conquerer Bayan, perhaps even the Great Khan himself, leaning on his carved rose-wood throne with his thin beard straggling on his breast, awaiting the return of his envoy.

'Places we know make us the people we are,' Marco told the Lady Kuan, as they lay perfectly still together. The City of Heaven, where luxury was so surely defined, the harmony between indulgence and happiness, had fashioned the lithe-limbed, green-eyed Kuan. But Marco himself was a composite of empires and deserts, from the quay at Venice to the never-dying lamp at the Holy Sepulchre, the natural wells of oil spurting out of the sands of Baku to the frothy sherbet sipped in cool courtyards of Baghdad, hawking on the high-lands of Pamir, limping for shelter from the sun and wind in the Desert of Lop, lost in the screaming port of Zaiton where men lived on frail sailboats, riding exhausted with Tartars across northern wastelands, drinking mare's milk until the skins were dry and they slit the horses' veins to drink their blood. A microcosm reflecting, like his father's gems, the play of light and shade in the mind of the Great Khan's empires and beyond. He was himself and all men. When he thought of it, he became dizzy, and all these split images revolved slowly around a still darkness in his mind, like the centre of a whirlpool, defined by fever emptying his vital fluids into the sheets of his bed as the caravan bumped painfully across Badakshan.

These thoughts—these memorials, I should say, with respect proper to the dead—I have reproduced from Amanda's note-books. There, as here, they have no strict chronology. It seems to me that she had begun to regard events as connected in ways other than a purely temporal sequence. 'When something happens, it exists forever, however brief the moment of occurrence. Time is only our own method of accounting for things, like putting objects in glass cases': these are her own words. It is grief to me to see them, and be unable to do them justice. I can only say that Marco Polo was as near to her as anyone, and Jerusalem as far as China.

In any case, her notes are incomplete. The snatches she consigned to paper are by reason of that very act faulty, hollow. Poor Ben, hoping to rediscover his wife in these relics composed among the vineyards and olive trees! Already it is like trying to step into an ancient civilization . . .

Instead of open carriages, delicate Chinese ladies with coloured parasols, I recall the old tin buses rattling through hot streets. The city that fashioned me straggled between the hills of Judaea, a provincial town in those days, a half-city, like the family heirloom burnished and put on display. At weekends in the summer I used to take the bus that crawled through the suburbs of West Jerusalem, collecting Hasidim with their baskets full from the dusty street market, and out to the north-west of the city. In the hills it was cooler, and the kibbutz nestling in the approach to the city had a natural pool among the rocks. Sometimes I would stay the whole weekend; on the Sabbath, when there were no buses, I could scrounge a lift from an Arab truck-driver, a peasant returning to his village with empty crates. At night I sat up late in the hills and watched the city from afar. I liked the kibbutzniks, many of them Africans from Tunisia or Algeria, or Sephardim from Baghdad or Yemen. One of these, a small, hard nut of a

87

man, became a friend. He was a Jew from the unlikeliest place, the uplands of Turkestan, north of the Hindu Kush, recovered, he said, from the Lost Tribes. There were a few Jewish settlements scattered there, near their ancient trading centres of Bokhara and Samarkand. Yakov had walked to the new land of Israel, he claimed, as soon as independence was declared.

'I wanted paradise,' he said, 'and I found a land gutted and bare. What you see here, we built with our hearts and our hands.'

'Do you still hope it might become paradise, Yakov?'

'Oh no, I ceased to believe in that. As soon as I had real work to do—this work—the dreams were no more than the illusions they really are.' I thought then of other dreamers, far to the east of us, following the road to paradise. If Giles had been a potter, like Yakov, or a carpenter or a farmer, would he be scrambling now over arid plains, chasing a dream?

Because of his expertise, Yakov had been employed as an advisor at many of Israel's archaeological excavations, reconstructing finished pots from chipped fragments. And so, of course—how easy and inevitable are these connected relations, as if ordained!—he knew Martha, who had worked in Jerusalem and at Caesarea on the coast. I expressed surprise, although I knew her fiancé was an archaeologist. Yakov looked at me curiously, but said nothing. How long had she lived in Israel, I wondered, remembering that I had taken her for a sabra. Yakov did not know, but told me her mother had been born in Palestine, in the days of the British Mandate. And her father? An Englishman, like myself, which explained her education and accent. These lucid answers were unsatisfying. 'Yes, but what is she?' I asked. She seemed to stand apart from any origins or background, as though a stranger, perhaps even an elf, had appeared unannounced one day with a baby in her arms. Her mother was killed in the fighting for independence, near Zefat; her father lived alone in

England. I told him we had met briefly in Jerusalem, and that I loved her.

'Everyone is in love with her,' he said, 'that is why everyone hurts her.' When he dispensed his scraps of hard-earned wisdom his bald brown head looked more walnut-like than ever. On a hot day the veins in his head would stand out when he spoke.

'Did you know she was back in the city?' I asked casually. As I had guessed, it surprised him.

'I thought she had left the country. I have not seen her for a year, or maybe more. We were at Caesarea together.' Yakov played with the leather thong on his wrist. Once it had been fine white snakeskin, but the earth of the centuries and his continual fiddling had discoloured and worn it. All his people wore one, he explained, as protection against snakebite. It was as much a part of him as the little flute he played in the evenings, with an inexpert grace. 'It would be good to see her again,' he mused. But I had no idea where in the city she was living, or even if she was still there. My small circle of acquaintances (smaller now without Ben and Amanda) was set and defined; for all its chaotic mixture, Jerusalem was a private city. To search her out would be an intrusion not of its privacy but of the laws by which it had defined our meeting, our brief, imagined liaison. She had entered my life by chance but deliberately, and left it with equal certainty. When she came again, it was her own choice. I found her sitting amid the semi-squalor of my tiny flat when I came home from work one evening.

'I thought you would still be living here,' she smiled, in greeting. 'The landlord let me in.'

'I wasn't aware you ever knew where I lived.'

'Oh, I make a pretty good spy. Better than poor old Saddle.' She had brought up the only thing which was between us, like an accusation, as if his crushed body was lying on the floor at my feet. She had made herself at home in my ramshackle living-room while waiting; I noticed a few

89

objects moved, books straightened on the shelf.

'Did you hear what happened to him?' I asked. When I had imagined our conversation on meeting again, it had been on a slate wiped clean. This, of course, was folly, for it was the city that threw us together, Saddle's city.

'Yes—like the hand of Fate.' Ah, how we still trust those fickle goddesses—they alone hold up the narrow space between the heavens and the earth!

'Are you staying in Jerusalem?'

'I am working in the north, by the Sea of Galilee—Lake Kinnereth, I should say. It's a small excavation, near Capernaum, a first-century town.'

As when Yakov had called her an archaeologist, it was incongruous to imagine that remote, composed figure grubbing around among rocks and tangled overgrowth. Knowing nothing of it, the business of archaeology resembled for me a scout-like activity, like bird-watching or collecting coins. 'I tried not to come back,' she said, 'although I knew it was unforgivable, after you helped me. I thought I could transplant myself, like a flower, and forget the old bed of soil. It was too painful, having to look inside myself. But it didn't work, anyway. I am visiting you as an exorcist. Will you be able to help me this time, do you think?'

Brilliant strategist that she is, her hold over me was fixed from then on. Perhaps I am too pliable, but the clay does not complain if the potter's hands are light and soft to the touch. She arrived on a Friday evening, just before the buses stopped running. For me, at least, the city was empty that weekend. The tin shacks of the slum district were endowed with poetic nobility, the minarets on the skyline the heights of our exploration. Martha lay unrolled before me like a map, every delicate contour newly-drawn. It was not possession, still less conquest. I knew there could be nothing without consent. She began to face herself through me; even now, having deceived me, she thanks me for it.

She was surprised and pleased to see Yakov again, when

90

we went up to the pool to bathe. She looked older, he said, but approvingly, as if she were a woman in his eyes for the first time. They said nothing, in my presence, about old associations, and for my part, I had no desire to penetrate too deeply. Where she led me by the hand, I would follow, and the rest could lie buried. I was never, like Amanda, a traveller on the ocean-bed of the unconscious.

Drying herself off after a final swim, Martha said suddenly, 'You must both come back with me to Galilee.'

'Why?'

'I need your help, Yakov. We have a good deal of pottery we can't do anything with. First-century, mostly local, a little Greek.'

'If I can get away from here,' he grinned.

'And how can I help?' I asked.

'You need a holiday,' she said, 'and I need your company. I would like you to see the dig.'

'I would like to also, though Ben would be more useful than me.'

Then she started to ask about him and Amanda. I told her they were searching for paradise, which was all I understood of the matter.

'Amanda said a little about it, the one time that we met. She said they were following Marco Polo, but it meant nothing to me. A lot of what she said was over my head.'

'She is a dreamer, and Marco Polo is the subject of all her dreams, sometimes even her dream *persona*. She has had this fascination for years, which used to drive Ben to despair, but now I think she has begun to dream even during the day.'

'But Ben, too, is a dreamer, I think.'

'Is he?' I was surprised, never having thought it of him. 'In his way, maybe. He is an academic.'

'Paradise I suppose I can understand,' said Martha, looking far beyond me, 'but Marco Polo—where does he fit in?'

This was not a thing I could explain. I suppose I had become accustomed to Marco, and thought of him as harmless, but

91

paradise was like a code-word to a secret obscured from me. In Giles' novel, *The Tragedian*, a character exclaims, 'The idiot Orpheus, holding out his hand to his lover! He didn't understand the paradox: possession gained, love-longing over.' But in his vituperative way Giles failed in this too. If everyone has his own paradise, his garden enclosed against a fallen world (and if mine, as he mocked, was the dullest of all) what drove him to the outer reaches to try and possess his own? In a madly logical way, it was a suicide, this self-delusion that somewhere, beyond Cambridge, beyond Venice, beyond Jerusalem, perhaps, as in Ben's medieval maps, on the very borders of the world cut off by a wall of fire, lay Eden. Well, he had a right to it, but no claim at all on Marco Polo, and none on Amanda. Martha still blames him for her breakdown.

'In a sense,' she says, 'he was more her lover than ever Ben was. He forced into her his own desires, and shaped her dreams to be like his own. But she couldn't live with it, and he never had to.'

Whatever the truth of it, this vision of paradise on earth was never a part of the original dreaming, as far as I can make out from her notes. That was Giles' own end and delusion; Marco Polo's, I am sure, was something quite different. But the two became fused, and Ben and Amanda followed Giles east, in Marco's fading tracks.

A week after Martha's visit, Yakov and I travelled north to Galilee. The kibbutz had released him, as they always did when he was needed, and I was able to take a little leave from the Consulate. We drove in an old jeep that rattled on the road like sea-shells in a jar; it was left behind by the British in 1948, and used on the kibbutz. The route to the north in those days was less straight than it is now, when modern air-conditioned buses hurtle up and down the Jordan Valley, ejecting soldiers now and again to man the anti-aircraft guns pointing across the river. We drove west almost to the coast, and up the Plain of Sharon to the furnace of Tiberias on the Sea of Galilee. What little history I know is Ben's, but I felt a vicarious thrill as we approached the town; somewhere on this parched road, between two hills, the horns of Hattin, the small heavy army of Guy, King of Jerusalem, was trapped and massacred by Saladin, laying open and bare the road to the Holy Sepulchre . . .

Some of this I tried to convey to my companion, but his attention wandered. The history fought so valiantly and cruelly on his ancestral land was no part of his own or his people's. Instead, he dwelt on a more recent past. We had stopped in Tiberias to fill the jeep's tank and shake the dust from our hair (how I wished we could plunge just once into the warm, clear waters of the Lake!) when he asked me, casually, whether I knew the circumstances surrounding the death of Saddle. I explained that I had been there and seen it myself: the ancient wall making fragments of his skull.

'Ah, so it is true, this strange way of death? I wondered, I confess, whether Martha had not invented it herself.'

'But why should she? Unless you suspected her of killing him and making up this alibi?' I joked.

'It has a kind of beauty, do you not think? The troubled, cruel man caught in the hysteria of people he hated, the city he feared . . .'

'Saddle, a troubled man, afraid of the city? I think you must be making more of him than there was,' I said, bewildered.

'No, my friend, alas, there is much that you do not know.' Yakov's English, interspersed with Hebrew words and expressions, sometimes even with obscure Daric exclamations (which he never explained) had a poetry of incongruity, a misplaced drama. Occasionally, as now, it raised the content to the level of Tragedy. Or perhaps my own self-importance endowed our actions with the significance of clues in a larger, cryptic puzzle.

'I know only what I seem to see,' I said carefully. 'Martha implicated herself, in Saddle's eyes, through her attachment to Mansur.'

'Mansur! So there was another, after all!'

'Yakov, you have left me far behind. What do you mean, another? He was her fiancé, when I met her.' A small voice inside me began to recite the line that Ben used so often to quote, from an epic poem on Charlemagne: The wall so firm in the days of my youth shows cracks and signs of decay . . . Yakov looked at me with sadness, an expression that did not become him. It was not a face intended for gravity.

'Perhaps I have said too much already. What Martha has not told is sacred to her, and not for me to violate.'

'How can you violate the past by telling it, so long as it is true? Maybe she tried to tell me herself, but could not.'

'The true version?' he said, speculatively. 'But Alex, you already know a version which is not untrue: the events you saw with your own eyes, your inward reactions to them, your emotions, your thoughts. They are not false.'

'Nor, it seems, are they the whole truth.'

'Is it for everyone to see the same version of events? Is the universe the same shape for all men? What I know is only an unliving shadow of what really took place. It may be different from your version, but no closer to the truth; after all, it comes even less from direct observation than yours, and more from what Martha and Saddle have told me.'

'Saddle? So you knew him also? Yakov, who was he? I thought I knew, but I can see I must have been wrong.'

'No, you were not wrong,' he said slowly, 'but you made the mistake of assuming that Saddle consisted only of that tangent where his life touched your own. There is always more, Alex, for everyone you think you know. That is why there are infinite worlds.'

'Can my world never be the same as another's, as Martha's, for instance? Tell me how Saddle appeared in your world.' Yakov climbed back into the jeep and started the engine.

'It is better,' he said, 'on the open road.' As we left the town and followed the road leading north along the lake shore, he began again. 'Saddle's father was a prominent member of the British community in Palestine. He was made Dean of St.

George's, the Anglican cathedral in Jerusalem—that must have been in the early Twenties. The young Saddle was born in the cathedral precinct, and grew up in the city. He told me he had been sent back to England to be educated; I forget which school, but it was his father's before him. When he left school, during the war, he was immediately recruited by British Intelligence and sent back to Palestine—naturally, he spoke excellent Arabic. His father died during the war; his mother was already dead. So you see, he was more at home here than anywhere else.'

'But he feared the city, you said.'

'It came to symbolize many things for him, particularly his own misery. You must know that he was never happy here, especially after his mother's death, which must have occurred while he was in England. But in a British Palestine he could manage. The Arabs, after all, were the workers and the servants—it was the Jews he hated and feared. When independence was declared and the British left, that is when he became afraid.'

'Why didn't he leave too, when the British army did?'

'You think it is so easy? Perhaps you will see yourself, one day. After all, what remained for him in England? And slowly the city becomes your theatre, and its horizons the extent of your vision. I have seen this myself, among others. Saddle, who had lived out most of his life in the city, became, although an alien, its most typical inhabitant.'

While the old Tadzhik spoke I reassembled the living Saddle from the fragments in my mind. I remembered the soft, greasy face, the prominent nose thrust too close to mine as his hands clawed at my shirt, the metallic breath that smelt of stale wine. I recalled how my contempt had suddenly turned to fear as he lashed out at me. In despising him still, it was partly myself I hated. His sudden accusations: until now I had taken them at their face value, knowing no better and suspecting no worse . . .

'I do not know when he became Martha's lover,' Yakov

95

went on, and as he mouthed them the words fell dully into place like coins into a slot. The deadly inevitability of it, now that it was out, hardly surprised me, though a moment later it felt as though a knife were being rotated in my guts. Increasingly I was learning that these events surrounding me, and these people, moved on a wider plane than I could visualize. I felt like a small boy lost at the seaside. Later, it was as if something very slender, like a twig, had snapped under a tremendous weight. Yakov, looking at me, said kindly, 'I can see that you did not know this. Forgive me, perhaps I should never have begun to tell you.'

'Please go on. I have to know.'

'There is not so much. She was young when she came back to Israel, but not so young. All the same, there was a wildness about her. She began working in Jerusalem. I don't know when she met Saddle, only how. I heard it from him. Martha had been out drinking with some friends—it was someone's birthday. She got separated from them, and I suppose she fell in with bad company. Saddle had been meeting a contact in the poor quarter where the Yemeni labourers live, among the building sites and tin shacks. He heard noises and found, in a dark alley blocked off by builders' rubble, a gang of young Sephardim standing around a figure on the ground. Martha was edging away from the body; she had broken his head with a brick, defending herself. Saddle arrived only just in time, fired a few shots in the air, grabbed her and escaped. After that I suppose he felt she owed him something; at any rate, she was in no state to refuse. She was grateful, at first, then regretted it and thought she might have done better after all at the hands of the Yemenis. He used to hang around the excavation site sometimes, when one of his contacts let him down, or he had nothing better to do. We could stand him no better than she could, but we did not have to bear more than the sight of him. When she tried to join the kibbutz, he would not let her. She had killed a man, and who was to say what evidence he might give if it came to trial? And besides that, I suppose, archaeologists do not live well, and she had to eat.'

'What a snake of a man! He was worse than I had thought!' The horror of her situation struck me quite suddenly. When Yakov spoke of it—I suppose because he loathed even the memory of the man—all this seemed black and white.

'Martha stopped working at the dig; at the time I thought it was to try and get away from him. But he had a hold which I never really understood. I cannot believe she ever felt anything for him.'

'I cannot believe it either,' I said, knowing that what we believe is subject to our will.

'For a few months I saw nothing of either of them. Someone said she was working as a waitress, or a dancer. One day a friend of mine saw her in the city, in a bar frequented by Arab workers. She looked dreadful, her clothes were dirty. When she got up from the table where she had been sitting with three or four men, he greeted her, but she walked past without acknowledging him. After that I went to see her at her flat, but she was not in. I obtained Saddle's address and sought him out, though I have no idea what I would have said to him. At that time he lived close to the frontier, in one of those tenement blocks where the poorest refugees gathered. I still remember the stink of cat's piss and rotting fruit as I climbed the stairs. It was a dark, decrepit place. His door was slightly open, but there was no answer when I knocked, so I went in. The place was in disarray. He had two rooms, a sitting-room where he also slept, in a cot stripped of its sheets, and a kitchen which also had a cracked dirty bathtub. He was sprawled in the tub, unconscious, half-dressed. There was no alcohol about, but I found a paper package with some white powder still inside. I know nothing of these things, and was scared. I found a telephone and called for an ambulance, then ran away. When I heard the sirens approaching, I felt guilty for running so I went back and hid around a corner, watching as they took him away. Later, I went back to ask the other

97

tenants if they knew what had become of the Englishman. They didn't, but one said he had seen a young woman go into his flat: Martha, I suppose. That was the last time I saw Saddle.'

'So he was a drug addict too. I suppose he must have found it easy to get hold of it, with his contacts. That must have been what she was doing in the bar.' Yakov shook his small brown head. This foolishness did not concern him, for he was as remote from it as the hills of his homeland. God had given him a pair of good hands and fine eyes; there was enough clay to work with and a sun to provide light—what did he need with the squalor of our tortured loves? There was much he had left unexplained. Where did I fit in with it, and the café where we had met, while Saddle sat hunched in his corner with Hardy? And, above all, who was Mansur? But Yakov knew no more, or would say no more. Since that visit to the flat he had seen nothing of Martha, and heard of Saddle's death only days before, when I had brought her to the kibbutz. It had been in the newspapers, but of course Yakov never read them.

There was little time for all this to sink in, as we began to approach the excavation site. After what Yakov had said, I was afraid to see her again. He had been right: it was a mistake to pry too deeply into the roots of present happiness. Enjoy the moment, accept what you have been given. I was now an initiate into mysteries she dreaded, and by virtue of that, perhaps also an accomplice. If I had known nothing, I would have been innocent. As we left the main road between the hills, to follow the dirt road that would take us as close to the site as we could go in the jeep, I realized that the ignorance Yakov had despoiled was Martha's own hope. By telling me nothing herself, she was not so much hiding from the past as safeguarding a future.

The dirt track came to an end on a rough plateau, almost half a mile from the site. A few cars were parked here—other than by helicopter, this was the only way to reach the place.

We would have to find a path down the side of the high ground we were on, across the valley and up a steep path to the triangular shaped hill beyond, on whose peak was perched the resurrected town. Our hill was higher, which meant we could see the archaeologists' campsite, just below the path leading up to the summit. From a distance the dirty white tents resembled a bedraggled flock of birds of prey, resting from the midday heat. Apart from the tents we could make out a wooden hut and a covered area, where tarpaulin held up by poles protected two long tables from the sun. Somewhere, I hoped, there might be a well, even running water. I do not know what I had expected, but on the kibbutz, rough-shod as it was, giant fans churned up the air in the breeze-block rooms. There seemed to be no one about, until Yakov caught my arm and pointed towards the summit. Little figures clambered over rocks, others seemed to be filling buckets and carrying them away. I could make out a kind of pulley system by which the buckets were sent down to a point lower than the summit, on the side of the hill.

'I can't see much from here,' I said. 'We'd better find the path and join them.' But Yakov sat in the jeep in a kind of trance, gazing at the site, as though a drama were being enacted for his private viewing. His eyes were keener than mine, but surely, at that distance, he could see nothing that I might have missed. I urged him away again.

'This has set me to remembering,' he said. 'I have not told you how I first met Martha. It was at Caesarea. There was nothing there except for the site, and a village nearby. I had driven down the coast from Haifa; the others in the team had already been working at least a week. I did not know the area, so took a more roundabout route than necessary, and found myself on a shallow hill, like this one but much smaller, overlooking the site—it must have been almost the same distance away as we are now from the site. I was in no hurry, so I got out of the car and just watched for a while. You know how it is—sometimes one has the inclination only to watch, and the longer one watches, the more compelling the sight becomes. After a short while I noticed that I could see no one digging, or doing any kind of work. There were only a few people in the team at that time, but they were all standing around in a knot, in front of a ruined building whose shape I could not quite make out. I always carried a pair of binoculars in the car, so I fetched them and took a closer look. You will think me foolish—I should have simply driven closer and gone to see. That was what I was there for, after all. But sometimes we choose the less obvious thing. Through the glasses I could see that the ruin I had been unable to identify was an old building, half-excavated, that had collapsed. Two men were attempting to shift some of the enormous stones that had spilled over from the structure, but it was obvious that it was in vain. Someone else was lying on his belly in front of the entrance to the building, his head just inside. It was suddenly obvious to me that the building—perhaps a storeroom—had collapsed on top of someone, who must be trapped by the giant blocks of ancient masonry. There was no heavy equipment on the dig—no bulldozer or dumper truck that might have helped clear the place. They were helpless, and I stood about half a mile away and watched.' I was caught by the drama of his simple account; he was a natural story-teller. 'I am telling you this,' he said, suddenly, 'because Martha, a much younger Martha, was one of the group despairing of the life of their colleague. She was sitting apart from the others, on a rock overgrown with weeds, looking out to sea. At the time, of course, I did not know her, but I could see at once that she did not belong there. Her act of sitting on the rock alone was of as great moment as the pathetic attempts to rescue the trapped man. Perhaps it was my remoteness from the scene that gave me a perspective denied those on the site: I was there and not there, a voyeur of the tragedy but not a participant. All I could think was what a beautiful composition it made, like a set-piece scene in a film—sudden drama, the scrabbling rescue attempts gradually diminishing into resigned despair, a lull as they considered what to do next, waited for help, and meanwhile Martha sitting moodily alone looking beyond the wrecked site, beyond the beach to the motionless ocean . . . In the tragedy there was a kind of perfection that made me reluctant to leave. I have never been able to explain it, or recall those shapes and colours exactly. It was a complete moment, as if composed by God, perhaps solely to show me a harmony in things.'

'What happened? Did help arrive in time?' I asked urgently.

'Oh, yes,' said Yakov slowly, still looking out towards the hill, but beyond it, south to the hidden shores of Galilee. 'Very soon, an ambulance arrived, and a truck with a crane, to lift the stones off the body. The archaeologist—whom I never met—had a broken leg and severe cuts, but that was all. I watched as they dragged away the masonry with ropes, after the truck had left.'

Later, when we were sitting in the moonlight at the long tables, I was sorry that I had missed what he was trying to tell me, by insisting on hearing the outcome. Perfect moments are unexpected and cannot be fashioned by one's own fancy. But I found it impossible to ask Martha about it too. Probably, her version would have been entirely different. It was perspective that made it beautiful and whole for Yakov, and in a way I could see that this was why he had not wanted to tell me about Saddle and Martha. It was too late to unknow what I had demanded to know, but I think I was especially tender to her afterwards. We spent a few days bathing in the Lake, on the deserted northern shore. It was so hot during the day that we spent almost all the daylight hours in the tepid water. At night we slept on the beach, and could almost reach out and clasp the stars. We were quiet, as if we had arranged beforehand not to examine ourselves. This also was a part of her; she seldom categorized anything, least of all us. There was little talk of love. Still, quiet waters, like the sun-absorbing Galilee. We could see straight down to the bottom, where the outlines

101

of the pebbles shone clear. When I said, 'I love you', the words were blasphemous to her ears, as though in the telling of it I had violated some secret unmentionable thing. With Martha, it has always been thus.

Each morning that he awoke in Kinsai, Marco said a prayer, to thank God for having brought him safely home to Venice. Then he looked about him, scrambled out of bed and realized he was not there but in the City of Heaven; the walls, though colourfully decorated, were not his own, the sparse, perfect furniture alien. From his window high in the Palace he had a marvellous view of the best quarters of the city, the elegant centre with the most fashionable shops, the widest streets, the most beautiful temples. These had grown up like flowers around the magnificent palace of King Facfur. On the other side of the building, he would have had a view of the park where the king had built pavilions and gardens for his people, the lake with its island of love in the middle, and the pleasure-barges that crawled back and forth each day like insects. And from a window between these two, he would have been able to see the mansions of the most notable residents of the city, perhaps even the yellow and white house of the artist Chao Meng-fu . . .

There was no city known to Marco that was less like Venice than Kinsai, but each morning he awoke convinced he was back in his birthplace. Perhaps he dreamt of Venice at night, and the dream passed with him from the frontiers of sleep to the first moments of wakefulness. Or perhaps he heard the water lapping against the sides of buildings, for the great river which flowed to the south of the city had been channelled into many tributaries which penetrated the quarters of the city, so that, like Venice, it appeared to have been constructed on a network of islands. But the streets and canals of Kinsai were wide enough for several carts and boats to pass alongside

102

each other. This wideness in everything, in market places and houses and canals and streets and bridges made the city very large indeed. Chao Meng-fu told Marco that if a man wanted to walk all around the city, including the lake, which was also fed from the great river, he would have to walk a hundred miles. He also said that in the whole city there were twelve thousand bridges, and most of them built of stone. Marco himself had counted the market places, each one not less than half a mile across, and each encircled by enormous stone warehouses where the foreign merchants stored their goods. He sent word to his father, encouraging him to open a branch of his business there; for a while the details of arranging this and setting it up allowed him an excuse to stay in Kinsai after his official business was long over. Naturally, the city was too large for a man to walk through, but a carriage with a coachman and a fine white horse had been provided for him by the governor. He loved to visit the markets, each one so similar and so different, and watch as the people quarrelled (but not, as in Venice, really meaning to disagree) over the price for roebucks and stags—which could be bought whole and carried home by the merchant's boy—or rabbit or game—partridge and pheasant, quails, capons, wild duck and geese. When the Lady Kuan was showing him the city he had insisted on being taken to the markets, and even on purchasing fruit and game, much to her horror (at first) and then amusement, for she had never been to market herself. To her surprise she found herself enjoying it too, and after that sometimes astonished her servants by insisting on doing her own shopping. (When this happened, it must be added, they always had to follow her out—discreetly, so as not to embarrass her—and purchase those necessary items she had forgotten.)

As the envoy of the Great Khan, Marco found himself the most honoured guest of the new governor. His lodgings in the Palace were decorated with a restrained luxury: a Tartar now presided where the lazy Facfur had reigned. Kiyu was the nephew of the victorious general, Bayan Hundred Eyes, a young protégé of the Great Khan, one of a troop of younger men he had promoted over members of his own family, whom he might have expected to use their positions of influence to sway others against him. Marco approved of the policy—had he not himself done well out of it?—but pointed out that the Khan's rivals, the sons of the brothers and cousins he had put to death, would be more, not less likely to harbour resentment against him if also deprived of high office.

'Firmness and strength, Marco: that is the Tartar way,' the Great Khan replied. 'Put your enemies down when you are able, and you will not fear them; show too much mercy, and your nights will be sleepless.' The Tartar morality would allow for no weakness. To be weak was a sign of cowardice, fear, a soul as cankered as a rotting peach. There was no danger of this in Kiyu, a bear of a man who impressed the Chinese by appearance alone—and also, it must be admitted, repelled them. He had a reputation as a magnificent horseman, although his enormous bulk seated on a horse was a comical sight. But he had twice won the long horse-race in the New Year Games. To Marco he showed the consideration due his rank and esteem in the eyes of the Great Khan, but not without a certain bemusement, as though he could not understand this friendship between the Great Khan and this pale, tall outlander.

Kiyu was grateful for Marco's advice, though it was unofficial: his responsibility had not extended beyond ensuring that the Great Council of the City of Heaven was established according to the Great Khan's instructions.

'These Chinese bewilder me,' the governor complained; 'when they speak in council, I do not understand what they want.' Conversation in council was held through interpreters, mostly Chinese, since few Tartars could manage the various complicated Chinese tongues. 'They speak with their mouths but their eyes say something different,' he went on, echoing Marco's own discoveries. 'How am I to govern them?'

104

'You must learn their ways,' Marco told him. How was he to do this? Well, thought Marco, you could fall in love with one of them, that is a quick and sure way. But, all things considered, it is one that a man would not choose. It is a road that leads into a strange country, where there are no clear frontiers, no guards at the border to tell the traveller that he has taken the wrong path and should turn back; there are mountains and valleys, glaciers and enormous flat lakes whose waters are so still that a man might think he was swimming in the air. This is the sameness of love, this lake, which may beguile or choke its victim in the saturation of desire. Far better, thought Marco, the painful loss of absence, for pain may at least be dulled, eventually perhaps forgotten . . .

Kiyu gestured at the expanse of the city that lay at their feet. They were taking the evening air on the outdoor terrace of the governor's house, set around a courtyard in the Palace. This was built on a hill, and the first-floor terrace gave the best view of Kiyu's domain. But Marco had no time for the view; he stared at the sky, slowly changing colour as the sun fell, from a pink wash to a deeper rose, then an ineffable moment when the light clouds, reflecting the sun, became a landscape in the sky, red and orange hills and plains suspended upside-down. As this faded the clear strip of cloudless sky in the distance shone like pearl, held between cloud and horizon.

'Is it possible,' Kiyu sighed, 'that I may grow to love a city such as this?' He had been regretting, since he arrived, the steppes of Uighuristan, where lately he had been grazing his horse, and sleeping by night on hard turf.

'It is not the city you will love,' Marco replied, 'but the things that are behind the city—the dance of the people, the reflection of light on the roofs, the sound of waters slapping the boatman's oars. These things will beat a rhythm within you; imperceptibly you too will begin to move to that rhythm. Maybe that is love; I do not know.'

'Are you dancing with the city, Marco?' Kiyu asked in his

105

direct way. But Marco did not know how to reply. Weeks had become months, and months almost a year. Soon the Great Khan would summon him to his presence, at the paradise he had built at Shangtu. This hung over his head, both a promise and a curse.

'It will be hard to leave,' he said slowly. He recalled Kuan's words to him: 'You are beginning to fall under the spell of the City of Heaven. Your limbs will soon be gripped by languor, the thoughts freeze in your mind. Curiosity has no home in Kinsai: it will seep away like water from a sponge.' Was he becoming torpid, like the happy people of the city? At first he had thought he had merely lost his way in love, straying off the path. He began to see that this was inseparable from the city: it had created these meetings with Kuan, these touching fingers and lips, these lies hidden from his friend, just as it created the giant lilies on the lake, the willow trees, the neat whir of carriage wheels on paved streets. If he were to leave Kinsai, the slow days of silk and light rain, of peaceful study in the Palace library (his grasp of the language improving as he pored over ancient rolls), could he become a different person? Or would the city and its people, green-eyed Kuan painting her toenails purple, lay a claim on him forever? If it was the same with every place, then a man's life was not his own, but a thing determined by movement, perhaps a chance wrong turning. Marco felt this was something about which he should warn his Tartar friend, but he could not find the words. Perhaps, after all, Kiyu did not mind, as his uncle and father did not seem to, or Kuan. But for himself, he began to think of each parting as an escape, each leave taken of a place a shackle loosened. To free oneself of the rhythm of each place, a man would have to be travelling constantly, lest he absorb even in one afternoon the smells and sounds that are the beginning of the grip. Or he would have to be like Aristotle, perceiving each possibility as actual, a mind holding all things, split into countless fragments.

When he thought of this, the caresses of his lover disgusted

him as the pawing of a beggar. Before his eyes would appear
first the clean white walls of his mother's house on the canal
front in Venice; then they would dissolve into the white-grey
of the sky. Peace came from watching the clouds on their
journeys across the sky. At such times, he would have the
illusion of standing quite still, while the universe moved.

5

Between the towns of Khanabad, on the Qondoz, part of the Oxus river, and Feyzabad, about a hundred miles away, east and slightly north, the highlands of Badakshan begin to swell and cascade among the tributaries of the great river. This country is an arm of the Hindu Kush, which sweeps westward from that point where China and India meet, along the narrow handle of north-eastern Afghanistan. The mountains of the Hindu Kush reach an average of 20,000 feet, although the whole area is influenced by the Indian monsoon climate; dense rainfall results in a thick vegetation across the whole of this country. Ben had expected the region to be sparser, like the high plains of Iran, but instead he found the mountains covered in foliage, like hair on an ape's body. Altogether the forests stretched over 7,000 square miles: mostly conifers, at 10,000 feet, but below that cedars, and below 5,000 feet a bewildering mixture of oak, walnut, ash, juniper, alder. And so tall—as if this were a land peopled by giants. In the forests of Central Africa, he had heard, travellers experienced the same phenomenon, of appearing suddenly Lilliputians. Marco Polo, of course, had described the mountains and their lush plateaux and pure springs with his customary tantalizing meanness: 'These mountains are also the home of saker falcons—fine birds and good fliers—and of lamer falcons. They abound in game, both beast and bird, and in wild sheep.' As if these attenuated words could contain the hillsides and valleys, the slopes crawling with living creatures! Ben had seen, in the short time

108

he had been in Badakshan, foxes and jackals by night, and during the day, from afar, wolves and wild dogs. Goats were commoner than men, and the wild sheep Marco had mentioned as an aside were the 'ovis Poli', that peculiar shaggy, horned sheep almost as large as an ass, that no European saw after the Polos, until the nineteenth century. Giles insisted that a bear lived in the forests just along the creek from the village, and tried to persuade the headman to organize a hunt.

For Ben, this stay with Tadzhik farmers in the highlands of Badakshan was like an anthropologist's holiday on a South Sea island. Even when he had been writing on the dispersal of the Lost Tribes of Israel in the Hindu Kush, and their vicarious influence on European Jewry in the Middle Ages (who, before him, had examined the obscure and fantastic 'Hebrew Letters' of Prester John?), it would have been unimaginable that he should meet their descendants. Perhaps a third of one per cent of the population of Afghanistan claimed Jewish descent: that Giles should have found this settlement and called him there from Jerusalem, was a thing that defied coincidence, a mad, terrifying clue, like a bolt of lightning exploding from a clear sky to strike a tree next to where he was standing. To Amanda, self-trained to expect and then embrace the quirky, nothing could be more natural. Ben explained it in academic terms:

'It is a "topos", a point of interaction between the purely human and the superhuman, or supernatural, if you prefer.'

'We must go, whatever it is,' Amanda insisted.

'It would be unimaginative not to,' Ben agreed.

'It would be worse than that—it would be wrong, sinful, like a denial of nature. It is obvious: here we are in Jerusalem, and Giles writes from the depths of the Lost Tribes, like desolation calling to redemption. Badakshan is the place where Marco Polo spent a whole year recovering from the fever. Two nights ago I dreamt of his leaving Hormuz, with Nicolo and Maffeo. He was already gravely ill: while they

109

rode out on camels he lay in a closed carriage. Even that must have been unbearable. By the time they reached Herat, he was well enough to sit on a horse, but the fever nagged, until he collapsed at Balkh.'

'The ancient capital of Bactria,' Ben murmured. 'But it must have been in ruins in the 1270s.'

'Yes, Genghis Khan had laid it waste, half a century before. But even the ruins of Balkh were as a city of Europe. It was there that Alexander married Darius' daughter. They told Marco that the mansion where they spent their wedding-night stood until the Tartars came.'

'Impossible! The Arabs took the city—in the 650s, I think—yes, 653. The palace would have been almost a thousand years old even then. They were exaggerating, Amanda, whoever it was who told him that.'

'Well, he wasn't paying too much attention. As they wandered through the ruins he suddenly clutched at a broken column, and slid to the marble floor. They hadn't rested properly since Herat, and the journey is hard, across the northern plains. But there was nothing much in Balkh, so they had to put together a stretcher on slides and drag him slowly east, to Talikhan. That was twelve days' journey, being carried like a pregnant Eskimo woman across the ice.'

Their conversations became more abstruse, until I could no longer follow them with interest. Amanda loved to talk about Marco Polo; she had plotted, in her dreams, almost every step of the three-year journey to the Great Khan's court. I thought Ben might have been jealous, as if Marco were a rival lover, but his fine hands rested serenely on Amanda's, eyes never leaving her face. It was then that they were happiest: she untouchable, radiant; his head slightly to one side, like a watchful dog. This was so frustrating for me that I suggested he take her to see a psychiatrist. He became suddenly angry:

'What the hell for? You seem to regard her as insane!'

'Not insane, but in danger of becoming unbalanced. This has become an obsession. She thinks of hardly anything else, as if everything that happens is significant only if it can be related to Marco Polo.'

'Try to understand, Alex,' Ben said patiently. 'It is an exceptional gift, like being a visionary. Her dreams are of such incredible intensity, and every detail is so . . . so plausible, so correct. At times it is like travelling in time to the 1270s. How can you call that madness?'

'Don't you see how blind you are being? If you weren't a historian, it wouldn't be fascinating in the least, it would be frustrating and tiresome, as it is for me, and then it would begin to scare you, but by then it would be too late. You're encouraging her, when you should be helping her to snap out of it!'

'But I don't want to snap her out of anything, and nor does she want it. We are happy, Alex. Maybe it's that you can't stand.'

'For Christ's sake, Ben! You are exploiting my sister! She isn't a circus exhibit, to go into trances and talk gibberish! You're using her for your own academic fantasies.' But at this a look of such pained sadness came into his eyes that I let the matter drop, and never mentioned it again. Ben understood very well what I was saying; perhaps he even agreed, but love would let him do nothing. I know—it makes one powerless even to decide, like a rust eating away at the sharp end of desire. Ben watched and presided over her gradual progression into the innards of her world. What more could he have done? It was enough for him to be with her, as she descended further into the cavern of incoherence, memory . . .

In the spring, the banks of the Oxus sprouted with narcissi and snowdrops, the delicate whiteness of the foothills a soft reflection of the snow on the higher slopes. Hard clear skies, like polished glass. Giles wrote: 'This is too beautiful not to share. I insist that you and Amanda come immediately. I am close to Eden.' He was fitter and happier than ever before, his spare frame well filled by the simple Tadzhik diet and the mountain air. He had stopped smoking, because getting cigarettes was too much trouble. There was so much to do! He envisaged an epic creation poem, a catalogue of flora and fauna, a celebration of the minute exploration of this strange country. Each day he walked in the forest, discovering trees and plants new to him. He spent the mornings feeding the hens, baking bread, weaving; he had even started to cultivate his own tiny patch of land. In the afternoons, he wrote, or read from his small stock of literature: Milton, Spenser, Thackeray, and some of the French Arthurian cycles, in translation. They thought it odd, his wanting the solitude of his own house, rather than staying as a guest of the headman. But after a few weeks one of the more prosperous farmers let him have the use of a small outhouse on the edge of his farm, and once some necessary improvements had been made, it suited Giles very well. The headman, a farmer who owned one of the few motorized vehicles in the village, and was by virture of this and his fields the richest, had been sorry to see him leave, though Giles often dropped by in the evenings to play chess, or join the singing. The solitude was inescapable, to some degree, for only one man in the village understood and spoke English, the rabbi's son, Asher, who had worked in Kabul and taken evening classes: he became guide, interpreter and friend to Giles. The Jews in the village spoke Daric, an eastern dialect of Farsi Persian, the others either Daric or a Pamiri dialect. Only Asher had seemed surprised that an Englishman should one day have appeared—on a bicycle that had come too far already and would go no further—in this small Badakshan village.

'In Kabul now there are a few Europeans, and even Americans,' he said, 'but here, in the mountains, we have never seen any.'

'The Europeans and Americans in Kabul are called beatniks,' Giles explained dogmatically. 'They come to Asia for the drugs, and for enlightenment. Most finish up in India. But few writers come this way.'

'And those who do, like you, because they lost their way.'

112

'It was providence,' Giles said solemnly. 'For this I have been in preparation all my life. We all seek, but it is only a fortunate few who are given comprehension of the end of their search.' These were wasted words, for the rabbi's son's English did not stretch so far as to embrace the abstract. Giles tried mentally to frame a metaphor involving a bus ride, but abandoned it. Silence was more fruitful. Instead, he thought of the preparation: the precocious, wasted undergraduate days; freezing rain in the canals at Venice (he had not expected it to be cold, even in January!); he and a lame pigeon keeping vigil in the greyness in front of San Zanipolo—but this was what writers did—and the slow journey to Jerusalem: sea-sickness on the Adriatic, dancing to shepherds' pipes on Peloponnesian hills; robbed and stranded, like a poor crusader, in Anatolia. In Jerusalem he would lie motionless on his bed and listen to the minutest sounds against the background of the muezzin's call. Hashish-loaded afternoons, and in the evenings, he read the 'Book of the Thousand Nights and A Night' while the pieces on the backgammon board clacked under dry fingers. The city cooled, colours changed; each evening like autumn in a forest. Houmus and lemon juice with unleavened bread, arak to wash it down. Through the broken shutters of his window he could see the moonlight on minarets, each crescent slicing opaque sky. The summer warmth suggested a pall of incense looming over the city.

In Badakshan the stars, souls of the dead, gleamed from a coal-black heaven. Night and day were separate, each heralded by a dramatic moment, each a new Genesis. Things were as clear-cut here for Giles as when he had been a child: work and leisure, dawn and dusk. He had planned to write a travel book, after leaving Venice. He had no clear outlines, or even an itinerary; the route he took would be as revealing as his reactions to places. But when he came to sort out his roughly-scribbled notes, they were as meaningless as hieroglyphics, a catalogue of railway stations, sea-ports, hot tarmac. In Jerusalem, other things intervened. For the months when he was a visitor (if never a tourist) there was no time, and his mind ached with the imprint of each step.

'I saw everything in Jerusalem,' he told Ben, 'not just every site with the remotest biblical or historical association, but each stone of the wall, each coffee-seller in the street. How I longed to write it all down!'

'You could go back,' Ben said. They had both told Giles what they knew of Saddle's death—assuming, as I had, that the melodramatic collapse of a certain stretch of wall in the city had ended his troubles, like a final curtain.

'All the more reason to leave, if Saddle is dead.' In Giles' mind Saddle's demise meant nothing: he was a metaphor, and they can be extended only so far. Saddle was Jerusalem, and when Giles left, he ceased to exist. In his rambling letters, initially from Baghdad, then from a nameless stretch of Iranian road, and finally from the village in Badakshan, he had wavered between self-doubt and enthusiasm for what he called 'My Project', about which he would be no more specific. Amanda thought he meant to travel east and further east, until he found the site of the earthly paradise.

'That is what he told me, when he came that afternoon, just before he left. He was more or less incoherent, but he seemed to know where to look.' (At this Ben muttered darkly about amateurs.) 'It must have been what he meant in that strange dream I had about him, in the cathedral, when he talked about the Grail.'

'He was always talking about the Grail, ever since he read Malory, at Cambridge, and I introduced him to Chrétien de Troyes. His ideas were always hopelessly confused.'

'Well, he's certainly off course. Surely no one imagined the Garden of Eden was in Afghanistan?'

'No, which is why we must be there to prevent him making a mess of it,' Ben said. It was in his mind that Giles was determined to base his next work on this theme, which Ben had for some time regarded as his own, a natural extension of

114

his work on the medieval Jerusalem. To be pre-empted by another academic would be galling, but that it should be Giles ... This graphomanic rivalry that drives men to undertake journeys that defy logic is incomprehensible to me, but I have been told often enough, by both of them, how limited is my horizon!

Giles had taken the overland silk route, but Ben, for all his faults, was more pragmatic. I think he was surprised that Amanda complied so readily with his insistence that they fly, rather than trail across the plains of Iran on horseback or in a caravan, as Marco had done. The two hundred or so miles from Kabul to Khanabad were endured on a train that burrowed in and out of the Hindu Kush. Amanda slept on Ben's shoulder, while he dredged his prodigious memory for the strands that would build up a composition of Eden.

Scripture, of course, was the first word where Eden was concerned, if no longer the final. 'And the Lord God planted a garden eastward in Eden; and there he put the man whom he had formed.' And from that propitious start man became too full of himself—pride goes before a fall, Augustine remarked grimly—and Eden could no longer contain him. Paradise is a later word, entering Greek through Persian: 'Firdawsa', an enclosed garden. 'A garden enclosed is my sister, my spouse; a spring shut up, a fountain sealed.' The words sprang unbidden to Ben's lips, as Amanda stirred gently in the crook of his arm. A fountain sealed: after the expulsion of Adam and Eve an angel stood at the gates of Eden, brandishing a flaming sword. In medieval maps Eden was often shown as a small square patch of land at the top, shut off from the earth by a wall of fire. The Arcadian innocence of Eden must remain uncontaminated, untouched by a fallen world. In Eden, St. Ambrose argued, Adam and Eve had been chaste, though they had wandered naked until their eyes were opened by the serpent's temptation. There's the rub, Ben thought: until they ate the fruit of the Tree of the Knowledge of Good and Evil, there was no good and evil, but only nature.

'Behold,' said God, 'the man has become like one of us now'—and like a god he was flung out of nature's sanctuary, to make his own judgements in a bruising, blemished world, where waters flooded crops, the sun parched and cracked the earth, germs distributed disease, bodies withered and grew tired from the work of mastering the land. If Eden existed now, it was enclosed against men, walled perhaps not by fire but by something insuperable, knowledge. A thing known cannot be unknown; it is like a ravished virginity. Ben understood suddenly the words 'carnal knowledge'. Once they comprehended what they were, it was too late to go back, useless to hide from God's approaching footsteps. Then why did God put the accursed tree right in the middle of the garden, like a red rag waved in front of a bull? It was an impossible challenge, like the secret society Ben remembered reading of, whose only stipulation for membership was that initiates had to stand in a corner for an hour, and not think of a white bear. Were even the seeds that God planted rotten, and man never intended to be a part of nature? As well, then, never to have fashioned him from the dust, as to instil within him, like a genetically-inherited fault, this knowledge that set him apart from perfection, but set him always in search of it because of that very thing, that he knew full well what it was. 'He hath made everything beautiful in its time: also he hath set the world in their heart, so that no man can find out the work that God maketh from the beginning to the end.' It was the ultimate irony, Ben thought, not without bitterness, to be able to see and comprehend beauty, but to attain and possess it, never and nowhere.

But man had tried, as Giles was trying now, with all the foolish determination of which the species is capable: Alexander, they thought in the Middle Ages, had reached the gates of paradise but found them barred to him; St. Macarius

116

went off in search of Eden and was discovered, a toothless, dribbling relic, only days' journey away, but as far as anyone. The last voyage to set sail in search of Eden was launched in 1721, but two generations before that the wise had given up hope of seeing it in its original state. Instead they took the scattered fruits of Creation from all four continents—for by then the New World was already known, and already discarded as a possible location of Eden, despite these strange new species, chocolate and tobacco and turkeys—and planted them together in a new paradise, the Botanical Garden.

Long before that, before the story of Adam and Eve was known to more than a few thousand Israelites, Europeans knew that it was to be found somewhere, this nameless perfection, and since the west was already known as far as the Ocean, the south was desert and the north frozen barbaric wasteland, it must lie in the east, beyond the Persians and Indians. And when they began the extraordinary process of grafting their history and myth on to that of the Jewish people, and Deucalion became Noah, they realized that the terse, bony words in Scripture describing Eden were amplified by the science of Herodotus and Strabo and Pliny the Elder. 'That is it which compasseth the whole land of Havilah, where there is gold; and the gold of that land is good: there is bdellium and the onyx stone.' Yes, indeed, there was gold and onyx, but how much more besides! Rubies and sapphires and chalcedony, whole palaces built from them, for they could be collected from the very river beds, and herbs and stones with all kinds of magical properties: they made one invisible, they bestowed light or heat or darkness. And creatures! Hippogriffs and dragons and many-coloured lions, unicorns and the phoenix born from its own ashes, pygmies and giants, winged ants that dug for gold, men with the heads of dogs, men with no heads, but holes for eyes in their breasts; sciapodae, the men with one enormous foot who lay on their backs in the sun, lifting the foot as a shelter; salamanders who could be flung into a fire and would not burn,

117

but turn white; and marvellous buildings, the chapel of glass that could expand to accommodate more people, the golden Palace of the Sun, and his fountain, too hot to touch during the day, and the miraculous palace commissioned from St. Thomas by the King of India, which God built in one night, after the saint had spent the money allotted him for the task on feeding the poor, and which later became the palace of Prester John, the Christian emperor of the East, whose tributaries included 72 kings, whose realms encompassed the sea of sand and the fountain of Eternal Youth, who feasted at his table thousands at one sitting, and commanded in battle the savage hordes of Gog and Magog. This land was surely a paradise, for here there were no venomous reptiles, no disease or old age, no fornication or adultery, no heretics. If only the Prester could have brought his armies to the help of the Christians in their struggle against the Saracens! Ben recalled a passage in Otto von Freising's *Two Cities*, where he reports a rumour of the Prester's attempt to cross the Tigris and Euphrates and march on the infidel from the east, but without success. So desperately did they want to believe in that Eden! At first in the Far East, or India, or even in the uninhabitable antipodes; then in Ethiopia or Abyssinia, at the source of the Nile, and even after that in America, where travellers in the early years of the seventeenth century found a tribe who preserved among themselves a tradition of a paradise to be found far to the west. California? Ben wondered sardonically, as the night train wheezed farther north, to those empty mountains so long discarded by Utopians. And now Giles, excitable, erratic Giles, revived the dusty memories: not as historian or archaeologist or anthropologist, but as a simple traveller. Ben dozed off, accompanied by pictures of parrots floating down the rivers of paradise in their nests, holding in their beaks precious gems.

It is hard to write of Ben at this stage. I suppose I have known him as well as anyone, better than most. For a few years—our own Eden, looking back on it—we were together oftener than apart. After that, he seemed to have grown more serious every time I saw him, and more withdrawn. But we do not change more between the ages of, say, fifteen and sixty than between one and fifteen, and even after all the years when we met barely two or three times, it was to me that he turned when most in need. Yet when it comes to paradise, and the journey to Badakshan, I might as well be describing an event that took place many hundreds of years ago, involving people unknown to me. If I cannot describe it, I believe that no one can, but even to Martha I am unable to open my mind; less because I am unwilling than because I am afraid to find it empty.

Perhaps I began to lose Ben when he fell in love with Amanda—how hard it is to conceive of any man in love with one's own sister!—but it was after they left Jerusalem that I felt abandoned by an old and familiar presence. When, much later, I brought this up with him, he simply shrugged and said, 'We both had lives, Alex, and they were bound to be different. You went your way, with Martha, and I mine. We couldn't be children forever.' I flatter myself, perhaps; his eyes were sad as he said it.

It may be that Ben kindled in the back of his mind the hope that there might be somewhere, unknown to generations of cartographers, a small region, perhaps enclosed by hills, or an island in the middle of a lake, as yet unexplored, like a garden with an angel standing at the gate; perhaps, like Nicolo Polo, he could not explain the impulse that locked his brain in that set path, so that circumstances combined to reduce every alternative to the one unimaginable, not to go, to turn back, only to dream. An aside from the prologue to Marco's account of his travels recurred like a creed: 'When the brothers came here, they could neither go on nor turn back. So they stayed for three years.' As if 'here' were not Bukhara, but only

119

Constantinople, or one of the Illyrian coastal cities. Nothing could be more natural, in Marco's 'Travels', than that two Venetian merchants should decide to live in the silk-ridged caravan city, where the Tartar Bakran ruled a mixed population of Turks, Uzbeks, pagan Tartars. Hardly a word about the logistics: how did they travel, under what conditions, who guided them, what did they wear, how did they communicate? And what did they do when they reached the gates of the city? It is these details that worry me, but to Ben and Amanda they were adiaphora, irrelevances. No matter how you got there, or how dangerous it might be, where you might have to stay—if you thought these essential trivia worth troubling over, you might as well stay home. Of course, I exaggerate: Giles had no fixed employment, and Ben was on a year's sabbatical of which the teaching post in Jerusalem had taken only a single term. But, if I am honest, it was not the Foreign Office that kept me in Jerusalem.

So it was the other three who squatted on low stools by the fire of the headman's house, absorbing the heat from under woven blankets, for the spring nights in Badakshan are cold. A large, low room, plastered walls, wooden untreated furniture, earthenwear jars filled with rice and flour and herbs: on the floor, home-spun rugs and sheepskins. The headman, as befitted his wealth and rank, had installed electric lighting in his house, which shone dimly. His family was large; after a while he scarcely noticed the strangers by the fire. There was singing and dancing, but Ijaz himself was too old; he played chess in a corner with his neighbour. Sweet woodsmoke filled their nostrils like a drug, stilling thoughts that beat in over-active minds. The rabbi's son came over to where they were sitting. He was welcome in the house, though it was a Muslim family, but of course he could not have supper there, as Ben and Amanda and Giles had done.

120

'Tomorrow will be a fine day again,' he said. 'If you wish, it would be a good day to see the ruins.'

'We have been looking forward to it,' Giles said. Religiously, he had refused to visit them until his friends arrived, contenting himself with glimpses stolen from between the trees, or a hilltop opposite. Asher could tell them little about them, and his father even less. Opinion among the villagers was divided, a few maintaining that they were haunted by demons, others that they were built by the original inhabitants of the land, before the Turkic peoples came in their waves across the steppes, before the Arabs brought Islam, perhaps when Bucephalus, Alexander's horse, was put to stud with the local mares, when the general himself rooted out the last of the Bactrian nobles to defy his authority, and built the gateway across two mountains to keep out Gog and Magog . . . Giles himself hoped fervently that the thing, whatever it was, was not simply an abandoned fort left over from European imperialist expeditions in the last century. His brief examination from afar had hinted at more: broken columns, pediments overgrown with weeds, something that might once have been a tomb. Ben would know, and if he did not he would have an opinion.

Now, his square-jawed face half-lit by the fire, Ben plucked at the loose threads in his blanket while he listened to Asher.

'There are other ruins, further to the north, if you are interested. I have not seen them myself, but my father says they are bigger than our own. All along the river there are ruins; this country was great, in ancient times.'

'How could we get there?' Giles asked.

'With horses—or by car along the road, and then walking. They are undisturbed, for no one lives there now, or visits them.' Obviously, he took Ben for an archaeologist, a reasonable conclusion. Why else would he be here, and so interested in ruins? Giles had arrived by mistake, on a bicycle, but he had taken a train from Kabul, and driven to the village in a hired jeep. Ben had been brought—with his wife—as an

121

expert. What kind of a pretence could he make, up on the hillside, he wondered now. He had no idea what he was looking for, but it could not be stones crumbling on a mountain. It was Giles who distributed confidence like cigarettes to weary troops, assuring, cajoling. You will love this place, he had told them: the cleanness of the air, the liquor, home-brewed in every barn. He had spent hours cleaning his meagre house, borrowing and scrounging, re-painting walls, to prepare for his guests. At the last moment Ijaz had insisted on looking after them himself: honoured visitors must of course stay with the headman. (Of course, he was immune to the sheep-odour that hung over the entire house, creeping like a virus from the skins on the floor, the cooking-pot, the leather he wore himself.)

The host came over from his chess-game. He had important news: an antelope hunt, on the mountain tomorrow. It was the least he could offer his distinguished guests. The solitary gold necklace at his hairy throat glinted in the firelight. Almost bald, stocky and powerful, he still worked every day in his fields, although he could now afford to hire enough labourers to do the work. He reminded Ben of a Tartar warrior; the bow legs would sit well on a horse. Somehow, Ben felt he would be insulted if asked to postpone the hunt in favour of exploring the ruins, but he did not want to offend Asher either, who had been so helpful to them. Eyes were on him as he framed a response—to be delivered, of course, through Asher.

The young Jew said, with a smile, 'The ruins will be there forever. In any case, you may get the chance to see them on the hunt. It is the same mountain as where the antelope live.'

'Then please express my gratitude, and say we will be honoured to hunt antelope with him tomorrow,' said Ben.

'All of you?' Asher asked, not looking at Amanda. Muslim women never hunted, but this one was a guest, after all. She said, 'Yes, all of us. I can ride better than my husband.'

He did not translate the last words for the headman. While

122

he was speaking, Giles whispered to Ben, 'Have you hunted before? I mean, on a horse? Foxes, or anything?'

'No, just rabbits, with a shotgun. But I can ride, just about.'

'As long as you can stay on. It's their show, really, though you may be asked to make a final kill, as a gesture of hospitality.'

Ijaz called over the younger Tadzhik men, who filled the room with laughter and shouts. Ben had the impression of square black beards thickening dark faces, white teeth, curly hair. They began to toast his health and the headman's, in anticipation of the hunt, in their colourless potent liquor. Asher said it was made of caraway seeds, but it looked and tasted nothing like the commercial kummel; it was yielding as water, but deceptive. After they began to drink, Ben remembered very little, except that the dancing began in earnest, and the huge wooden table was pushed into a corner and the tiled floor pounded by booted feet until he was sure it would crack and the tiles split. Ijaz turned off the electric lights and lit old-fashioned torches whose flame leapt in time with the wild Afghan music. This was the rhythm of the ancient hills of Badakshan, the last country Alexander tamed, a music older than the muezzin.

As Ben danced with a succession of Tadzhik women—their proud, dark faces hard to distinguish in the enigmatic light— he sometimes caught sight of Amanda's marble skin, and her rain-grey eyes, like the palest of emeralds. They moved as if in the dance of a puppet-master; now closer, now further again. When the music changed and all the dancers gathered in two lines, holding hands, he found himself opposite her as they flowed like waves towards each other. Passing, he thought he felt her fall, and reached out to catch her in his arms. She whispered, 'After this, I may never know whether I am awake or dreaming!'

He said nothing, but held her tightly through the rest of the firelit evening, until they went to bed. At around this time, I myself heard of the legend that when the dance-music begins

123

on the shepherds' pipes and timbrels, the very mountains hear and strain to follow the notes, and trees wave their branches slowly in accompaniment, as if in this unwritten human music there is something deeper than the fingers of the players, the crafted instruments themselves, something that ties a cord around the people and the land until they become almost indistinguishable, like the lost harmony of created nature.

Amanda remembering Badakshan: lapis lazuli perched on the brown soft ears of women, fat-tailed sheep in the sun, straggling like refugees, the untrammelled river, speaking its own language to the ruddy fields.

Unimaginably early Ijaz crept around the house, waking the hunters. It was still dark outside, and would be for a few hours yet; the antelope lived high on the plateau, almost a day's journey away. Giles stirred from the sheepskin rug where he had fallen asleep when the dancing finished, without bothering to go home. He wolfed down barley cakes, sitting cross-legged, wrapped in a woollen blanket. Beside him, a pocket edition of *Le Morte d'Arthur*. The hunters stretched and talked quietly, as if the expedition were a secret kept from the rest of the village. There would be a dozen, with the three guests, Ijaz leading, two of his sons, his wife's brother and his sons, a neighbour and the teacher at the village school. Each brought his hunting spears; Ijaz took some from his own small armoury for Ben and Giles. He hesitated, and seeing Amanda (dressed in breeches and an Afghan shawl) gave her his own. One of his sons brought in a pair of hounds, the beautiful silky Afghan breed, murmuring to each other. Outside, the horses were being saddled; Ben could hear their gentle snorting. The scene moved in slow motion, but sure, each actor catching an invisible camera at the most perfect angle. Snatches of the tunes they had danced to reverberated around Ben's mind, softly, unfocused.

'A cup, before we leave,' Ijaz said, passing around earthenware bowls. The liquor tasted furry in their mouths, but lit

124

tense stomachs like a lantern in a cave. And suddenly they had left, as naturally as if Ben were mounting his bicycle to pedal through the waking Oxford streets on his way to work. Amanda had been right: she rode better than he, and thanked adolescent afternoons at riding school, and hacks through country parks. Giles had learned to ride in Turkey, out of necessity, he admitted, but it served him well here, and this was not his first hunt. The path along the river glistened with moonlit dew, and sometimes an otter stirred the waters gently. Huddled into their shawls—it was cold, and they would climb higher before dawn—the hunters resembled nocturnal wandering beasts. Watching Amanda's slender back in front of him, feeling the spears in their leather sheaths strapped to the saddle by his knee, Ben imagined them a party of scouts from the army of Darius, feeling their way up the mountain, to outflank the Macedonians trapped in the valley below, unsuspecting . . .

Dawn came imperceptibly, stretching the sky with painful slowness. Lemon tinges on the horizon, sickly moon fading like a light bulb. Darkness seemed to have blanketed smells as well as sight, so that suddenly the earth and shivering leaves emerged complete before them, heavy with odours. Ben felt exposed and small, gripping the thick flanks of his horse inexpertly. Ijaz and the teacher led the way, then, in single file, Amanda, Ben, Giles, Asher—the strangers' mouthpiece —and the other villagers. Suddenly Ben felt tiredness like a heavy weight around his neck, and wished he were as separate from this as the birds watching them. (To his surprise he saw swallows, which reminded him of the jejune bird-paintings in Egyptian pyramids.) The only sounds on the path were the horses' hooves against the stones, and the padding of the loose-limbed hounds running alongside. Ben began to nod in time to the hooves as if hypnotized, and Giles, noticing it and afraid he would fall asleep, moved closer and began to talk in a low voice: whatever came into his head.

'This path climbs around this side of the mountain,' he

explained. 'Before we reach the antelopes' habitat, we have to leave these trees behind.' Already the deciduous trees were getting sparser, sticking out of any spot where they could force down roots. Giles pointed out, in addition, rhododendra and ferns. Amanda turned round at the sound of his voice, her face flushed with excitement.

'Ben, this is almost exactly the path! I feel as though I know every inch!'

'What path?'

'The one Marco took, of course. They sent him up into the mountains here, to cure his fever. Don't you remember: "Messer Marco vouches for this from his own experience"?'

'It is true,' Asher said, 'that the air here is well known as a cure for diseases. A generation ago, you would have found little wooden huts by the side of the road, especially higher up on the plateau. Sick people were brought to them for a week, or a month, to recover from fever.'

'Is it still done?' Giles asked

'It is done occasionally, if we cannot obtain the right medicines quickly enough. But even in Khanabad now the hospital has everything one could imagine,' he said with pride.

It was light now, like a grey-white sheet held out above the valleys. They had left the river behind, and the lushest of the vegetation. The gully path swelled gently, as they approached the half-way point, where the mountain flattened out slightly into a wide grassy ridge. Now they could ride two or three abreast, which made conversation easier. By the time they came to the ridge, the sun was high, and shawls were discarded. Ijaz, at the head of the little group, called a halt. They would rest before the final ascent. Handing out the flat barley cakes and skins of warm milk to the hunters sprawled on the grass, he found a few words for each of them: for Ben, encouragement, praise for Amanda's horsemanship; Giles he clapped on the shoulder like an old friend, and joked with one of the boys, not yet eighteen but already as knotty as a tree

126

trunk, who was whittling at a piece of wood like a cowboy. Giles lay back, letting his eyes drift from the spectacular view of the Oxus valley to the cloud-blotched sky. Tall grasses waving gently like banners above their heads; far below, the spine of the river arching away from them. The company was as good as any he had known in his life, the situation, poised like a scene at the end of a reel in a film-show, as perfect.

'Do you still wonder why I called you here?' he murmured. 'I have been so happy here. The air may also cure diseases, but certainly it helps me to think, and to write.'

'What are you working on?' Amanda asked. 'The travel book?'

'Maybe it is a travel book,' Giles considered. 'No, it isn't—it's a novel.'

'Set in Badakshan?'

'Not especially. It will start in Jerusalem. When I was there, it was impossible to write, even to think about writing. But here, I feel as though I could do all the things I have ever desired to do.' Again, he recalled sleepless nights, walking among hovels in the dense Arab streets, recoiling from contact with limbs that sprawled at him from doorways: beggars, fleshy prostitutes, arak-soaked pimps. 'I knew you were both there, on the other side of the city,' he sighed. 'It would have been easy to see you, and Alex. But I couldn't find the courage. I hated myself—what would you have thought?'

'You only hate yourself now, looking back,' Amanda said. 'You didn't when I saw you, just before you left—or when I dreamt about you. And no self-pity, either.' (Well, that was something he never sank to. As Ben said, a true egomaniac never pities himself. Something to be said for it.)

'How did you know about Alex?' Ben asked him. 'He heard about you from the Intelligence chief, the unfortunate Saddle.'

'I know. Poor Alex—I am afraid he became involved against his will. Saddle had been the lover of the girl who came to

127

your flat on the same day that I did, and the day he himself died—Martha Pollock. I don't know how they became involved, but it became unpleasant, by all accounts. He was a wretched man anyway, a drug addict, something of an alcoholic. He lived in squalor, and wore dirty clothes. At first I think she despised him, though he must have had some hold over her; but she is a good person, and was unable not to pity him.' (Even now, it is hard to write these last words—they come so slowly, so reluctantly from my pen!) 'He improved for a while, but then got worse again. When I knew him he had begun to drink again, and was sometimes violent.'

'But how did you meet him? He thought you were a Palestinian terrorist, according to Alex.'

Giles smiled ruefully at this, as a man will who has made a ridiculous mistake in the past but has learned to view it without rancour.

'That is naturally what Saddle would say. He was a spy, after all. What better way to denounce us, and scare Alex into the bargain? The fact is that he was perfectly suited to his job. He knew Jerusalem better than anywhere else; he was born in the Arab quarter, off the Nablus Road. He knew where to find the dirtiest whores, the meanest contacts. Subterfuge came easy to him, for he had long abandoned looking straight-faced at himself, or at anyone. The incredible and ironic truth is that deep down Martha pitied him, and that nagging chink widened, until she found herself immobilized by pity. When he was at his weakest, lying unconscious on the floor, or slumped in the arms of a fat whore in a café, then she could not make herself leave him. Later, when she had taken him to bed and sat with him while he recovered from his bout, then he was too strong for her, and though she hated him for his ingratitude and brutality, she could not go.'

'She did not seem to me to be the kind of woman who could care for a man without a spark of good in him,' Amanda said. Giles shrugged and chewed a grass stalk.

128

'Perhaps no woman can. As Ben would tell you, there is no soul so lost that it has not a residue of good, like silt at the bottom of a pool.'

'Souls come from the good, and are in essence good themselves,' Ben said. 'Augustine would say that the only real soul, the only soul that has fulfilled itself in essence, is the perfectly good one. Saddle's viciousness and drunkenness do not make him bad, just less good and therefore less real, because further from the good. Evil is not a positive force, like good, but a lack of something, like blindness, or a grey day instead of sunshine.'

'I doubt whether Martha rationalized it quite like that, but at any rate, she was unable not to see the possibility that he might improve again.'

'But where do you fit in, and Alex?' Amanda wondered. Before Giles could reply, it was time to move on, lest they waste too much of the daylight. Asher caught Amanda's arm to point out the hawks—sakers, goshawks and even higher up, eagles. She recalled in intense detail the hawking on those upland slopes, as the tiny caravan dragged Marco into the pure air; he had been too unwell to join in, but Maffeo, with the help of Yusuf, the one-eyed Syrian (whom they retained after deciding to abandon the ships at Hormuz) had bought a fine hawk in the town and now caught rabbits and smaller birds for the pot. Giles, wiping perspiration from his nose, continued to speak:

'I lived in the Arab quarter, just outside the Damascus Gate, in Jordan. To keep myself occupied, and to be able to get along better, I took lessons in Arabic with an elderly imâm. We used to meet in a café on the street of the Chain: he drank coffee and smoked a hookah while I grappled with the squiggles. I think he learned more English than I Arabic. His friends were often there, also elderly Jordanians for the most part, except for one, who was by coincidence (or something) an Afghan. I chatted with him often, and went to his house, where I met his son—Mansur.'

129

'Whose name you gave, with a telephone number, just before you left.'

'Yes. We became friends. By this time I had learned of his involvement with the PLO, but it was too late to disown him, even had I wanted to. What could I do? Perhaps I even sympathized with his cause. At about the same time, I had come across Martha, at the house of the imâm. Her mother, you know, had taught her both Hebrew and classical Arabic. We used to go to the Archaeological Museum together, where she would tell me about each item in exhaustive detail.' (Cool corridors, white linen curtains blowing gently inwards in the breeze through open windows: Martha's soft hand resting on hard-edged marble; Giles too, helpless as a fly trapped in amber. Yakov's words: 'Everyone is in love with her.') 'You must understand, I was lonely in Jerusalem, and confused. The heat and the people frightened me; I had arrived in summer. When I walked out of my flat, down a set of outside steps, I trod in rotting fruit, and at once the odour of melting overpowered me: melting tarmac, the sides of buildings too hot to touch, people melting before my eyes. I seemed to see only elderly, crippled Arabs, men with cataracts, hobbling women bent under great loads, in creased baggy layers of clothing like sacks, hems dragging on the ground. Beyond tourism, I had no business there—but I could no more identify with the parties of wealthy Americans one saw filing into the Church of the Holy Sepulchre, and straggling out again, blinking like voles. To meet Martha and Mansur was to gain allies. They knew the city, especially Mansur.'

'Alex seemed to think they were engaged, Martha and Mansur,' Ben said.

'Yes,' Giles said sadly, 'I am sorry for Alex, truly. He had no part in this, but he ended up being hurt. I used to visit Mansur often in his father's house. Once I came at my usual hour in the evening, unannounced, and surprised him with a group of young men I did not recognize. They wore black and white head-dresses. One of them leapt up and grabbed me, and I

130

think would have been happy to have had me bound and abandoned in a cellar or a dark gutter, but Mansur held up his hand. "This is my friend," he said, in Arabic. "He is your friend too." Then he said to me, in English, "What you have seen you cannot change." "But I see nothing," I replied. "Look down." They had amongst them a small wooden box, inlaid with red and gold thread. It was open, and inside it lay a dismembered hand, fingers outstretched. The nails were crooked, and not too clean. It had turned white, except for where the severed tendons were still stained dark red. "This is not my affair," I said, to reassure them. Mansur shook his head. "You cannot escape it. But if you share with anyone else what you have seen, we will have to do the same to you as to this informer." After that, he made me leave. I saw him only infrequently from then on, and he never alluded to that evening, but it made no difference. I was an accessory not only to a crime but to the cementing of a brotherhood, or something like it. All these men had bonded themselves to one another with the murder and mutilation of an informer. This is something that remains until death—for me and for them.'

'But how did Saddle come to know of it?' Ben asked. 'Something must have implicated you in his eyes. It must have been that.'

'No, he never knew. Saddle never knew anything, except where to get hashish on the Israeli side, unless it was from the Israelis themselves. He was their man, more than England's. But he knew I was Martha's friend: he saw us together, and had me followed. That was after she had finally left him, on my insistence. I don't know the exact circumstances, which she refused to tell me. But he followed her doggedly, completely indiscreet, uncaring whether she saw him at it or not. I suppose he was in utter despair. She used to frequent a certain café in the afternoons, and he began to follow her there and sit at a table in a corner, staring, or sometimes pretending not to notice her. He never dared make a scene in public. She simply ignored him, as best as she could. One day Alex happened to be there, and began to talk to her. She pretended she was engaged to a Palestinian named Mansur —she had heard me talk of him, and the name came into her head—to enrage Saddle, or, more likely, to tell him, indirectly, that it was no use his pursuing her any longer. But she miscalculated: he confronted her in private, tailing her to her home, and threatened her. He lost control and became violent. She only escaped injury by calling neighbours. Saddle had already denounced me to Alex, out of jealousy; now he threatened him, denouncing Martha too as a spy. On that same evening, he died.'

'And Martha?'

'She became afraid, for herself and for Alex, whom she felt she had deceived and harmed. I suppose she thought that by leaving she could break all that had happened. Of course, she never suspected that Saddle would claim to know a Mansur who was being watched as a terrorist. But I think we were all lucky that he came to such a miserable end so soon.'

Amanda's grey eyes held his for a long moment. Later, she said to Ben, 'Both of them ran, when it mattered; the girl especially. She used Alex only to ward off Saddle.'

'Well, she was not to know that Saddle would turn on him, simply for having spoken to her. And his threats were empty—Alex told us that nothing ever happened after his death, no inquiry, no investigation.'

When I heard Giles' story, after his death, I wondered whatever had become of the dismembered hand. Did they keep it in the wooden box inlaid with red and gold thread, or bury it? Was it sent to the man's family, as a warning? I ask idly, but not in vain. Mansur, I later discovered, disappeared and for a long time was feared dead, or to have been caught and tortured by the police: such things happened. In fact, he left Jordan and settled in Lebanon, where he became an active figure in the Palestinian cause, for which he eventually died. I found all this out by accident. But it seems to me now that the

132

rigid dead hand was the only stable, fixed element in all this. We flitted in and out, neither belonging to nor understanding the world of severed hands and informers. Perhaps it is safer: Saddle, who understood but never belonged, the most unfortunate of all of us, was our victim.

Giles' reminiscences occupied them until, early in the afternoon, they reached the point where the conifers stopped growing. Now the path narrowed again and became almost too steep for horses. A hush came over the small group, which caught up even the two newcomers. Ijaz held up his hand again, and Asher whispered to Ben and Amanda, 'When we pass that outcrop ahead, the path will come out on to the start of the plateau. That is the home of the antelope.'

They emerged on to the sun-absorbing plain like sailors landing on a new-found island. The suddenness of the transition from mountain rocks to grassland was a fresh discovery each time, even for the Tadzhiks, who knew this country from ancestral memory. Wind at first so strong after the sheltered gully path that it almost blew them from their horses. And the plain stretching, meaningless, as far as could be seen, although this was not even yet the summit. A gentle slope carried the plain upwards to where the mountain became rock once more. The snowy peak winked down at them, an ancient god in sunlight. Here and there a spring of mountain water appeared, and shrubs. Amanda, who had been there before in other company, knew where to look.

'See, Ben! The whole country lying before us.' She gestured at the valley where they had begun the day, and the Oxus glittering like a snail's track. But there was little time to admire the view, for suddenly, a second before they came into view, Ijaz cried some warning or prophecy, and a group of antelope strode across the plain to their left. Then everything happened at a terrific speed, so that describing it afterwards Ben mixed up the minute actions and sequences in a jumble. Like Tartar warriors the Tadzhiks spurred their horses to a gallop, drawing spears from saddle-sheaths in one long, flowing

133

movement, but so that they were balanced perfectly in the
throwing hand. The beasts, sensing imminent danger, were
gone as quickly as they had arrived, and the twelve hunters
after them, the younger ones leading. Ben was surprised to
see Giles leaning forward in his saddle, fair hair fanned in the
wind, spear poised, a veteran. For himself, he took longer to
react, and then first looked round for Amanda, who was
laughing in excitement. Then Ben too was caught up in the
chase, and lost thought and sight and hearing to concentra-
tion on the moment. A fleeting awareness of grass like the
white sea's hair; sweat on the horse's neck; perspectives
shifting violently. The plateau rose and fell, turned this way
and that, the sky looming before wide-open eyes, clammy
grip on spear-shaft. Dogs snapping at the antelopes' heels.
Then, like a suicide, a light brown body hurling itself across
his path—throw! throw! But too late—head it off now, follow
its twisting run. The experienced hunters worked as a team,
choosing a single animal instantaneously and closing on it,
throwing from each side. The dogs, incredibly swift, did their
work soundlessly.

When his spears were used up, Ben drew apart, and
noticed to his surprise that Asher, Amanda and a few others
had already stopped hunting. Asher bent over a fallen antelope, not yet dead. He turned to Amanda and said something,
and she walked a few paces away while he finished the kill.
Suddenly Ben became aware of the stillness on the plains.
Hunters returned in pairs from all over the plateau, as if by a
pre-arranged signal. Giles, accompanying one of the sons of
Ijaz, was flushed with excitement. He grinned wildly at Ben.

'I saw you get yours, Ben! Well done!' Only then did Ben
begin to gather up the fragments of the so recent past and
reconstruct events. He was riding hard to keep up with Ijaz
and the teacher as they rode down a beast, one on either side.
The teacher shouted something in Tadzhik and Ben saw the
antelope turn suddenly, losing momentum for an instant, and
the hunters close, and then realized that he was in front of it

as it leapt up in the turn, trembling, with his throwing arm erect, but still it was Ijaz's spear that caught the beast first, even as he was manoeuvring his horse, and once the antelope was hit it was an easy kill, shuddering in front of him. That moment, seeing its wide-open eyes, lasted forever, until through no willing of his own Ben felt the spear leave his hand and thud into the proffered neck. Others had seen it too, otherwise he would have been sure it was another man, and not himself, who had made the kill.

The hunt had lasted a fraction of a minute, to the participants, but the sun was dropping as they hauled the bodies of the slain antelopes—five, in all—into a mass near the centre of the plateau: as if sweeping garbage into a neat pile. The Tadzhiks stood over them while Ijaz said a prayer of thanksgiving, and Asher enquired, too solicitously, after Ben's welfare. The beasts were slung on poles, which had been brought along in sections for the purpose. Ben would have liked to be able to stay a while longer on the windy grassland, but their business there was over. All the way down the mountainside the Tadzhiks sang: at first simple hunting or battle paeans, tuneless and festive, but as the dusk threatened the singing became melodic, calling to the hovering night. They took the same path down the mountain, until they came to the ridge where they had rested before. Then Ijaz called Asher to him and consulted, and the Jew took over the lead. At one point they left the path to head across rough sloping ground between the cedar trees, until they found another path that seemed to lead through dense woodland. As the sun left, flanked by bands of amber sky, they came upon the ruins Ben and Amanda were to have seen that day.

Who knows, even now, what hopes they once defended, or whose dreams? Perhaps, as I write, they have crumbled away into the very earth. Ben was able to say, after scrabbling around for a while, 'They are Islamic; the bee-hive tombs give that much away.' But he, supremely learned, touching the porous stone, comprehending arches and muted columns,

135

stood on the outside of a darkened window. Giles, seeing in his square features an unexpected fineness, his scholar's hands brushing earth from the deathless stones, felt suddenly sad, as if he had been looking down from tall windows on the destruction of the fortress, and had done nothing. But, as Ben said, this mountain fastness never fell to siege or demolition, like the city of Balkh despoiled by Genghis Khan; rather, it was forgotten by generations that no longer needed it, or thought they did, like an old book passed down in the family. It had been fine, once. There were fragments of a mosaic floor, a marble fountain head, some pieces of carved sculpture. Among these the villagers sat like children in a playground. They had made a fire and began to roast one of the beasts for supper. The water skins, filled at a mountain stream, were passed around. Learned thoughts and fragments of verse came unasked into Ben's mind—mourners at a funeral—but he left them unsaid, and waited patiently as the smell of roasting meat wafted towards him.

Over supper, moonlight; and stars like an army encamped. The singing continued, and Giles, lifted outside himself, swung gently to and fro, sometimes joining in, but softly. Amanda looking across at him with affection. Ijaz, proud as a war-leader, sucking on bones. On hunting-days, he wore gold arm-bands, rings on his fingers, and in one ear: '. . . the gold of that land is good; there is bdellium and the onyx stone.' Silence clawing at the edges of their huddled noise, the silence of the mountains that is oblivious, and unknowing.

'This is a time for dreams,' Asher said to Ben. 'It is mine one day to go to Jerusalem. I envy you for having been there.'

'One day you surely will,' Ben said, and thought of the man, David Al-roy, who for a while in the middle of the twelfth century was regarded by the Jews of Baghdad and Mosul, Bukhara and Persia as a saviour, perhaps even the Messiah. Captured by the Caliph of Baghdad, he escaped

136

miraculously (like Dionysus from Pentheus' prison), and flew unaided through the air. For a while he gave hope to some of a glorious return to their city: on a certain night, the Jews of the Lost Tribes were to go out on to their rooftops, whence they would be lifted up by an angel of the Lord as by an eagle, and flown to the city of peace, Jerusalem.

'Many years ago, when I was perhaps four or five years old, a Jew from the village set out for Jerusalem,' Asher said, reflectively. 'He was a potter, exceptionally skilled. The village was sorry to lose him, but although everyone told him he was a fool, he insisted on going just as he was, without money or transport. We never heard from him, so I do not know whether he made it safely. Indeed, I hardly remember him at all, though my father still has some fine pots he made, and candlesticks.'

When Ben told me this, I wished that Yakov could be there to hear also. Even he, unsentimental old man, would be moved; maybe he would even have written to his old friends in Badakshan. But I suppose that when one finds something like an end to striving—which Yakov, simple potter, declined to call paradise—there is no need to tread backwards into caves long since left behind. (May I know for sure, one day!)

They left behind them bones and offal, ruins among the ruins. On the last stretches of the mountain path, lit by the hunter's moon, Amanda almost fell asleep, as Ben had done hours before on the way up. This time he cantered forward and took her hand, and the headman's horse picked its way carefully over the rocks. The gentle slopes swelled like a stomach, and stretched themselves gradually into the fields and meadows of the village. Still a mile or two out, the headman's farm workers rode out with torches to meet them, and take from their shoulders the weight of the slaughtered animals—like the companions of a Roman bride greeting her after a moonlit ceremony, invoking Hymenaeus, guiding the couple to the marriage bed.

Images before sleep: Asher warming bony hands by the fire, Giles' straw head leaning close to the intricate, grimacing chess pieces. The regular rise and fall of a hound's sleeping breath, fiery patterns darting over his white coat.

6

even after their return, it was not a Venetian canal that
Amanda saw but the wide, clean channel of water
running beside the Kinsai streets as the ceremonial
barge, rowed by a score of liveried sailors, bore Marco
Polo away from the city. At last, the Great Khan had summoned him. In Marco's baggage, the thick report he had
compiled for the Great Khan (a copy had been translated into
Chinese and left in the Palace library), the seal of office which
he must return, and gifts pressed on him by his Chinese
friends: from Chao Meng-fu, an exquisitely painted bamboo-
roll; from his wife, a cluster of her dark, sweet hair. He had
taken from her dressing-table a small bottle of the perfume
she used: it smelt of the woods after rain, oozing freshness.
Much later, when he tried to recall her presence, he would
feel soft wisps of hair drifting across his face, a tiny hand
resting in his. This was a hard parting, and a moment swollen
with import. The curious crowds gathered to see who the
royal official in the barge might be was reduced in his sight to
one, the green-eyed Kuan, standing up in her carriage seat.
She had said, 'We will not meet again,' and he had smiled and
told her not to be so sure of that. As the flat craft swam
through the canal gate and so out of the city walls, he
remembered how he had said the very same thing to his uncle
Maffeo, as they pulled out of Venice, ten thousand years and
miles ago.

That parting had lasted two whole years, from the time
when they came back unexpectedly from the Great Khan's

court with letters for the Pope, and Nicolo caught up his son in his arms and looked at him as if for the first time, and his father, Marco's grandfather, told him that they had buried the wife he had left behind. There was rest, and feasting, and meeting of old friends and business partners, and indecision, since they had learnt that the Lord Pope was dead and his successor still unchosen. Two years of quiet business, as the Polo brothers built up their trade—easier now, with their fame as adventurers—and Marco dreamt of the places they described. Mafeo would pace up and down on the balcony outside their house (they were able to move to a larger one, on the Grand Canal) and occasionally beat the flat of his hand on the marble columns.

'How much longer, Nicolo? How much longer can we wait for the cardinals?'

'They must decide soon. You know we have to wait until then.'

'The Great Khan will have given up waiting for us, by now. Do you know how long it has been since we left his presence?'

'Five years, give or take a month. He is a patient man, and understanding. We would do him wrong, if we left here without a papal envoy.'

But eventually the pacing up and down got to Nicolo too, and one day, while they were entertaining an important customer, he stood up and announced that the waters of the town were making him ill; he longed for wide, wide steppes, mountains, wild grass and skies filling unimaginable horizons. And Maffeo laughed and shouted, even in the presence of the distinguished customer, that the Romans could elect a Pope whenever they wished, but they, the Polos, could wait no longer to see the greatest land in the world. Then it was as if a taut rope had been cut, and everything seemed to happen very quickly: the business put in trust, half the assets made over into gold and gems to be taken with them, a farewell banquet, and suddenly a moonlit night in the lagoon, waiting to set sail at dawn. Of course, once they had reached Ayas in

140

Armenia, they heard that a new Pope had been elected, their old friend Tedaldo of Piacenza. Maffeo joked that they must have forced the cardinals' hands, by setting out before the election was completed, but Marco preferred to think that this was God's blessing on their voyage—and had their every step not been blessed? Those were miracle-days.

As in Venice, Marco had lingered too long in Kinsai. When the Great Khan's summons arrived, it brought a kind of relief, as well as sadness. The weeks and months in the City of Heaven had been unearned, and ever since the day when he had first been taken to the court of the Great Khan and knelt before him, and Nicolo, bowing, had said, 'This is my son, and your liege-man,' each day was consecrated to the service of this mightiest of rulers. Now, the Great Khan received him again, in his own city of Shangtu, in the palace he had built for himself. Except for the different location, he might never have moved since Marco left his side: he sat erect on his marble throne, his thin legs drawn up under him and resting on a footstool. As always, he looked beyond the shoulders of the people who surrounded him, with the faintest trace of a smile on his face.

'Great Khan, I beg forgiveness for my delay,' Marco began, bowing deeply. From the right of the throne, where a knot of favoured Tartar courtiers stood, Marco saw the eyes of his uncle glowering at him.

'Few men are loath to come to paradise,' said the Great Khan. 'It must mean that you have much to tell me about your travels in Manzi. I look forward to hearing you.'

He was referring, when he spoke of paradise, to his famous gardens at Shangtu, the sixteen square miles of parks and meadows attached to the great palace, the royal hunting ground. Marco suspected this was an ironical allusion to Kinsai, which the Chinese called the City of Heaven. On the very day of his return, Marco went out riding with the Great Khan. On the crupper of his stallion the Great Khan carried a young leopard, which he released when they entered the

141

wooded areas. They rode behind it while it hunted down a stag, and sent for bearers to carry the victim away to the mews, where it would be fed to the falcons. The Great Khan tired easily, at his age, and suggested a pause for refreshment. In the middle of the park, enclosed in a grove, he had built a summer palace constructed of bamboo canes. Marco had seen it before, but never failed to marvel at the combination of craftsmanship and artistic genius. The canes were built on a series of gold pillars, each one twisted in the shape of a dragon; they were treated with a special varnish to make them waterproof, so that even the roof could be constructed out of them. Each was fifteen feet in length, and the width of three hands outstretched. They were held together with nails, and the whole was thus both solid and flexible: a guard against the weather, yet capable of being struck like a siege tent and moved to a different place, or stored in the cellars of the palace. Like a tent, the bamboo palace was held in place by ropes pegged into the ground, as well as by the columns. Every summer, when the capital city became too humid and the air too grimy, the Great Khan moved his court to the palace. But his most intimate friends and advisors, and chosen members of his family moved into the bamboo palace, which was set in place at the start of the season and dismantled when he left. It was here that he now took Marco, where in the heat of the day they could drink iced rice wine. The Great Khan spoke first:

'In your absence, Marco, I have appointed a new governor of my city of Khan-balik.'

'May the heavens bless his face.'

'This was not an easy choice to make; initially, I considered your father Nicolo.'

'The honour is surely too great!' Marco blurted, in surprise.

'That is what he said also, and refused it. But I knew already that he was a wise man. The worthy Maffeo, I think, would have accepted.'

142

'My father refused? Great Khan, on his behalf I beg your pardon for this insolence.'

'Granted,' replied the Great Khan mildly, 'but as you will be aware if you consider for a moment, I am hardly insulted by such matters. There are many men who deserve the honour and would be glad of it, but your father is wiser. In his position, I trust you would have done the same.'

'I do not know,' Marco said slowly. The responsibility of envoy had sat heavy on him in such alien lands: the post of governor was as a mountain-peak. Besides, as he said, he and his father were foreigners.

'We are all foreigners,' said the Great Khan. 'I do not say this abstractly. Ahmad was a foreigner, and the man I have chosen in his place is also one, though a man of ability. A Saracen is as much a foreigner to the Tartars as you are, and no more to the Chinese than I. It is not a simple thing, to reign over a strange people, and maybe an unsafe thing.'

Marco recalled words from long ago, learnt perhaps at the school in Venice: the man who finds his homeland sweet is still young and tender; he to whom every soil is as his native land is already strong, but he is perfect to whom the entire world is as a foreign land. But all he said was, 'Are you afraid that his authority will not be respected?'

'Then I would not have chosen him. This man has his own authority. But it is not enough, on its own; remember Ahmad. In your country, Marco, I have no doubt I would be reckoned a cruel man. But if I am sometimes harsh, I have no wish to make men afraid.'

Marco thought: all this is nothing; it is not for me nor any one man to control the rhythms of a city and a people. The stewardship of Ahmad, and the reign of the Great Khan, are moments in the life of the city, the bricks, the river, the trees.

'If I were to refuse an honour such as this,' he said, 'I trust it would not be through fear of the consequences of rulership, but for this, that anything I might do would be like a footprint

143

in the sand: the imprint of my will, until the purifying wind comes to brush it away, leaving no trace.'

'Perhaps, Marco. I know you are a pessimist. But perhaps the opposite is also true, that each act of the will, each moment of suffering imposed on the city—who knows, each moment of happiness, too—is a permanent thing, frozen in ice. Is a thing that lasts only an instant of our time less important than a war that drags on for ten years? How do we comprehend this decade, that instant? By a measurement of the bodies in the sky—from sunrise to sunset, from one moon to the next. But our measurement is arbitrary: the act itself, a kiss, a snatch of music, a horse-race, a stab to the belly of a man, these are not determined by time. That is merely the order we have imposed, to set events in a sequence we can understand.'

'Then a man dying with a spear in his belly will be in agony forever,' said Marco in a whisper.

Looking up to the Great Khan's face, he saw it impassive; even the eyes gave no clue. Only the slight twitch of a muscle above the left eyebrow gave any indication that he was alive. Marco was reminded of those people of India known as yogis, who lived among the Brahmans of Maabar, on the warm east coast. Once he had met a yogi who claimed to be 170 years old, and Marco could see that his body, although withered, was healthy enough to support him for many more years. They ate only healthy foods, such as a drink made of a mixture of quicksilver and sulphur, which was taken twice a month to promote longevity. Some of these yogis went about stark naked, since they saw nothing in the body to be ashamed of. 'We go naked because we want nothing from this world,' they said. 'We are not ashamed to display our member, since we do no wrong with it. Why should we not show it, when you show your face and hand, which you do not use in lechery? You are only ashamed to show your member because you use it in lechery.' Moreover, these men ate no flesh, since they refused to kill any living creature, nor even any fresh plant. Marco saw a yogi go to the sea-shore to relieve himself, and when he had done it in the sand he washed himself in the sea, and then took a stick and crumbled the excrement into the sand, so that none was visible. Afterwards he explained to Marco: 'Excrement breeds worms, but the worms, once their food was dried and consumed by the sun, would starve to death. Since the substance issues from my body, I would be responsible for the death of these creatures. For even the worms have what you call a soul.' Marco could not imagine the Great Khan, who was after all a Tartar warrior, parading naked, or going to these lengths of purity. But he would surely be interested in them. Perhaps one could be persuaded to visit paradise, and explain their philosophy to the Great Khan. They would surely be able to help him find the truth concerning the nature of time, for they were reckoned to be the wisest of all men in the world.

When he came to think of it, Marco was glad that his father had refused the office of governor of Khan-balik. This post, which had lain vacant for a year since the revolt against Ahmad, was perhaps the highest in the Great Khan's bestowal. As Nicolo told him, he was only a merchant, though an experienced judge of men and a widely-travelled one. But although he would surely have avoided the fate of Ahmad, it was better not to put it to the test. Marco was away when the end befell Ahmad, but Nicolo had been in the retinue of the Great Khan and was able to tell him something of it.

'He deserved what he got, although maybe not in the way it happened. He should have been killed by the Tartars, not the Chinese; that was a disgrace, for a conquered people to be able to rise so easily against their lawful masters. But wickedness has its own reward.' When Nicolo spoke of lawful masters, he exaggerated the case, for the only law that made the Tartars masters of the Chinese was the law of arms. But

145

who could have much sympathy for a people who held their freedom so lightly as to shun the science of war? Nicolo and Maffeo, who had met barely a handful of Chinese, shared most Tartars' contempt for them.

'The Great Khan thought highly of Ahmad,' Marco said.

'Be careful what you say about that! The Tartars now believe he had bewitched him, to blind him to his wickedness. Oh, he had charm, there's no doubting it; many Saracens do. He was a fine-looking man, until dissipation spoiled his face, and as strong as a bear. But the power went to his head. At first, it was lechery. Any woman who took his fancy, he couldn't resist seducing her. And if she was married, or someone's daughter, he would simply bribe the man, or, more usually, threaten to expose him to the Great Khan for some misdeed. He had dossiers compiled on the private lives of most important men in the city. If he couldn't find anything with which to threaten him, he would invent a conspiracy, or plant obvious bribes on him. He only lusted after the women of the higher classes of Chinese, and never after boys—which is unusual, for a Saracen. You know how the Chinese fear the Great Khan; he simply played on their fears.'

'And none of this reached the Great Khan's ears?'

'How could it? He had twenty-five sons, some of them as bad as their father, and an army of secret agents. You know how seldom the Great Khan is in the city—perhaps three months in the year. Ahmad had only to ensure that for those three months no petitioner or official from the Chinese could get near enough to the Great Khan to expose him. Even if one had, would he have been believed? Anyway, Ahmad put trouble-makers in prison, or had them executed. You know how the administration works, Marco. Scores of secretaries and bureaucrats at work recording hundreds of decisions and policies every day. How can the Great Khan check each one personally? Even important ones get lost, or go through the hands of subordinate ministers. A man like Ahmad could hide from him whatever he chose, so long as he did nothing

146

too obvious. Once, he had a man executed, a commander of 10,000 men in the army, to whom the Great Khan was quite attached. The man's daughter had been ravished by one of Ahmad's sons, and he was terrified it would get back to the Great Khan, because of his influence. So he fabricated a conspiracy against the throne, made the unsuspecting man the figure-head, and cut his head off. Then he was able to write to the Great Khan, with great regret, informing him of the justice meted out to the traitor. Would you believe it, he even warned the Great Khan against making friends of the Chinese! He carried on with this kind of insolence for twenty years.'

'How did they overthrow him? With the help of the Tartars?'

'No, surprisingly they did it on their own. If they had gone to the Tartars and asked for their support, they might have earned some glory; perhaps fewer of them would have died, as you will hear. After all, Ahmad was a Mohammedan, from Persia. The Tartars had no great love for him, although he did not dare to bully them as much as the Chinese. The plot was a simple one, led by two Chinese commanders, a Chenchu, a commander of 1,000 men, and a Vanchu, a commander of 10,000. In a month when the Great Khan was away at Shangtu, they agreed to murder Ahmad, which they could do more easily than most, since by virtue of their office they lived in the barracks next to the new palace. At a given signal all the Chinese in the city were to rise up and slaughter any bearded men they found—that is, any Tartar or Saracen. They even planned to light beacons alerting other cities, where the Chinese would do the same. In one night, they planned a full-scale massacre.'

'They should have had more piety, and respect for the lord who had so honoured them as to make them commanders in his armies!' Marco said angrily.

'They were too ambitious, anyway. The Chenchu had good cause to hate Ahmad, since his mother, wife and daughter

147

had all been ravished by the man. But he would not let his rage stop there, and wanted to destroy the whole empire single-handed. On the appointed night, the two men took a small detachment of their palace guard into the Great Khan's throne room. Vanchu sat on the throne, dressed in the Tartar fashion, and had all the lights lit in front of him. Then he sent a courier to Ahmad, whose house was in an annex of the old palace, telling him to come immediately, because Chingiz, the son of the Great Khan, had arrived in the city and wanted to see him. Ahmad was puzzled, for he knew that Chingiz had been away in the north and was not expected back, but he did not dare disobey the order. He went alone, in day clothes and unarmed. On his way through the gate that connects the palace of the old city and the Great Khan's new palace, he met Kogotai, the Tartar commander of the city guard. "Where are you going at such a late hour?" he asked conversationally. "I have been summoned to the presence of the Great Khan's son," Ahmad said hurriedly. "Which one?" asked Kogotai, for he knew that none of them happened to be in the city at that time. "Chingiz has just arrived." "Impossible! He could not arrive so secretly that I would know nothing of it!" cried Kogotai. "I was surprised too, but I do not intend to refuse his summons," Ahmad answered, and went on. Kogotai decided to follow him with a small patrol. If Chingiz really had arrived, it would be as well to do the honour of providing an escort. Now Vanchu and Chenchu had not really thought beyond killing Ahmad, and alerting their own detachment of Chinese to murder as many foreigners as they could. When Ahmad entered the throne room, he saw the marble columns gleaming in candle-light, and the braziers lit all the way down the hall, and the banners of state unfurled. In the half-light he could not make out the identity of the figure on the throne, but he saw the Tartar costume, and knelt before him in his distracted state. Then Chenchu stepped out from behind a pillar and cut off his head with a single stroke of his sword. As this happened, and he was holding the head in his hands,

148

Kogotai came into the hallway, and saw immediately what had happened. His guards rushed forwards to seize Chenchu, while he himself unslung his bow and transfixed Vanchu to the throne with an arrow. The Chinese guard had advanced at the signal, but now found themselves faced by the Tartar patrol, which although outnumbered, will always be more than a match for the Chinese; they were slaughtered to the last man, and the signal to rise against the bearded men never given. In the morning, Kogotai had Chenchu tortured until he revealed the names of the others who had been involved in the plot; he had these all executed, and sent for the Great Khan.'

'The admirable Kogotai is well known for the diligence and zeal with which he guards the city,' Marco said wryly. Of course, he had acted quite properly in the circumstances, but Marco suspected that these would never have arisen, nor the Chinese been provoked into such a state of despairing outrage, had Kogotai and other Tartars not turned away from witnessing Ahmad's deeds. Though he commanded 12,000 regular troops, he seemed to fear crossing the governor as much as anyone in the city.

'When the Great Khan arrived, he was told by Kogotai that two Chinese had murdered the governor, but that he had taken care of the incident. The Great Khan then asked why this had occurred, unknowing of Ahmad's vile behaviour. None of the Tartars wanted to tell him, although they knew very well. But they were afraid: not of Ahmad's sons, who were as unpleasant as the father but lacked his charisma and personal influence with the Great Khan, but of their lord himself. For they knew that they should have told him long before of Ahmad's doings, but had, like Kogotai, pretended not to see them. So they looked at their feet, and muttered about the lunacy of the Chinese. And then your own uncle Maffeo, who had travelled back with me in the Great Khan's retinue, got up and hurled an accusing finger at the Tartar lords. "Are you afraid of him, even in death?" he shouted

149

angrily. "Does the viper still bite when its head has been cut off? Or are you ashamed at your own part in this?" They began to stir at this, and protested that the whole thing was nothing to do with them. Maffeo turned to the Great Khan and said, "My lord, we are all to blame. This execrable man deserved his fate, but it should have happened sooner!" The Great Khan asked him coolly what he meant, and we all began to tell him of the outrages he and his sons—not all of them, but at least seven were as odious as the father—had committed against high-born ladies of the city and their families. And Kogotai admitted that he had heard of a considerable treasure that Ahmad had amassed through extortion and blackmail. The Great Khan sent men to ransack his house and bring all the treasure they found before him. While this was done he said nothing to us, but paced up and down the great colonnaded hall, black eyes flashing angrily. He stopped before Maffeo and said, "Foreigner, you are my friend, for you have shown more courage and honesty than my own lords." And you yourself know what honours he heaped upon your uncle, including the command of a squadron of Tartar cavalry—a strange destiny for a Venetian jewel-merchant!'

'How much treasure did they find?' Marco asked. Nicolo, with his business brain, would have calculated its worth, and stored the information.

'Unimaginable amounts! Countless boxes of gold and silver jewellery, onyx and sapphires, rubies, chalcedony, emeralds and jade! In addition to all this, there were chests of the paper money that is used in Chinese cities—Ahmad must have extended the range of his activities well beyond the city of Khan-balik. Then there was furniture, and statues, a stable of thoroughbred stallions, a collection of priceless suits of armour, although Ahmad himself held no military office. Truly his wealth was beyond reckoning! The Great Khan took some of it for himself, such as the horses and furniture. The paper money he sent back to the cities of origin, and the rest of the treasure he stored in a public treasury. Then he estab-

150

lished a commission of inquiry to deal with the complaints and grievances of those whom Ahmad had harmed during his stewardship of the city. All those who had suffered, or their families—many had been left orphans by his perverted cruelty—were encouraged to come forward and give evidence, so that restitution could be made from the treasury. A year after the event, the commission is still hearing cases against him.'

'What happened to Ahmad's family?'

'First of all, the body of the evil doer was dug up from the honourable place of burial where it had been laid by his sons. It was flung into the streets of the old city, in the worst quarter, by the river and the warehouses, and torn to pieces by the stray dogs that live there. Those sons who were reckoned to have been as bad as the father were flayed alive, and the others dismissed from the sinecures given to them by their father. Their treasure and property, where gained illegally, was confiscated. But the Great Khan did not stop with the accursed family, for he blamed the entire Saracen community in the city for abetting Ahmad's crimes, and anulled all their privileges, especially those allowing them to take as many wives as they wished. So now, although individuals may still be honoured, the Great Khan holds the Mohammedan race to be utterly contemptible.'

It seemed to Marco that this, of the whole episode, was the part which gave his father the greatest satisfaction. Still, however, the Great Khan showed no inclination to show his personal favour to Christianity. Marco only once mentioned Ahmad in his presence, for he knew that Kublai held himself partly responsible for his misdeeds, for having chosen him as governor and having given him total control of the city. Marco visualized the torture of Ahmad's sons in the courtyard outside the palace, and the Great Khan watching, and it seemed that with each blow of the iron-tipped thongs, he felt the pain himself, although, as usual, he showed no emotion.

So it was with a sense of relief that Kublai Khan accepted

Nicolo Polo's rejection of the office of governor, though of course he did not voice it. Indeed, from then on he seemed deliberately to overlook those closest to him, or those most capable, when it came to making appointments of the greatest importance, as if he were shielding them from exposure to a responsibility he had found to be corrupting.

He told Marco, 'I no longer care to see any of my favourite sons in positions of authority, or my closest advisors. The government of my empire largely runs itself; there are more valuable things for you to do.'

'But a government left to itself may produce men like Ahmad,' Marco said, greatly daring.

'Ah, you taunt me, Marco. I have learnt much since then—after all, it was many years ago.' (He looked the same as when the Venetians had first set eyes on him, but he moved more slowly and with great precision. Marco had changed more: years had amplified his frame; his beard was thicker, but his straw hair sparse.) 'It would not be possible for another Ahmad to exercise such power. The safeguards are more effective, and besides I seldom appoint men of such talent to high positions. The empire grows old with me; its pioneers and great men are of the past. Mistakes are made, of course, and no longer glorious ones, but that is unavoidable, and in any case not very important. Administration is a dull business, best left to dull men.'

'Then your empires will never increase, and your treasuries dwindle where once they swelled.'

'If I ever knew how to increase my empires, I have forgotten,' said the Great Khan, spreading his hands wide.

He no longer hunted actively, but sometimes, as now, he took a favourite falcon with him when riding in paradise, and derived pleasure from watching its flight, and the capture of smaller birds or rabbits. 'Something is thus gained, and something lost. Perhaps even what treasures I have slip a little further from my fingers each day.' At first Marco thought he was referring to his advanced age, but he smiled and said,

152

'No, it is not age. It is another thing—perhaps despair. A thought comes to me sometimes, unwelcomed: does it matter, after all, who rules over these lands? A single hand, or a dozen, or none? Whoever it is, he will never comprehend their extent, for they change every day, as people do.'

'That may be so,' said Marco, 'but at the same time I have found that although I travel a great deal, I see fewer people, because they have begun to repeat themselves. Maybe there is a limit to the number of shapes a human may take.' The Great Khan nodded slowly, and the problem seemed to absorb him for some time.

'For you, the possibilities in my empires have contracted; for me, they are expanding. Every day the man who brings me my clothes in the morning, my chief falconer, even my sons, they all change. One day I notice the shape of a smile, but the next day it is gone and the nose seems to have assumed a different proportion, or the eyes a new angle, so that each person resembles not even himself. Are there endless people in the world?'

How could this be, Marco wondered, when the Great Khan was now almost inactive, and spent more of his time here in Shangtu, or in the palace at Khan-balik, where he had a favourite garden, while he himself travelled more than ever: Manzi, Tibet, Lesser India, the northern plains beyond Karakorum? The Great Khan still demanded to hear the reports brought back from his journeys, but Marco had the curious feeling that these places were now more remote for the traveller than for the listener. In the city of Zaiton, recently, he had accosted a man he was sure he recognized from years back, to find it was after all someone else. Once he had followed a Chinese woman in a carriage, breathless with excitement: surely, the sleek hair, that contained sweep of the arms, the delicate mouth? But if it was Kuan, it was another. Had he seen all that one man could see of the Great Khan's vast empires? Were all the possibilities exhausted? Marco could describe to the last detail the road from Khan-balik to

153

Shangtu, but it was the same as the road to Kinsai, or Kara-Jang, or Sa-chau.

One face Marco saw repeatedly, but in his mind: a middle-aged man, grey-bearded, clear-eyed, in a dusty black robe, a European. A certain stretch of mountain road, square city gates ahead. Eagles circled almost out of sight: the man had pointed them out. At first he thought the name was Aristotle, but then he remembered it: William, William of Tripoli. He could no longer recall exactly how they had met, or what they had spoken of, but suddenly it became very important that he should, though he could not say why. And he began to think of going home, and saw white walls, the sun shining on dull waters, and spires like needles in the sky.

The Polos' departure came about thus. For Marco, it was like a crossing-point, reached one day, perhaps one night while he slept, traversed blindly, covered over later so that no moment could be traced when he knew that the Mongol life was over. The realization was simple, like a consent granted, and after that only the opportunity was required.

When he spoke of it, his father nodded and said, 'This has been in my mind too. We have lived here, as I reckon, for seventeen years. Maffeo and I are now old, but not too old to travel, if it is soon. You are a man of middle age, but not too old to begin to live anew in Venice. If a man is rich, a beginning can always be made.' But Maffeo said nothing for a while, brooding instead.

Later, he came back and said abruptly, 'No. For one thing, the Great Khan won't release us. By now, he relies too much on us to do without. Since Ahmad, he trusts few people, and we are among the few.'

'We can only ask his permission,' Nicolo said. 'If he refuses, so be it.'

'There is more, which isn't easy to explain,' said Maffeo

154

gruffly. 'Here, I have become something. We were well off at home, but not remarked upon, and no different from so many thousand others. We crossed the world's span, for no reason or cause that we have been able to tell anyone who asked, but it was a feat never before accomplished, and maybe that is enough. We brought something new to these lands, which were greater by far than our own before any of our people knew of them. Nicolo, you know me well: no one will ever take me for a Tartar, and that in any case is not what I want. You will say, we are Venetians, and it is wrong and unnatural to pretend that we belong here. But what is Venice to me now? Whom do I remember there? Can you think of anyone you care to meet again, any place you cannot bear not to see? We may not be too old to survive the journey, but to take things up once more, for that it is too late. We can expect a seat in the sun, and a useless one in the council chamber.' He paused, pacing about and playing with the beads around his neck, as he did when nervous. 'I don't have your son's talents, God knows, but what little I have, I have put to good use here. I dare say I won't be much missed when I die, but maybe something will remain of me—nothing I have built, no scheme of government I have devised, no victory in war, but something of whatever I am. The Great Khan was good enough to take what I have offered, and ask for nothing else, and for me, that hallows this place.' He spread out his arms, as if to embrace the marble and gold palace of Khan-balik, where they stood. 'This city, these walls, are hallowed, in a way no other place can be. That is all.'

This was a brave and rather wonderful speech, Marco thought, as he listened in silence. But he could see that his father's mind was decided, as his own heart was, and he could remember no occasion on which, at the last, Maffeo had prevailed over his brother.

'As to the first objection,' Nicolo said quietly, 'It is true that we have come to be valuable to the Great Khan, a thing we could have predicted. But as you know, this has brought with

155

it the envy of others of his own race and tribe who have not come so close to him. If we are old, the Great Khan is older, and when he dies, his successor, whoever he may be, will not protect us from enemies now impotent. These have been good years for foreigners, and we have been fortunate, but when they come to an end, it will be bad for us. A business-man must look ahead and see these things. As to your other words, Maffeo, there is no answer. I am sorry. It is hard for a man, when the heart and the body are no longer together.' And he put his hand around his brother's shoulders with a tenderness that Marco had never seen before, and which caused a prickling behind his eyes.

Because he knew with an inescapable knowledge that they would leave the paradise they had found, alone of their people, Marco looked for no opportunity, but made a note in his heart, when he passed a certain temple, or watched the waves of the sea, that it was the last time. But Nicolo was busier. He began to associate with the three ambassadors of the Levantine Khan Arghun, who had arrived at Shangtu while Marco was away. Arghun's wife Bolgana had died, and her last request to her husband had been that he should re-marry, but only a princess of her own tribe, the Bayaut, who had provided many capable ministers for the Great Khans. The envoys had come to find a suitable princess, and ask the Great Khan for permission to take her away.

This, naturally, took time, for it was necessary to make the acquaintance of a great number of noble families, and study their marriageable daughters. These ambassadors, whose names were Uladai, Apushka and Koja—good Tartar names, which made them popular—were immediately respected for their charm and good breeding. In their turn, they were delighted with the Polos, especially when they learned how influential they had become. Indeed, it was partly through the introductions made by Maffeo to certain noble families that the Princess Kokachin's father was approached and her hand requested. Maffeo, an honorary commander of Tartar

156

cavalry, spent increasing amounts of time with the old soldiers of the Great Khan's youth, drinking and exchanging stories. Of these, he had plenty, and invented more. Marco often saw his father in discussion with the envoys, but they broke off conversation whenever someone approached. He thought little of it: the envoys would soon leave with the bride, and he was making his own preparations for a journey to India, to study the Brahmans of the Kingdom of Maabar.

It was not until his return, eight months later, and the celebratory feast given by the Great Khan in his honour, that he remembered the envoys, and then with a sudden start. The Great Khan, eating sparingly, as was his custom now, had ears only for India, and the gods worshipped in its monasteries. Those of his entourage who were within earshot had made their own judgement on Maabar, having heard that the horses reared there were so stunted that the kings were obliged to spend the larger proportion of their annual revenues on importing war horses from Arabia.

'In the sacred places of these monasteries stand idols of their gods and goddesses,' Marco explained. 'Now for the most part they remain on good terms with one another, exchange words and endearments, and have intercourse. Then the land prospers, and the rains come in season. But sometimes the monks report that the gods and goddesses are displeased with each other and will not join in intercourse. Then no one in the Kingdom carries out any business, and the king shuts himself in his palace in fear, because it is in the copulation of the gods that the Kingdom is blessed.'

'That is natural,' said the Great Khan. 'But what recourse do they have to petition the gods to favour them?'

'Young maidens, expert at dancing, are sent to the monasteries to dance naked in front of the idols, and thus arouse the gods. I was fortunate enough to witness this myself. While they dance, they sing, and beg the god to observe the beauty of the goddess, her hair, her breasts. Then one girl lifts her leg higher than her neck and performs a pirouette on the

157

toes of her other leg. This requires enormous strength, Great Khan, for there are many gymnasts who cannot do as much.'

'And are these girls specially trained for the art?'

'Yes, but I was not permitted to visit their schools. After the performance in front of the idols, I took one girl aside and questioned her. She made a wager that I could not pinch her skin anywhere on her body, and she was right, as it happened, for their skin is kept so hard and taut by the training that until they leave the service of the gods and are married, there is no loose flesh anywhere on their bodies.'

The Great Khan was musing on these words when the guard at the entrance to the dining-hall (not the palace seating hundreds, but the private hall in the bamboo palace) announced the arrival of the envoy called Uladai. The talking stopped, but momentarily, for such interruptions were only to be expected, and there were always so many envoys and couriers. Most of the party had probably forgotten the Tartar from the Levant, who bowed deep before the Great Khan in mud-splashed boots and a head-dress seamed with dust. But Nicolo, leaning forwards slightly to catch the words exchanged, and the Great Khan himself, had not forgotten.

'You have returned sooner than expected, Uladai,' the Great Khan said. 'But be welcome, and take a seat.'

'We were forced to turn back, Great Khan. The roads have become impassable beyond the Desert of Lop. Before the mountains of Pamir, we were lucky to escape with our lives, and many of our party died on the long road back.'

'But it is the summer!' one of the barons exclaimed. 'How can the roads be impassable?'

'There are armed bands everywhere,' said Uladai. 'The kings of the Great Plains are at war, and this has made the roads unsafe. Soldiers become impatient with large parties of civilian travellers.'

Marco, sitting by the Great Khan, felt him stiffen, a movement almost imperceptible, but as significant from him, as for another it would have been to have leapt up from table, scattering silverware. Following his eyes, he saw them focus on Nicolo Polo, who stared back expressionless. What passed between the two of them? Only because he was his father did Marco know, without even being aware of it, that it was a kind of recognition, or a tacit understanding. It was not only Marco, newly arrived from India, who was taken by surprise by the envoy's words; most of the Tartar barons in the Great Khan's entourage heard for the first time of this war in Uighuristan. But nothing seemed clearer to Marco than that his father, the taciturn, elegant merchant, had caught this delicate rhythm of high politics or diplomacy as surely as a musician will hear an unfamiliar tune and make it a part of his own repertoire. As for the Great Khan himself, Marco sometimes found himself thinking of him as one of those magicians who are able to tell what is happening in another city, or even another part of the country, even though he is sitting in the same room as his audience.

The Great Khan said now, 'We have heard of this war, Uladai, and regret your misfortune. You may be assured, it will not last another summer.'

'But in the meantime, Great Khan, the Khan Arghun's bed lies empty. We dare not delay longer, so grievously was he hurt by his wife's death, and so eager to marry again.' The same baron who had spoken before shrugged at this, as if disbelieving the envoys' plight.

Chingiz, the son of the Great Khan, said, 'There is no other way to travel. Either wait for the autumn, when the campaigning will stop, or risk the road now.'

'The campaigning stops in autumn because the roads become impassable, and the steppes freeze solid,' said Marco's father in his solemn voice, an interruption so unexpected that all faces turned towards him. His words were respected because of his closeness to the Great Khan, and because it was known, even to the younger men who had not been at court when it happened, that he was a Frankish wise man who had crossed the whole world, and returned again to

159

prove it. And Marco, studying Uladai's face, saw expectation in his eyes, perhaps hope, and understood.

'Your party cannot cross the mountains in winter, if an army cannot,' Nicolo continued. 'However, there is another way.' Knowing he held an audience, with the torchlight making patterns on his drawn old face, Nicolo gave pitch to his voice, like an actor. How many times in his career had he cajoled, persuaded, bluffed with men whose purses could starve him, or make him a prince? Thus had the Venetians, patient as ants, accumulated their bazaars and markets and quarters, their rents and customs in cities conquered by others, from one end of the Mediterranean to the other. But never from such a lord as this. The humorous coconut face of the Great Khan was turned towards him still, but without discernible expression. Behind the tiny flat eyes an image was retained, more powerful than this torchlit evening in the bamboo palace: the Great Khan saw through the merchant's eyes as he stood on the quay at Hormuz, his robe clinging to his back in the humid, rotten heat, looking beyond the makeshift boats, the sun-haze on green waters, to a point where sea and sky merged and became lost. He had seen this again, when they visited together the great port of Zaiton, and instead of remarking at the streams of colour, the pullu-lating junks with their precious cargoes, Nicolo's eyes had followed only the sea-gulls, drained with envy of those birds for the wisdom of travels only guessed at.

The Great Khan, nodding slowly, said, 'The sea-way. You are right, Nicolo, that is another way.' A murmur began to spread among those at table: everyone knew the sea encircled the world; did the Frank expect a man to sail right around it? Was he not content with crossing its width on foot? Chingiz voiced these thoughts:

'That is impossible, father. They would never reach land safely—it has never been done before.'

'By ourselves, we would perish,' said Uladai, taking his chance. 'But the Polos are experienced voyagers, the most

160

knowledgeable in the world. With them, we would be safe, and the Great Khan's kinswoman, the Princess Kokachin. I beg you to let them accompany us to the West.' This, of course, was presumption on the part of Uladai. All knew how firmly the Great Khan loved the Franks and how faithfully they had served him over many years, longer than the time it takes for a new-born baby to grow into a man. But few of them knew, as the Great Khan did, that this journey was also in the hearts of the Polos themselves. He recalled what he had told Maffeo, when he had come to him in private, nervous but fierce, to entrust him with this secret, that his brother and nephew were planning to leave his side. 'In truth,' he had told him, 'I do not know what I shall say when the day comes. It will be like losing an arm, to let you go; but if the branch is dead, the tree does not mind losing the weight.'

'What do you say, my counsellor Nicolo?' he asked him.

Once again, the old men understood each other, and the Venetian replied, 'I ask that we may, at the least, undertake the voyage with hope.' The Great Khan's agreement was granted on the condition that the Polos would return when the mission was completed, but all four of them knew that this was a mere form of words, perhaps for the benefit of the rest of the court. Maffeo, of course, did not profess his own preference to stay, for he understood the demands of loyalty. As for the Tartars, even those who had been friends to the Venetians were amazed that all this could be thrown away on a whim, the wish to feel the sea under the planks of a ship, the earth moving to the rhythm of one's own feet. So there was scorn from some, and astonishment and hilarity, but no comprehension. And, as Nicolo had predicted, not all were sorry to see them leave. Marco wondered at the tide of fortune that had enabled Uladai to make his strange request (saving them the difficulty of having to ask the Great Khan themselves for his leave), and although he never discussed it with him, he long entertained the suspicion that the wars of

161

Uighuristan were a thing about which his father knew altogether too much.

This is what Amanda dreamt after their return from Marco Polo's travels. What Marco saw, Amanda realized too: paradise on earth does not last forever, even for Adam and Eve, who had more of an opportunity than most, even for Gilgamesh, who was allowed, in the Sumerian epic, to re-tread history and consult the only survivor of the Great Flood. 'There is no permanence: only the nymph of the dragonfly sheds her larva and sees the sun in his glory.' But it was Giles who was most concerned with this. I wish I knew now whether he thought he had come to the end of something in Badakshan. A hint from a letter he wrote long ago, in Venice, may tell me. He talked of much that did not interest me, such as Perceval and the Holy Grail; now, a few images stand out: Perceval standing fully-armed in the Great Hall of the Fisher King's castle, battered sword dangling by his side. From the great sick-bed of the King, a shrivelled hand beckoned, and he was led into the ailing presence. With every echo of his armoured foot on the flagstones, the same question repeated in his mind: why me? The ravaged land, the blighted herds of cattle, the starving peasants, women wailing inside the castle, tearing out thin handfuls of hair, all waiting, sick with waiting for the healing power of the Grail. Perceval, the seeker, powerless and unknowing, but chosen. 'Understand this,' said Giles. 'To seek and find the Grail is insufficient in itself. Perceval had to know how to use it, what the purpose was. It is not the thing itself that heals, it is the question asked of it.' Whenever I think of Giles—always with longing, missing him—I hope fiercely that he found his question, sorry that I was not there at the end, to be sure.

162

Giles never did anything half-heartedly. He caught a chill, riding out in the cool dawn, and came back to do a day's work in his little allotment, pushing himself beyond the limits of his endurance. When Amanda saw him in the evening, he was feverish, but he insisted on staying up to write. At midnight the lamp still burned in his uncurtained window, his silhouette hunched over the table. They tried to persuade him to rest in bed for a few days, but it was unmanly to him, in the sight of the hard-limbed Tadzhiks. The sickness persisted, and the doctor warned against staying up. He mentioned pneumonia, and recommended the hospital at Khanabad, but his English was so poor, and their understanding of the dialect so shaky, that Ben and Amanda were as unclear after he left as before. They put Giles to bed, and Amanda sat up with him through days and nights, cooling his forehead. Villagers brought dubious potions and remedies—one, as Amanda said, might have worked, but each wanted to outdo the other in curing the famous guest, and they fought each other in Giles's throat and stomach. Ijaz came to visit, but could not speak with him (and what advice could he have offered, who had never been sick for a single day in his life?); Asher brought his chess set, knowing Giles' predilection, but the patient could not concentrate. After a few moments he would suddenly overturn the board, or sweep the pieces aside into the lap of the silent, uncomplaining Jew.

While she watched over him, Amanda continued to dream. She saw four sparse walls, fresh-painted like those in Giles's house, a simple bed, a frost on the ground outside. Bundles of coloured silks and other cloths were strewn on the floor like offerings. Outside, Maffeo and the boy they had hired for the horses saw to their stabling, while in the dark room Nicolo watched tight-lipped as his son twisted in delirium. His eyes were the colour of the foul, rain-drenched canals of Venice. In a corner, Yusuf rocked back and forth on his heels, chewing bloodless lips. A steady, colourless rain fell.

'We must get him higher up into the mountains,' Maffeo

warned, stamping his boots on the beaten earth floor as he came in, shaking water off himself.

'When the fever has broken. We cannot move him till then.'

'St. Mark rot the guts of that doctor! He assured us the boy would be well enough to travel.'

'Pray for health, not damnation,' said Nicolo quietly. He hardly moved for the whole of the night that the fever held Marco, leaning slightly forward in his chair to be able to hold his son's hand. He was known as an unemotional man, but he had mourned his wife's death, when he returned to Venice. It was more than half repentance, of course, for deserting her for gold. It was not his fault, as he explained to everyone: they could only go east from Sarai, cut off behind by local wars that made travel too hazardous. She would be looking at him now, wordlessly, as he made the same mistake again. East, east, always further east; for what? A man can spend only so much money in one lifetime. She had always said, and others too, that he followed Maffeo too readily. Well, the two of them knew the truth, that his quietness was not weakness, and the last word was usually his. When he thought of this now, pressing the hot sick hand in his own, it was more than he could bear, recalling the arguments at Hormuz, all of them exhausted by the heat, barely containing rage while Yusuf stood apart, squinting from his one eye. This stage of the journey was his responsibility, though Maffeo would not let him admit it. If they had followed his advice, they would have long since been in Aden, perhaps in Ethiopia itself, instead of this mountain village in Badakshan.

In the night, Maffeo was awakened by Yusuf's petulant shuffling about. Propped on one arm, he watched as the Syrian dipped his hands into a jar and transferred their outlines, covered in blue paint, to the walls. Fragments of conversation from Mosul, months ago: 'Why are the doors of all the houses painted blue?' 'If you go inside, you will also see blue hand-marks everywhere. It is the sign that guards against evil.' The rough scrabbling hands disturbed his sleep,

164

but in the morning Marco's fever had broken. He found his brother pitched forward in his chair, head in his hands. At last, he had allowed himself to be dragged into sleep.

Later, climbing the mountain in slow stages—Marco could ride, but Nicolo never took his eye off him, just to be sure—Maffeo waited impatiently for the chance to try out his new falcon. According to legend, Alexander himself had hawked here. He was sure the headman in the village had cheated him on the sale, but at least they had been able to buy food from him too, and shelter for the night. A whole caravan would have met with stones and closed doors: they were unused to strangers here, but three tired men and a sick boy were no threat. But it would be hard to find another party to join, so far from the main trading route as they were. It was a thing to worry over later, when Marco had recovered in the clean air, bathed in the mountain streams. Spring was the best season in Badakshan. Delicate white flowers blown unresisting on to the water, carried lightly downstream.

Being ill, Giles said, was like swimming endlessly in heavy, cloying air. Even concrete shapes became formless. The familiar things he wanted to latch on to—books, a saucepan, a chair—became suddenly as insubstantial as images. It was this slide into semi-reality that Giles feared, and fought by refusing to admit to himself that he was ill, and, once he found himself bed-bound, by getting up too soon. I suppose they could have prevented him, but who can say how someone else is feeling? So when he came in the morning to call for Amanda and Ben at Ijaz's house, saying, 'I am going for a ride, perhaps into the mountains. Will you come?', Ben looked at him slowly with wide-open eyes, but said nothing.

'I don't think that's wise,' said Amanda, motherly.

'I'm fine now—no fever, regular pulse, no dizziness. It's a beautiful day, and the air will do me good.'

'Well, I can't come,' said Ben. 'I've too much to do here.' He was now often to be found closetted with Asher's father, the rabbi, from whom he collected scraps of oral history and tradition. He foresaw his densely-packed notebooks transfigured into fresh-printed typeset between glossy covers: the first truly comprehensive study in English on the Jewish diaspora of Central Asia.

'Amanda, you wouldn't let me go off on my own, would you?' Giles teased, knowing she would not. He got his way, and that, Ben said afterwards, made him master of his own fate. Much later, Martha was to say that it would never have happened amongst Italians, or Frenchmen: there would have been arguing, and perhaps tears, but not this frozen politeness, this false maturity that sent a friend off into the mountains when he was too weak even to be outside. It is ironic to think of Giles dying of a stiff upper lip.

Because of Amanda, his death, which of course I know only second-hand, is inseparable in my mind from the sickness of Marco Polo. I cling to it like Kublai Khan, trying to plumb the depths of a soul. In the small white-washed room, smelling of earth and cobwebs, crazy blue hands stared down at him. His body felt so light that it swirled around the room, leaving his mind and sickness lying on the bed. It floated, lighter than air, through the open window and into the springtime, upwards on wind-currents, helpless as a kite. Beneath him the river and the mountains danced wildly, daring him to join in. And meanwhile, back in the house, his abandoned mind entertained images that crowded impossibly into the room: his dead mother as he remembered her most clearly in the last years of her life, standing motionless on the columned balcony of their house, greying hair loose around her shoulders and eyes fixed on the gulls as if they brought news from far away; his grandfather, Nicolo's father who had lived with them while Nicolo was away, too old by then to engage in trade or even politics. He sat silent over him now, his eyes hideously shrunken. Nicolo and Maffeo were there too, but distorted; his father's head distorted so that his nose seemed to poke into the blankets when he leaned forward in the chair.

Maffeo was laughing, but noiselessly, his red face thrown back and mouth hugely open, showing yellow teeth. Marco tried to ask him what the joke was, but no one seemed to hear. He shut his eyes to block out these ghosts, living and dead, but in the darkness of imagination the images that visited him were worse, nightmares married to childhood tales. A painted dragon breathed fire over an entire forest and a city, scorching them in minutes and laughing at the shrieks of dying people and animals. Enormous winged ants, ugliness magnified in every detail, crawled on the floor dragging on their backs dwarfed human bodies. Men appeared in place of his father and uncle with the heads of dogs, slavering at the mouth. Their green eyes were almost as slits. He screamed again and again until these images were aborted, and Maffeo stepped forwards and held his sweating shoulders down. He could smell the comforting rain-earth on his breath and body, and the screams became whimpers. Nicolo was saying something, but the words emerged fragmented, with no connection to the open mouth, the moving lips and tongue. He could not hear the words for the rain that hissed outside in the darkness. At times he would lose all power of sight and hearing, but his sense of smell became sharper, like a new means of communication. Then he would only hear, but blindly: dismembered voices, Yusuf spitting into the corner where he still crouched, the rattle of cockroaches on the hard floor, the rain like careless drum-beats on the roof, and always the wind, the endless wind . . .

In the morning, when the fever had run its course, they left the shepherd's hut, to climb the healing mountain. Rain-fresh leaves dripped on the river and the muddy path. But it was cold, so cold! Marco's pinched face, the colour of silver birch bark, was framed in layers of blankets. Giles' face also, the morning he went riding with Amanda, though even to himself he would not own that he felt the cold. His fair hair, Amanda said, was translucent against that sharp paleness. beautiful, for once, like a flower in the last moment of its

167

blooming, so fragrant and delicate that the lightest touch will scatter the petals. Who needs such beauty, in death?

The spring air aggravated Giles' weakness, so that after only an hour he was coughing like a consumptive. They stopped to rest, but he shivered on the dewy grass. Amanda, putting her arm around him, felt his forehead damp and hot. When he laughed, his breath rattled in his throat. She wanted to turn back then, but he insisted he would soon feel better. He shivered even in the crook of her arm, hatless in the wind. As she led him back to the horses, she felt his tears on her shoulder, and was afraid she had let him down. He should have made it up the mountain, even if it killed him, she said later. But it was coming down that did that, the horse stumbling and throwing him on to the path, a heavy rib-breaking fall made worse by his condition. If he had been fit, he might have been able to stay on the horse. She brought him bleeding to Ijaz's house, and gradually, in the last hours, the entire village gathered under the windows and in the doorway. Ben intoned, in a deep voice, as much of the 'Requiem' as he could remember. Giles was not a Catholic, but it was what Ben would have wanted for himself.

It does not fall to everyone, to die where he is happy; and Giles was seldom happy. I have the details in front of me now, in the letter Ben sent. But at the time, they meant nothing to me, and now it seems too late to study them afresh, for I have my own imagined version, my picture of the low-ceilinged house, the colourful woven rugs on the bed, Asher standing over him slender and gaunt, like a medieval pilgrim. Giles' eyes, the lightest chestnut-brown, whites streaked with red. How often had I seen them so! He was never robust: sometimes, the morning after a heavy-drinking night, he would resemble an albino, skin stretched taut over his cheekbones, eyes, from a distance, like rubies.

There was more to be said, even after his death. Months after, I stood with Martha at the quayside on the Grand Canal, awaiting the return from paradise.

168

'They wanted it to be as far as possible an echo of Marco's return,' I explained. 'Hence Venice, rather than flying straight to England, or going on immediately to Santa Clara.'

'How sad! Do you suppose, if Giles had not died, that they would have gone on and on, until they reached Peking, or the sea?'

'I don't even think it was Giles' death that prevented them. Ben is at last concerned about Amanda's health—her state of mind, rather.' His letter was in my pocket, but the words rattled dully in my mind, like confirmations of something vague and inexpressible I had known for a long time, perhaps forever. She needs rest, Ben wrote; it has been too much for her; her dreaming gives her no peace. She seems always to be asleep, even when walking, eating, sketching in the forest. It is only at night that she is awake, and she loves with an intensity that frightens me. Why do you load all this on me, Ben? I warned you, and you accused me of making her into a mental patient. Well, if that is what she is to you now, it is you who made her so. There is no history of it in our family, no record of Marco Polo.

'Giles would have wanted them to go on,' Martha said, and it pressed a bruise in my head, recalling an intimacy the two of them had shared without me. How hard it is to reclaim a soul from memory—even a willing one! What she had not told stood between us, an ugly brackish pool. Both of us were afraid of the water. Again, as in Jerusalem, I would have to wait for whatever came from her. Dense, fat Venice at the end of the tourist season, churches beginning a glorious sleep . . .

'When you told me about your English friend, back in the Café Jaffa, I was suddenly ashamed. It was a sign that I should tell the truth. But then, if we believed in such things, there would have been many. And not telling is almost enough, sometimes, to make it not true—that was all I wanted, to make my life unreal.' It— living with Saddle, zombie-like.

'You could have left any time you chose, Martha. You

should have left him as he left his victims, with blood welling from a hole in the side.'

'For what?' she cried in despair. Then, quietly, 'I did leave, eventually. But there was no Mansur to take up with. I invented that, talking to you in the café.'

'So it was Saddle, even then?'

'I am sorry I never told you, Alex. Every time I should have done, I was too weak. I suppose you found out from Yakov?'

'I squeezed it out; he didn't want to tell either.'

'You deserve better than me, Alex.' But I never wanted anything better than the cold stones on the canal-side, the pigeon-droppings on church walls, her hoarse voice and hair of pressed lavender. 'Whatever Yakov said, try to forget. Oh, I am sure he told the truth. But if only it were so simple!'

'He told me a series of events. Only you can tell me what happened.' For a long time she just looked, first at me, then at the canal, as though the dark water contained not only reflections of present images but even that which made them, the host of unutterables, memory. When she began speaking, I had to lean close to hear every word.

'The beginning does not matter. It could have been that, or something else, at that time or another. These things are not important. I hardly remember seeing him at first, only smelling; the sweat trapped inside his grey suit inching further along the seat of the taxi, the smell of his quarter: cats, unwashed clothes, arak, nameless foods rotting. Then, later, it was a face like any other; ugly, but not more so than most. His hands were hairy. When he spoke, it was a struggle against himself. The public school expressions he must have picked up from his father even before going to England, the harsh Arabic of his environment. He hated the words he spoke. At first I hated him for not letting me go, and because I was ashamed to be seen with him. As for what happened between us, shame would be inappropriate.'

Here I wanted to stop my ears, or run off, jump into the water, but my diplomatic face betrayed nothing.

170

'It was too easy to despise him, Alex. When he made love, which he did not do so badly, it was with himself, not me. At times, he even cared for me. It made him feel better to have me there, and be seen with me. Even when he was violent with me, and threatened me with exposure to the police, or some such thing, it was himself he shouted at—as if I were a mirror. He was always alone.'

'How can you forgive him for mistreating you?'

'Forgive?' She looked at me, puzzled. 'To be able to forgive, you first have to judge. I don't know—maybe I deserved that: living in his squalid flat, watching as he smoked himself into stupefaction on the dirty floor. It wasn't a one-sided thing, Alex. I wasn't his prisoner, I was—well, perhaps his conscience. It was something he had to put up with as well, not just me. The first time I told him I was leaving—not just him, but Jerusalem—he began to cry, like a child with a broken toy. He sat down on the sofa, with the stitching splitting and the stuffing coming out from under him, and put his head in his hands, moaning. I looked towards the door, and thought, "It is as easy as this; I will walk out now, and never see him again." But it is not so easy, Alex, when it comes to it. After all, his life was worth something, too, worth saving when he drank himself unconscious, nearly drowning in his vomit; when he tried to kill himself by cutting his wrists in the bathroom. What might he have done to himself then, if I had left, or to someone else? I would have been responsible for more deaths than that poor Yemeni boy. That evening, when we were lying in his bed under the window, and I could just about see the stars beyond the bricks and roofs of the building next door, I was sorry I hadn't taken my chance, and I cried too. Then he was tender, and I was suddenly glad. Would it have been worth it—my freedom, against giving him an hour of tenderness?'

'Yakov told me how you went back to his flat, after he had found him unconscious, and called an ambulance,' I said, as confirming her words.

171

'That was after I had left. I did eventually, you know. Giles persuaded me. I met him one afternoon, when he came to the dig, to look around—I suppose he'd seen everything else by then—and because I was English they made me speak to him. I liked him, he was so awkward but wanting to be kind, and he was interested, although he didn't know any ancient history. He said he'd been to the Archaeological Museum, but hadn't been wearing his historical glasses. So I promised to show him around, and he was good company. At first he was very mysterious about himself, but finally he admitted he was trying to write a book, but that Jerusalem deadened him. I suppose we shared problems, different as they were. He told me about you and Ben and Amanda, and how he knew you were there, but couldn't make himself visit you. He was almost ashamed to admit that he really wanted to see you, as if writers had a duty to their work to be unsentimental in real life. Anyway, when we met I already knew who you were. I could even have told you where to find Giles.' She looked up suddenly, to cut off my obvious question. 'Oh, don't make me explain why I didn't, Alex. Selfishness, perhaps. I was afraid to lose his unhappy company.'

'But Mansur? Did you know him, or did you just make him up?' I asked, remembering Saddle's brooding presence at the back of the café, the dense book open but unread.

'There really was someone called Mansur, someone Giles knew, whom I had met once. Any name would have made poor Saddle angry, which was what I wanted. Maybe I was a little drunk. I thought, if I didn't stick a name into the conversation, he would just take it out on you. He never said anything, when he followed me, but I knew it would come to a head, and it did that very afternoon. I took a roundabout route home, but he was there, waiting at my door. He said, or rather whined, "You can't do this. You can't leave me to watch while you go after other men." "You don't have to watch," I said, trying to be angry. "Anyway, it's none of your affair." He wouldn't let me through the door of the flat, but

172

pawed at my arm. I could see he had been drinking. His teeth gleamed, but dirtily, like metal. I had never hit him before, not even in retaliation, and then I had to make myself do it, because he was too drunk to be a real nuisance. It turned my stomach, when I slapped him, and he looked at me in disbelief, and I just walked in through the door.'

'I don't understand how you could even pity him, Martha, a man like that.'

'No, you don't,' she said briefly. We were both quiet, just standing and waiting. Then she went on, 'I didn't allow myself to pity him, for that moment. It is a matter of control. When he overdosed and had to be taken to hospital, and I stood for hours in the dull corridor, white as a burial chamber, then I lost control, and pitied him, and they led me to his bedside, even though I didn't want to see him. Giles helped; he made me stop pitying.'

'How? How did he help?' I asked, too urgently, recoiling as soon as the words had left my mouth. She put her hands over my ears, mockingly.

'Not in the way you imagine.'

Kissing Martha, with the rich tones of church bells like a theme tune: that is my memory of the return from the search for Marco Polo. A clammy greyness, quays empty, slippery from overnight rain. Ben and Amanda rocked and plunged in their gondola in gun-metal waters, chopped up by the wind. His hair was longer, and the new beard greying. Smiles, a firm hand-clasp: eyes of desolation. Amanda shivered, and Martha put her arm around her for comfort. In that moment a warmth embraced me, seeing the two women of my life together. There was not much luggage, and the hotel was near. I had booked them a room on the same floor as our own. But something seemed to be missing, and I was reluctant to move on until I was sure what it was. The others stood apart, waiting for me to pick up the bag at my feet. The gondolier waited too, maybe expecting a further tip. Ah! the tears: painfully vivid, I saw the second-class compartment of an

173

Italian train—how many years ago? In fading light Amanda, younger then, her figure fuller, and shyer, recounted in every detail the ship that had carried the Polos home to Venice; the gangplank, the rough Tartar robes, Venetian loafers pressing forward in curiosity, laughing, an unexpected greeting from the town that had forgotten them, a pouch held around his neck emptying precious gems on the cobbles, and mingled with them, Marco Polo's tears. I picked up the bag and hurried after the others, trying with each step to leave the memory further behind.

It was over dinner in Venice that Martha's disparate pieces were stitched together for me, and Ben reported Giles' contribution. (All the while, I was thinking: was I there, while this was happening?) Amanda was not hungry, and would eat only fruit. The zestful waiter brought a delicate knife and fork, an orange on a silver plate. The fork plunged into the top of the fruit, and with a sweeping movement of great virtuosity the knife described a single circular incision, so that the peel fell like a snake to the plate. Images retained: the startling white of the waiter's shirt, Ben's calloused hands on the clean linen around the neck of the wine bottle. (Champagne, I had suggested beforehand, but Martha said: 'What is there to celebrate?')

'I have been telling Alex a little about Saddle, and Jerusalem,' Martha said. Again, it was as if I had been too young to remember, or back in England at the time. 'Alex, when Saddle accosted you at the Tomb of the Kings, and gave you such a shock, he was partly right. He had been collecting intelligence on Mansur for the Israelis, and through that had come to know of Giles' presence in East Jerusalem. I know this because Giles himself told me. One evening, he was late for a meeting, and when he came seemed nervous. He told me that Saddle had been to see him that afternoon. "I was sleeping, and either he didn't knock or I didn't hear him. Anyway, I must have left the door ajar because when I opened my eyes he was standing there, like a dream. When he spoke his front teeth seemed to hang over the lower ones. He told me he had reason to suspect I might be in danger, for associating with a known terrorist, and when I asked who that might be, he just smiled and asked if I was denying that I knew Mansur. He only stayed about half an hour, but he showed me some horrible pictures—photographs, he said, of some of Mansur's victims: dismembered corpses, and bodies with scores of lacerations. I was only half awake, and had a splitting head-ache. Before he left, he said he smelt hashish, and offered to get as much as I needed, in return for a favour." Giles was lucky; he was probably incapable of answering any questions at the time. He used to smoke quite a lot in the afternoons, you know—except if he was with me.'

'And did that convince you to leave Saddle?' I asked.

'Yes. I had visions of the hospital again, and that smell of sterilizing solution, and the white-painted bricks that signi-fied hopelessness.But instead of Saddle in there, I kept think-ing of my friends—Giles, and lots of people I had known, like Yakov, who had nothing to do with any of this. But it seemed that everyone was involved, because of me, like King Midas, but everything I touched decaying instead of turning to gold.'

There was more of this, about rows with Saddle, and changing flats, and conversations with Giles, and his decision to go off and test ancient theories about the earthly paradise. Ben became interested, and asked precise questions, which of course Martha could not answer, because Giles was never precise. All this seemed to me like looking over old examin-ation papers, at school: stale problems unanswered, mis-understood. All the while Amanda played with her redun-dant cutlery, making lines in the cloth with her knife, and staring beyond the table, to the canal. Already, this made no sense to her, struggling to recall the old unfamiliar Venetian words, unused for so long. Shangtu, Kinsai, Zaiton, the Great Khan: put them out of your mind, Marco, for you are back at home; half of your lifetime is over, meaning nothing to these people . . .

175

e did not loiter in Venice, where even the postcard-sellers were beginning their seasonal despair, but took an ill-matched series of trains across the Romagna to Tuscany, and Santa Clara. Martha went back to England, sloughing off like an extra skin the Jerusalem years; she vowed never to return. She would live for a while with her father, in the house amid the patchwork of Sussex fields and hedges. On the train Ben brooded like a Stylite, and Amanda gazed at the wheat fields and olive groves from the dusty window. Unfamiliar sights, travelling backwards. They existed, perhaps, only for her.

The house which Ben and his brother had inherited, jointly, from their Italian aunt had been repainted and furnished in his absence. His brother, the taciturn Simon, who seldom stayed, had driven Ben's car down from England and left it there when he returned—with the fresh pale walls and the brand-new refrigerator, marks of his presence. The hill was streaked with evening fire when we arrived. For some reason the olive groves reminded me of the furze and gorse of an English moor. After Israel, maybe nothing would look the same again.

Santa Clara still clenched the hill-rock into which it was built, just as it was when I had first seen it. The warm red of Tuscan brick, roads of saffron dust: old sights, once dearer to me than any. I remember that we simply stood in the path outside the house for a while, as if unbelieving. From the house one could see across the whole valley; on a clear day, even the village on the next range of hills, so alike and so different. For me at least, the house still held some of the qualities of a secret garden, the nursery of our youthful aspirations. We settled in easily, although for what none of us could say. Ben took on himself some of the massive calm of the place, the old farmhouse and the trees in the garden; during the day he would shut himself in the outhouse that had once been a workshop and into which he had dragged a desk and chair. We knew he was working on his book, and more than once he spoke with his editor from the University Press on the telephone, but when I walked past the hut I would see him sitting with his beard cushioned in his hands, staring across the valley. We hardly spoke to each other during those days.

As for Amanda, she saddened and bloomed at the same time, drifting slowly away from us, from the earth. I remember her sitting at the big table in the upper room, absorbing the cool deep space behind her. Maps were spread on the table, of India, Mongolia, China. Her hair fell in heaps over her shoulders and on to the pages of close handwriting. She drank jasmine tea, holding the china cup painted with roses in two strong hands. Roses on the cup, and dog-roses climbing the wall of the house, and up over the terrace. Sometimes there would be snatches of song: her own tunes, but borrowed words: 'A damsel with a dulcimer, in a vision I once saw . . . his flashing eyes, floating hair! Weave a circle . . . and close your eyes with holy dread, for he on honey-dew hath fed, and drunk the milk of paradise.' We discovered strange pictures, unsigned but so clearly her own, sketches of towers and palaces of unrecognized design, rare flowers and bamboos, totems with the faces of Turkic gods. She was transcribing her dreams into pictures, as well as words. How did this happen, this freeing of the gravitational pull that drags us to this earth, these parallels of time? Why the Venetian traveller, the dealer in gems and trader in fabulous stories? Between them there was nothing: she, a young wife, beautiful in a statuesque fashion, happily married and well-off; he, seven centuries older, foreign, unwashed, used to silence, darkness, smells—a medieval clarity. She breathed his ancient, distant air, chewed on meats prepared in oriental kitchens. Sometimes she would feed us small details, describe a wedding in India or a hunt on the steppes; afterwards Ben consulted books with trembling fingers, and found the exact words in the 'Travels of Ser Marco'. Martha has too little patience with Ben, thinking he misunderstood Amanda. But what was there to comprehend? Even in his embrace she could disappear from sight. He was confused, feeling himself abandoned for a ghost. He recited to me verses from the lovely Provençal poem, 'La nostr' amor vai enaissi, con la branca de l'albespi . . .': 'The way our love goes is like the hawthorn branch trembling on the tree at night in rain and frost, until the morning, when the sun sheds its light over the green leaves on the branch. I recall a morning when we made peace from war, and she gave me so great a gift—her full love and her ring. May God let me live long enough to have my hands once more under her cloak!'

'It is not war that comes between us, Alex, but a dreadful silence that I cannot penetrate. It is like a window, with nothing on the other side, not even air.' A piercing irony, that: the historian unable to touch the very fabric of his age! Let no one say that he did not try, but that he had not fed on honey-dew, nor drunk with her the milk of paradise. And increasingly he began to suspect that poor self-despising Giles had. For myself, I had never understood the ravings about the Grail, and Perceval healing or not healing the Fisher King, nor what connection this had with the sober Venetian. It was likely, Ben said, that Marco knew, perhaps had read some tale of King Arthur and the Grail. It was the most popular literature of the Middle Ages, even in Venice, where bezants and galleys had dulled the edges of chivalry. And Amanda confirmed this, with the confidence of intimate acquaintanceship:

178

'In Genoa, after he had been taken prisoner in the sea-battle, commanding a Venetian galley, he shared his confinement with the writer Rusticello,' she said, as if relating the events of her childhood. We were sitting on the terrace at noon, sharing in the stillness of the land, like a great lake. (Ben would probably have preferred to be out in the hills, hunting rabbits with his neighbour the wine-grower.) 'Now, of course, no one would know of him if it were not for the chance meeting in a Genoese prison, but at the time—I forget the year ('1298', Ben interrupted softly, unlistening)—he was celebrated for his romances. I suppose he saw in Marco the novelty that Arthur or the Matter of Troy had lost. It didn't work, of course,' she smiled sadly. 'Stories are better told than read, and no one was interested in the real Orient—just in dragons and the sciapodae and cenocephali and the Fountain of Eternal Youth, and magical gems. There were gems, but Marco was raised by merchants, and knew the magic came from the beholder, not the stone.'

Amanda was wrong, for it so obviously did work, the thin web in which Rusticello the Pisan had contained the life of Marco Polo. Mostly it kept people out, showing the skeleton of the itinerary but no flesh; Amanda the web trapped, closed off against the world. After a while, like an insect, she ceased to struggle. Some words of Rusticello's to Marco intrigued her, spoken as they were languidly, as the prisoners leant out over the bay window to see the Tyrhennian waters far below. They were well treated, and as gentlemen had the pick of the rooms, even if they were barely furnished, with bolts on the doors. Marco was sometimes reminded of a room high in the tower of the royal palace of Kinsai, where he used to squat with the young Tartar governor among delicate painted silks. A prisoner then, like now, but held in bonds of contentment, soft, passionless. Rusticello said:

'You have travelled so far, and seen so many wonders, that you are like a writer of epics. For me, to write about the noble Arthur and Lancelot, or about Aeneas and Antenor of Troy,

179

or the great paladin Charlemagne, is to live in those days again, so that my life is broken up by many others which are only imagined, and so different to my own.'

'But I do not write; I am simply a merchant.'

'Simply! Marco Il Milione—that is what they call you here, because the number of your stories is endless. You provide better entertainment than a troop of musicians or actors! But you do not need to imagine—you have known the people you speak about, and the places. Do you also feel that your life is fragmented, so that one part seems to have been happening so far away that it is as if there were many worlds, and not one?'

Marco frowned, for he felt a discomfort whenever the storyteller spoke of these things. He touched on a nerve, and Marco, an honest man, realized that the nerve twinged because what Rusticello said was true. When, in the evenings, the prisoners talked in groups around the fire, and begged Marco for more tales of the East, he held their attention like a god. Perhaps some or all did not believe him; perhaps they were right. He sat and talked, but afterwards could not remember the words he had used, and for some hours would sit quietly, unable to join in the games or the music, or to sleep. Far removed he would sit, unsure whether these men were real, or he. How could both be, when his seventeen years held no meaning for them? This was a discomfort he had felt for the first time on arriving back in the Venice he barely remembered, when he had stood on the cobbles in front of San Marco and wept. The others had assumed his tears sprang from joy at seeing his homeland again, but he had continued to weep at unexplained moments: at a banquet in honour of some city dignitary, in the council chamber, in church. On none of these occasions was he able to explain his tears—not even now to Rusticello, groping clumsily through the web of fables.

'The Great Khan often asked me to speak to him of Venice,' said Marco, 'and now, people want to hear about the Great

180

Khan and his cities. How can I speak to both? I must forever describe worlds unimagined.'

Rusticello nodded, but Marco saw that he did not understand, just as the Venetians did not; perhaps even the Great Khan had never understood. They had not the language to follow him, for in words the mountain ranges and moonlit sands were the same, on the Mediterranean and the China Seas. And this meant, of course, that he was alone among both peoples, among all peoples: one who has seen, but cannot tell.

'It is a problem of communication,' Amanda said, and now I know that she spoke, as it were, the words that were in Marco's own mind. 'Rusticello was an experienced enough craftsman, and knew what his public expected. Marco too, in his own way. But together, they could not sell his Travels.'

'Were they too fantastic even for medieval readers?' I asked.

'The opposite,' said Ben, 'not fantastic enough.'

'Kublai Khan, dear as he is to me, is not Prester John,' Amanda explained. 'His armies do not march behind the Cross, searching for a place to ford the Tigris, to attack the Saracens from the rear, and avenge the insults to the Holy City.' (Here, of course, they had lost me: Ben was later to relate the first appearance of the mythical emperor of India, in the pages of the German chronicler Otto von Freising, where the writer passes on the rumour of a defeat inflicted on the infidel near Samarkand, and the advance of the victor, with his army ablaze with anticipation for Jerusalem.) 'That is what Europeans wanted of Marco—mythical gems, paradise and Prester John.'

'And why not. What was Marco interested in, besides profits?' cried Ben in exasperation. 'What did he leave us? Hints, shadows. "After twelve days the traveller comes to a fine city, which pays tribute to the Great Khan." Is that all? Twelve days of what? Whom does he meet, what language do they speak, what are their thoughts? Describe the cobble-

181

stones, the trees, the bricks!' He was shouting in passion now, as if Marco were present with us to defend himself. 'How dare he presume? Does he deserve to take possession of your mind, Amanda?'

'It is no use, my dear,' she said calmly. 'Because he speaks sometimes, it does not mean he will do so always.'

'God knows, I do not expect answers,' he went on, quieter. 'No one can, from that distance. But an understanding of some kind—we have a right to it, surely.' He was like a man who has lost a relative in a disaster, and looks around for blame, or science, to explain it. It was the first time he had let his anger show, since Jerusalem, though Amanda told me that every night he moaned and cursed, blaming himself for Giles' death.

When my holiday ended, I was sorry to leave Santa Clara. On an impulse I wrote to my superiors requesting a post away from the city I loved, but I was not yet senior enough to deserve special treatment, and returned in mid-autumn to Jerusalem. Links like tendons held me to the past, to England: Ben wrote dutifully, and eventually an abstruse volume appeared, dedicated to Giles. I wrote awkward love letters to Martha, some of which I sent, and she offered in return terse details of a new-begun life. It seemed easy for her to start again (she had taken a job in publishing); she was younger than Marco Polo when he returned to Venice, and had lost less. But she could not unlive memory, and there was me, after all. Perhaps, had I been sent elsewhere, we would gradually have stopped writing, and I not taken a week off in the spring to visit her. I went to Oxford also, and while Amanda worked in the garden with her collection of medieval herbs, Ben told me he would be coming to Jerusalem again in the summer, to examine manuscripts in the library of the Greek Patriarchate.

When they came, towards the end of May 1967, I could not see them at once. It could hardly have been a worse time: relations with Nasser had deteriorated to the level of imminent war. The Jerusalem Brigade, reservists whose duties were to defend the Jewish part of the city, had been mobilized. Diplomats agreed that war, if it came, would be in the Sinai, but the Egyptians were hoping that King Hussein would take advantage of the Israeli army's absence to attack Jerusalem.

'If the Arab Legion is sent to East Jerusalem,' the consul said, 'the Jerusalem Brigade will not be able to hold them. A few outdated Sherman tanks in the hands of amateurs—that's all they have.' He was a veteran of the independence struggle, convinced since 1948 of the Legion's invincibility. When the Egyptians closed the Straits of Tiran to block Israeli shipping on the Red Sea, every yard of the border of the dismembered city was manned on both sides. At that time most nations maintained consular buildings on both sides, staffed largely by the same people, who drove daily across one of the U.N. checkpoints. Ben, as a foreign scholar, had almost diplomatic status; his research took him into the Old City on Jordanian soil, though he lived at the Hebrew University campus in Jewish Jerusalem.

As Israeli jets took off to bomb the Egyptian airfields, there was little reason to expect that anything drastic would happen in Jerusalem to relieve the tension of two decades. Citizens were advised, in the case of emergency, to go to the basements and cellars, but food was still plentiful. Most men of military age had already been called up. But surely Hussein would not commit himself until he saw the outcome of the war in the Sinai: everyone agreed to this, at the gathering at the American Consulate, on the Nablus Road in East Jerusalem, just outside the narrow demilitarized zone. I was there, with Ben and Amanda, who had refused to stay at home in Oxford.

'There will be skirmishes, I expect, at the crossing points. But the Jordanians won't try anything, with the U.N. installed here,' said an American official.

'What about an Israeli attack?' Ben suggested, and the diplomat guffawed politely.

183

'These are reservists, you understand. They might be able to hold a defensive position, but the odds are against them.'

'And where would they find the extra men they would need?' another demanded. 'They'll need all they have to hold the Egyptians—and keep an eye on the eastern border.' Ben deferred to experience. He was out of place anyway, the guest of an American scholar he knew who was staying at the Consulate. I watched them stroll off together into the past.

'To be sure, Bar Kochba's army was the last Jewish army, as such, to assault the city,' Ben was saying, 'but in terms of fighting in Jerusalem, you may be overlooking the Jewish inhabitants of the city at the time of the crusaders' siege in 1099.'

'I didn't know about them,' the American, a classicist, admitted. 'But what part did they play in the siege? We're talking about a Jewish army, after all.'

'The Egyptian governor of Jerusalem armed all inhabitants, Muslims and Jews,' Ben explained. 'The Christians he had mostly expelled, lest they sabotage the defence of the city. These were orientals, of course—Melkites and Jacobites, a few Copts and Latins.'

'So the Jews helped the Muslims keep the Christians out of their ancestral city?' said the American professor, bewildered. 'I don't know how you find your way around in the Middle Ages, Ben. I'd get lost, for sure.'

'Oh yes,' Ben said calmly, 'I've seen it happen.'

My own consul drew me discreetly to one side.

'No panic, Alex, but we're advised to stay on this side tonight. I hope you don't mind.'

'What's happened? Have they closed the crossing to neutrals?'

'I don't know, and mind you, this is unofficial. But the word is there'll be action tomorrow, and this is the safer side.' He looked happier than I had ever seen him: at the prospect of war, or its anticipated result? 'Accommodation can easily be arranged here, and for your sister and brother-in-law, of course. Just until we see how things stand, you know.'

'For how long, sir?' I thought of my friends on the kibbutz, many of them manning the bunkers along the frontier. The kibbutz itself would be in the war zone.

'Oh, it won't be too much of a wait. We anticipate a bout or two of shelling. If anything serious breaks out, the U.N. is sure to move in and call for a ceasefire. Nothing to worry about, really.'

'If you don't mind, sir, I'd rather get back tonight. I'm sure my sister feels the same.'

The consul shrugged, and looked indifferent. He trusted the Jordanian defences more than the Israeli; we had seen the streets full of Arab legionnaires, in khaki uniforms with British helmets, and British-made rifles. Ben, when told, insisted on trying to get back.

'I don't fancy being shelled by either side, but it would be less ridiculous for a historian of the crusades to be hit by Arab than by Jewish bombs,' he said. 'Besides, my papers are all at the University. I really must get them safe before this starts.'

We were the only ones to leave. The streets were deserted and unlit; a blackout had been enforced. We had left the consular car at the Mandelbaum Gate where we had crossed, and walked the short distance to the American Consulate. Not a hundred yards from the Gate, a lieutenant of the legionnaires stopped us.

'Where are you going?' he demanded.

'We are English,' Ben told him in Arabic. 'We're going across—we've been at the American Consulate.'

'No,' he said firmly in English. 'No one can cross now. The border is sealed.'

'I am an official of the British Consulate,' I protested. 'My car is at the border, and I demand to cross. You can't keep us here.'

The Arab grinned, and said, 'You'll be safer here than on the other side. It is too late, you should have left the city

185

before now. In any case, your car is no longer there. It has been requisitioned.'

'That is an act of aggression against a neutral power!'

'All cars have been requisitioned. They will be returned when it is over.'

'When what is over?' Ben asked. 'Will there be fighting in Jerusalem?'

But the legionnaire had already said too much; suddenly he forgot his English. His patrol escorted us back to the front of the Consulate in silence. On the doorstep Amanda said (speaking almost for the first time that night), 'I don't want to go in there again.'

'Then let's not,' said Ben. 'Where else can we go, Alex?' Bravado, or the still night swelling around us, made me play along.

'The Old City. Where better than behind Suleiman's walls?'

The Damascus Gate, the Bab el-Amud, dwarfed us, but inside its bulk the streets were as busy, or as quiet, as on any night. The great walls enclosed this eerie, imperfect city like a paradise garden. Following the split cobbles I suddenly remembered the evening of Saddle's death, not far from there. Then, as now, it was difficult to breathe in the pounding air. We saw soldiers sitting on steps or at café tables. They were as unsure as the civilians who tried not to notice them, as if the darkness of the blackout could hide rifles and grenades. Subconsciously I preserved fragments of conversation and laughter, perhaps aware that they would remain crystalline, the last moments of the city as I had discovered and known it. I think we sat down at one of the cafés where by day one can hardly move for the crush of people; if we spoke at all, I do not remember what was said. The city absorbs, drinks even our words.

Although knowing it would be shut, we headed for the Holy Sepulchre, and sat in a stone niche outside the southern façade. Grim, beautiful stones, worn by pilgrims' tears. There was no one there but an elderly Greek priest, locking up a

186

side-chapel. Greeks, Syrians, Armenians, Copts: what would they do, these familiar aliens, when fighting broke out? (It would of course, as I knew suddenly and certainly.) Their churches had survived the bitter street fighting of 1948, and their ancestors the changing fortunes of Christians and Muslims since the first capture of the city by the Arabs. For all I knew, they had their own catacombs and warrens beneath the walls, sanctified by the prayers of centuries. Just for a moment as we sat there, I had a minor vision, nothing to be compared to Amanda's dreams, or even Giles' winged fancies, but strange enough for me. I saw the whole city, its diverse shrines and mosques and cafés and street-corners, even its people, as one, a single mass, like one shaft of pure sound reverberating equally within each holy place, a sound so powerful to human ears that the very walls dissolved. All diversity became a single perfect building, architecture trans-figured, like a unique colourless pearl. (Thus, perhaps, Ben's medieval mystics understood their heavenly Jerusalem.)

'We had better find somewhere more permanent than this for the night,' Ben said, shattering the trance.

'More than just the night, if there is fighting tomorrow.' We had not voiced this till now: we were outsiders caught in an unknown city. When it came to a crisis, East Jerusalem might as well have been Peking, for all that I lived and worked not two miles away.

'Surely there will be public shelters, if there is to be shelling,' I said, unconvinced. Ben snorted impatiently in reply.

'Pointless to look for that. Who knows how long this will last, or if it will ever happen? I know people in the Old City. We'll have to try them.'

'What people?'

'Oh, just people. You know, librarians, and monks— people I have met in my work.'

'Could you find them now?'

'Of course.' He took his bearings, and led us back down the

Via Dolorosa. We came to a set of shallow steps built into the wall, climbing parallel to the street. It was surely the very wall that had collapsed—how many months before?—on an evening when souls had danced before my eyes like atoms, in a Jerusalem that seemed to have vanished.

'Where are we going, Ben? There's nothing up here.'

'Yes, there is. Don't you know the pilgrimage route?' At the top of the steps we turned to the left and stumbled along an unlit alley, where garbage bins had spilled their contents along the wall. There was a low green door at the end. 'If this is locked, there's another way,' Ben muttered, 'if only I could find it in the dark.' But it was open, and we bent our heads in turn to go through, emerging into an open space on the rooftops. Even in the dark, the round-topped, sun-baked cells told me where we were.

'The Ethiopian monastery!'

'Naturally. I imagine it will be as safe as anywhere.'

'I've never seen it at night,' Amanda said. 'It looks like the surface of the moon.'

Ben, pointing to a low wall enclosing some shrubbery, said, 'This is where the Ethiopians believe the thicket grew in which the ram got caught, when Abraham was about to sacrifice Isaac.'

'I thought the sacrifice was supposed to have been on Mount Moriah.'

'Well, yes, in Jewish tradition. But you know, many of the early Christian pilgrims believed that happened on Golgotha. Even in the thirteenth century you find pilgrims being told that.' Seeing me look doubtfully at the bush, Ben laughed. 'You know, Alex, you don't have to worry about sorting out all these traditions into a uniform pattern. Belief doesn't work like that. Suspend your rationality, and enjoy the diversity.'

'Doesn't that diversity invalidate the belief? I mean, both places can't be the real site. And the same with Golgotha and the Garden Tomb. You have to believe one or the other, or neither—you can't have both true at the same time.'

188

Ben looked at me curiously, but before he could reply Amanda murmured, 'Many things are true at the same time, if you don't worry too strictly about time.'

'Everyone worries about time, I mean in the sense that it governs actions.'

'God does not,' said a strange voice that had not been there before. 'Nothing matters less to the Eternal One.' It was one of the monks, tall and shapeless in his pale robe, dark looming out of the darkness. 'He hovers above time and change, like a moment preserved forever.'

'And so,' said Amanda, 'everything happens at just the right time, if you are God.'

'Everything happens at the same time,' the monk said softly. 'For us, things happen; for God, they are. We can only see them gradually unfold, like a flower blooming and dying.'

'I believe Kublai Khan said the same thing once, but the words escape me now.'

'You must forgive an ignorant man,' the monk said, 'but I have never read his works.'

'Oh, he didn't write them down, he couldn't write.'

'Kublai Khan was a Mongol emperor of the thirteenth century,' Ben explained solemnly. The monk laughed, a good-natured but unusual sound.

'And why are three Americans looking for a Mongol emperor in our monastery?'

'Oh, we aren't looking for him, he's easy enough to find; it's Marco Polo one has to search for,' said Amanda, but the monk did not catch this because Ben said quickly, 'We are English, not Americans.'

'Ah, delightful! When I was young, in Ethiopia, I saw your King and Queen. They walked through my town, shaking everyone's hand. She was a most beautiful lady.'

'Thank-you', Ben said graciously.

'But you must be lost. It is not a good time to be lost in Jerusalem.'

189

'Can I speak to the abbot? He knows me, I have worked here. I am a historian.'

'Ah, yes. The abbot is at his prayers.' The monk did not indicate that he thought it a strange time to pay an unexpected visit. 'You can wait in here.' He showed us into a large low building, and lit an oil-lamp for us.

'This is the chapter house,' said Ben, like a tour guide. It was pleasantly cool inside, and bare. Benches lined the walls, and above them were painted figures. In the oil-lamp's glare these were lurid: bright colours, green and red and blue predominating, naïve open faces, childish poses. Above each figure was some writing, but unintelligible to us, of course. 'Those are past abbots. Unfortunately I cannot read the script.' I sat on a bench opposite the abbot's great wooden seat, and wondered what it was like to be a monk here on the rooftops. Ben explained that the monastery, which had the appearance of birthlessness, had been there since the fourth century. The Ethiopians claimed their conversion to Christianity from the eunuch of Queen Candace to whom the apostle Philip had preached, on his return from Jerusalem. There had been disagreement about the allocation of chapel space in the new Church of the Anastasis (now the Holy Sepulchre), according to Ben, and the Ethiopians had been left without any altars inside the church, so they had built their small monastery in a position to overlook the open dome of the church. (Now, of course, it was overshadowed by the new, closed dome.) Ben told us a good deal else besides, about councils and orthodoxy and a monk called Nestorius, and how many natures Christ had, and whether his nature was the same as his will. Apparently it was this that had really split Christianity, centuries before minor upsets like Luther and Henry VIII. But although he became quite animated, it seemed less important than the calm smile on the monk's face as he had appeared out of the night to talk to Amanda. (She was smiling too, as Ben spoke, but she must have heard even less than I. What was all this theory to her,

190

who had known Nestorians in China?)

It was very late when the abbot came in, but he recognized Ben at once and kissed him warmly in greeting. Ben explained how we had been trapped on the Jordanian side, and introduced us. The abbot was old, like an ancient olive tree. He stooped slightly, but strong white hair stood up off his shrunken scalp. His hand, when I took it, was dry, a bag of small bones. I forgot his name as soon as Ben mentioned it (my habit, unfortunately, with foreign names) but in any case he was simply 'the abbot', as if he had been born with the title. Ben knew him only slightly, having visited the monastery to study the frescoes in the church, and some archives. Indeed I was surprised, when I came to consider it, that he had led us here, rather than a place he might have known better, such as the Greek Patriarchate. But we were made welcome, and taken to the tiny guest-house. After all, monasteries had a duty to care for travellers, like Homer's heroes. Seeing the narrow hard bed and rough blanket, I was suddenly tired, and looked forward to sleep. Ben exchanged a few words with the abbot, and lay down in his clothes. Amanda and he were given the room adjoining mine, but I could still hear her outside as I went to bed, her rather deep, soft voice, the abbot's slow English. They were watching the stars together, but I could barely hear their words. After a while, I thought that he had left, or fallen asleep where they sat, but then I heard the unmistakable sound of an old man's cough. For all I knew, they sat up talking all night.

Monks rise early in the morning, but I slept on undisturbed. When I woke, breakfast and linen were waiting for me on the table. Amanda strolled in, fresh-looking.

'Awake at last? Ben's gone to the church. Do you want to come and look at the paintings?'

'I've seen them before. Let's find our friend of last night. Do you suppose he's busy?'

'He's sitting outside in the sun. Come on.' But as we crossed the hard earth of the compound the sky shook with

191

the first blasts from the artillery pieces that had stood poised and pointing for weeks; war had come to Jerusalem. Amanda grasped my arm instinctively, and later I found that I had bitten my lip so violently that it bled.

Slowly, with exaggerated calm, the monk stood up and put down the can with which he had been watering a small tree. He crossed over towards the church, calling out, 'It is far away, there is no need to be afraid. Come into the church.' By the time we reached it the first bouts of shelling had drawn responses, though I could not tell whose the first salvo had been. About fifteen monks had gathered in the church, which must have been the full complement, for it was almost full. They looked like the dark angels of oriental Christian painting. Ben came over to us.

'It has started, then,' he said unnecessarily. Unbidden, the monks took their places. The early morning service had ended long ago, but the abbot began to lead us all in prayer. The language held me so that I was unable to concentrate. How many years since I had knelt to pray! For a moment I was transported back to school assemblies; the benches here were arranged like pews in an Anglican church. But above our heads, instead of gilt names carved on to rolls of honour, the startling brown faces of the Holy Family flanked by unknown saints. They stared from one wall to the other, oblivious, from round, innocent eyes. In the midst of the gunfire from the Mount of Olives behind us to the heights to the west, they stared, like large, trusting dogs. Paintings to sate the eye, and for the nose, the smells of henna, incense, oil-lamps. Thus, as a child, had I imagined Aladdin's cave.

After what must have been an hour the abbot stooped over us.

'Naturally, it is out of the question for you to leave the monastery until this is over. Please regard yourselves as our guests. You may stay here, or in the crypt underneath. It will be perfectly safe.'

'It seems that the Israelis are not bombing the Old City at

192

all,' said Ben. 'Can't we go outside?'

'If you please,' the abbot shrugged. 'We are not in the firing line, but we are beneath it. There may be mistakes . . .' He shuffled back to the altar.

'Surely there will be a ceasefire before the troops engage,' Ben said.

'That depends on how the war is going in the south. I don't believe the Israelis will try to do more than hold their line here, unless they manage to break through quickly in the Sinai.'

This is, of course, what happened, although we knew nothing of the progress of the war until the Israelis entered the Old City, two days later. Afterwards, an Israeli aide in the Defence Ministry told me of their constant fear that a ceasefire would be agreed before they had had time to make a significant territorial gain. But as that first day wore on, it seemed clear that there would be no fighting in the city walled against the world. We became bolder, and sat out in the compound. The view we might have had of the city's rooftops was denied by the high walls encircling the monastery. The tiny church nestled against the east wall of the greater Church of the Holy Sepulchre. All we could see were occasional flashes, and clouds of smoke, drifting and dissolving. Ben was transfixed.

'If it comes to a siege,' he speculated, 'I wonder where they will try to break in. The geography is no different from 1099. Then, the crusaders had difficulty establishing a bulwark anywhere except on the north—Godfrey de Bouillon finally broke through just east of the Damascus Gate. The whole army was in desperate trouble: undernourished, short of horses and supplies, dispirited. They had taken Antioch by sheer luck, survived as far as Jerusalem by a miracle. The siege seemed interminable, the chances of success minimal. Some of then drifted off to the Jordan, to perform the rites of pilgrimage before going home in despair. One night the ghost of Bishop Adhemar, the pope's own legate who had died at

193

Antioch, appeared in a dream. He told the entire army to lay down their weapons and march barefoot around the walls, fasting and singing hymns. Only through this act of repentance would the pilgrimage attain its goal.'

'Like the Israelites before Jericho,' said Amanda.

'Exactly! They were the New Israel, before the walls of the New Jerusalem! The old city had been destroyed by the Romans, its temple and rites humiliated. The Christian city was lost—imagine the impact of the loss of the New, unsullied Jerusalem! Don't you see? It was not just a city that had fallen, not a church or a tomb, but the very vision of heaven! Ah, the piety, the poor, brutal piety!' Even as Ben spoke the skies pounded, like a manic drum-beat, a new crusade. Amanda, frowning, turned to him with a familiar distance in her eyes.

'But what of the paradise on earth? In the Middle Ages they thought Eden was far away in the east, just as Giles did. Jerusalem might be the goal, but surely it could be reached only through Eden.'

'Giles found no Eden,' said Ben quietly. 'He was searching, even on the day he died. Better to forget the terrestrial paradise, as those theologians did who placed it far out of human reach, on a peninsula walled off by a sheet of flame. You must see, Amanda: Eden is of the past.'

'Oh, for you, perhaps, and for Alex, who thinks it ended when you left Cambridge. But Marco still thought it could be found, even in a world without magical gems and the Tree of Life. He thought it could be discovered in the variety and sameness of people and places—in flesh and in bricks.'

'In Kinsai, with the soft Chinese? Or Shangtu, a human contrivance? You will not make me believe in Eden, Amanda, not even Marco will.'

Portentous words, spattered with distant gunfire! Even as he spoke they were ravaging the hope and stay of centuries. The suburbs on both sides of the border were sustaining fearful damage, while we sat at peace with the Ethiopians in

194

the untouched heart of the city. So easily did Ben reject his own quest, their fateful stay in Badakshan. But the monk of last night, who of course knew nothing of this, said, 'You speak of Eden and Jerusalem, a garden and a city. Why should the two be so opposed? A garden may flourish within walls. Our ancestors here believed that the monastic garden was the re-creation of the lost Eden.'

'You see, Amanda? A re-creation—that means it was first necessary to lose it. By its nature it has to be copied, made again.'

'Perhaps that is the wrong word,' I interrupted nervously. ' "Symbol" would be better, or "metaphor". I can understand Jerusalem being the metaphor for holiness, or even salvation.' Ben looked at me in surprise, but Amanda hugged me excitedly.

'Yes, oh yes! And if you allow Jerusalem to be a metaphor for your pilgrims and crusaders, why not Shangtu for Marco Polo? Why should all medieval people have expected the same paradise? And why not Badakshan, for Giles?'

'Leave Giles out of this.'

'No, he is part of it, he should be here. How he would enjoy this!'

'He had his chances, Amanda; he messed them up here, and escaped to find an Eden as far away as possible. It would be too easy, if that were all that was needed.'

How merciless Ben is, I thought for the first time, and how demanding. He had constructed mental channels to aid his own understanding, and expected others to use them too. What he found unforgivable was not Giles' needless death, nor his failure to enjoy his talent, but his failure to make something of Jerusalem. For Ben, every journey here was a pilgrimage accompanied by grateful thanksgiving, every hour in the archives a ritual bathing in the Jordan. But Giles had lain in his squalid unhappiness, not written a word, stopped thinking altogether. He had drifted, like Marco Polo in Kinsai. Amanda, of course, with her peculiar sensitivity, understood.

195

She could forgive, as Ben could not, the confusion of the symbols, Jerusalem and Eden. Indeed she welcomed that very confusion. Had Marco not shared her illusions and her despair? In the afternoon of that first day of enforced seclusion, to the sound of guns and the exhortation to the faithful from the loudspeakers installed in al-Aqsa mosque, Amanda slept in the little Ethiopian church. She dreamt, naturally, of Marco; but not of return and disillusionment, or the latter days with the ailing Great Khan, but rather of the untravelled, undefined Marco.

The Polos were rich pilgrims. They owned their own small merchant fleet, and had no need to buy passages on a cramped lower deck. But money could not provide everything. It was needed these days to gain access to the holy sites in Muslim territory—which meant Jerusalem and Bethlehem, the Jordan and the Galilee, everything except Acre and the narrow coastal strip—but it could not make the Holy City itself Christian again, it could not spread over it the ineffable aura that the first crusaders had known. The New Jerusalem was in the hands of the enemies of Christ. As the Polos climbed the slopes of Montjoie (so named because it had given the earliest pilgrims their initial, unrepeatable sight of the Holy City) Maffeo wept with grief and joy. The Muslim guide, who had seen this so often before, hung discreetly back. Now that they controlled the city, the Muslims had taken over the tourist trade also. Pilgrims were permitted into Jerusalem only to visit the Holy Sepulchre and Calvary, and sometimes by special arrangement some of the other churches that had not been converted into mosques. The regular fee could be supplemented by any amount thought appropriate, depending on how much one wanted to see. The pilgrims were accompanied by the Muslim guide in groups all the way from the border of Christian territory. In general, it worked

196

well: the Polos had heard the usual stories of pilgrims cheated and robbed, but as their friend Tedaldo the papal legate at Acre had told them, this has been the case even in the days of good King Baldwin. And the Sepulchre and churches themselves were not assaulted as they had been by the mad Caliph al-Hakim, long before the first crusaders were born.

The pilgrims entered the city through St. Lazarus' Postern, in the spot where the New Gate now stands, leading to the Christian quarter. This was now empty of Christians, but for the few priests serving the remaining churches. And of course, over the Sepulchre itself the miracle still bore witness to a deprived generation, in the Easter lamp that burst into spontaneous flame every Holy Saturday night. It was part of the Polos' commission from the Great Khan to bring him some of this fire. The pilgrims advanced in small groups to enter the chapel built around the tomb itself: there were twelve marble columns, one for each apostle, a cupola above the chapel, and on top of that a silver figure of Christ. The whole of the outside of the chapel was faced with marble. As each pilgrim entered the sanctuary, he kissed the stone of the tomb. Marco could see where countless pilgrims' mouths had worn the rock smooth. He had heard that before the pilgrimage was regulated carefully when arrangements were left very much to the individual, pieces of the sacred tomb itself had been secretly chipped off and taken by zealous pilgrims. Now there was hardly a moment when their movements were not watched by a priest or canon.

Unexpectedly Marco was seized by a kind of nausea, and quickly left the church to sit in the clearer air outside. He realized that it was neither sickness nor despair that had come over him, but rather a fear. He watched the straggling pilgrims bow their heads before entering the church, and waited to see them again when they came out. He studied faces and expressions, looking carefully into the eyes of each, noting the lines around the corner of the mouth, the involuntary squint as they emerged from darkness into sunlight. In each face that entered, different as they were in shape and degree of ugliness, he saw anticipation, or hope, but something else on coming out, his own strange fear. Later he remembered that the faces had turned towards him (or perhaps he imagined it), as if demanding a thing lost or unredeemable. This still did not explain the fear, until he remembered that here was the vision of paradise, the city of God. Faces that had looked on Jerusalem and remained unsated. What more was there to be given than this, he wondered? He did not speak of this to anyone.

Maffeo, who had wept on seeing the city from afar, sniffed loudly as they left, and said, 'Rather poorly looked after, in my opinion; it cannot compare with our own St. Mark's. Such a shame, but then the whole kingdom has been run down. I shall tell Tedaldo we were disappointed.'

Marco thought: I imagined a city swirling on clouds, radiant as a jewel, crystal-clear. I pictured jasper, and onyx, gem-studded walls and twelve gates of pearl. Here was brick and dust, half-starved dogs, cobbles running with slime. Paradise must lie elsewhere.

For an epilogue, a pilgrimage of another kind. After Amanda's funeral Martha arrived in answer to my call, and to see the notebooks for herself. She forced us to make desultory trips to Florence, Siena, anywhere that was not Santa Clara, the poisoned little village. On one such excursion, in an empty winter Florence, we stand in the church of Santa Maria del Carmine, to look at Masaccio's frescoes, as once the four of us had done after missing a train. Parts of the church are covered with scaffolding and boarded up for reconstruction, like sticking plaster on an injured limb. It is cold, and Ben wanders off after a single glance; he has seen the frescoes too often, too many frescoes, and said too much. Martha points to Adam and Eve in the Garden of Eden, one of the scenes by

198

Masaccio's contemporary Masolino.

'They look like Roman aristocrats.'

'Now look at Masaccio's expulsion scene. See how different!' This scene entranced me years before, when I was interested in art. Adam and Eve are banished from the Garden by an angel who brandishes a sword. They are exquisite nude forms, drawn proudly: the agony on Eve's uplifted face, hands covering new-found nakedness, Adam hiding his eyes in despair. The angel's face is terrible and calm. Where have I seen such faces before? Cordite-choked streets, spent cartridge cases, vehicles smouldering and abandoned. From somewhere comes the sound of singing. Jerusalem recaptured, the battle fought around the monastery subsiding into smoke. The abbot with expressionless face hands over to Israeli soldiers the legionnaires who had sought refuge in the last hours of the battle. Ben running wildly through the narrow streets, eager to see everything at once, talking constantly. Everywhere the angel, Adam and Eve.

'What a pessimistic way of rendering the beginning of man,' says Martha. A kind of understanding dawns with those words, as though it has waited for articulation for this very moment. Suddenly I wish I could tell Amanda, but it is too late, and I never told her anything when I had the opportunity, but instead thought her insane, loving her all the time and pitying, but uncomprehending.

Martha is here, so I put my arm around her and whisper, 'Not an end, but a beginning.' The road to redemption begins here, at the point where Eden is sealed off by the flaming sword. Knowledge destroyed it in a blinding flash, showing the ravaged earth beyond, the toil and absence, the loss and weariness on the faces of Adam and Eve, surrounded by mad, silent nature. They are alive at last, freed from the immortality of Eden, of plants and animals: possibilities exist, branching off like myriad paths.

Emerging from the musty church into the square, we squint like Marco Polo's pilgrims.

'I think you are right, Martha,' says Ben after a while. 'We really ought to do something with those notebooks.' She turns to me smiling triumphantly; I have been trying to persuade her to leave them alone. There are pigeons loitering here, as on the quay at Venice when the Polos disembarked with pouches stuffed with gems hanging underneath their cloaks. Amanda said, 'It is a problem of communication.' The tears Marco shed over Venetian stones are the clue none of us could follow, his tears and the tears of Adam, weeping as he leaves the Garden. It is hard to disown my tears now, recalling the two still figures, Marco and the Great Khan, facing each other over the chessboard, across the continent of Asia. A million Tartar empires, a million Kublai Khans, a million Marco Polos—or perhaps none: Marco's words to the Great Khan. Ah, the tears, so much more precious than the gems sparkling in the sunlight! At last I see, they were for her.

When we get back home, I decide as we follow the line of bare trees and turn towards the river, I will read the 'Travels' of Marco Polo.

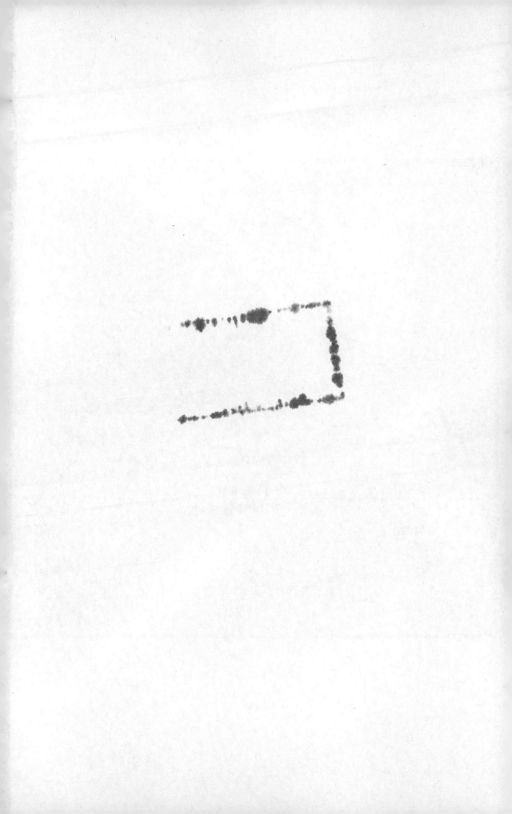